PRAISE FOR THE QUEEN BEE MYSTERIES
Plan Bee

"An entertaining amateur-sleuth mystery starring a fascinating protagonist whose amusing asides about family and friends make for a jocular small-town tale. Fans will enjoy the dynamic duo [as they] work Plan Bee in the case of the murdered sibling." —*Genre Go Round Reviews*

"You will not want to put [*Plan Bee*] down until you find out whodunit. I love, love, love this series. The characters grab you immediately, and Story follows a wonderful, winding cozy path. Run, don't walk, to your favorite bookstore and get your hands on this new title—and if you haven't read the first two, pick those up as well. Then sit down in a comfy chair with a warm blanket and cup of tea (with honey) and enjoy." —*Cozy Corner*

"Story and her comedic sidekick, "Pity Party" Patti, know how to delve into clues and uncover the most unlikely suspects using unconventional methods and flying by the seat of their pants. This is a very funny and entertaining mystery that will have readers laughing until the very end."
—*RT Book Reviews* (4 stars)

Mind Your Own Beeswax

"Reed pollinates this novel, like its predecessor, with a smart story, characters who leap off the page and, of course, interesting material about beekeeping. It will keep you busy." —*Richmond Times-Dispatch*

"The characters are as colorful as the rainbow . . . With the perfect blend of humor and drama and a gutsy heroine . . . Readers will be thoroughly entertained by this madcap mystery." —*RT Book Reviews*

continued . . .

"Story Fischer is one of the spunkiest heroines of a cozy mystery that I have had the pleasure of reading! I love the character's strength, her fearlessness, and her smarts . . . A delicious series that is a sweet treat for cozy mystery fans!"
—*Fresh Fiction*

"The prose is witty, charming, and peppered with beautiful imagery, the plot is rich and complex, and the mystery is cleverly constructed and skillfully written, tying past events to the present in a way that adds import and intrigue to both. Story makes for a fabulous heroine and an engaging narrator. Strong, smart, snarky, and positively bullheaded in her independence, she's a character for whom readers can't help but root . . . Run out and buy yourself a copy."
—*The Season*

"The second in Hannah Reed's terrific Queen Bee Mysteries that serves up all kinds of interesting beekeeping information and honey recipes, a wacky and totally likeable cast of characters, and a frenzied hive of story activity . . . I loved *Buzz Off*, the first in the series, and this one is even better."
—*Cozy Corner*

Buzz Off

"A great setting, rich characters, and such a genuine protagonist in Story Fischer that you'll be sorry the book is over when you turn the last page. Start reading and you won't want to put it down. Trust me, you'll be saying 'buzz off' to anybody who dares interrupt!"
—Julie Hyzy, award-winning author of
Grace Among Thieves

"Action, adventure, a touch of romance, and a cast of delightful characters fill Hannah Reed's debut novel. *Buzz Off* is one honey of a tale."
—Lorna Barrett, *New York Times* bestselling author of
the Booktown Mysteries

Berkley Prime Crime titles by Hannah Reed

BUZZ OFF
MIND YOUR OWN BEESWAX
PLAN BEE
BEELINE TO TROUBLE

Beeline to Trouble

Hannah Reed

BERKLEY PRIME CRIME, NEW YORK

THE BERKLEY PUBLISHING GROUP
Published by the Penguin Group
Penguin Group (USA) Inc.
375 Hudson Street, New York, New York 10014, USA

Penguin Group (Canada), 90 Eglinton Avenue East, Suite 700, Toronto, Ontario M4P 2Y3, Canada
(a division of Pearson Penguin Canada Inc.) • Penguin Books Ltd., 80 Strand, London WC2R 0RL,
England • Penguin Group Ireland, 25 St. Stephen's Green, Dublin 2, Ireland (a division of Penguin
Books Ltd.) • Penguin Group (Australia), 250 Camberwell Road, Camberwell, Victoria 3124, Australia
(a division of Pearson Australia Group Pty. Ltd.) • Penguin Books India Pvt. Ltd., 11 Community
Centre, Panchsheel Park, New Delhi—110 017, India • Penguin Group (NZ), 67 Apollo Drive,
Rosedale, Auckland 0632, New Zealand (a division of Pearson New Zealand Ltd.) • Penguin Books
(South Africa) (Pty.) Ltd., 24 Sturdee Avenue, Rosebank, Johannesburg 2196, South Africa

Penguin Books Ltd., Registered Offices: 80 Strand, London WC2R 0RL, England

This is a work of fiction. Names, characters, places, and incidents either are the product of the author's
imagination or are used fictitiously, and any resemblance to actual persons, living or dead, business
establishments, events, or locales is entirely coincidental. The publisher does not have any control over
and does not assume any responsibility for author or third-party websites or their content.

PUBLISHER'S NOTE: The recipes contained in this book are to be followed exactly as written.
The publisher is not responsible for your specific health or allergy needs that may require medical
supervision. The publisher is not responsible for any adverse reactions to the recipes contained in
this book.

BEELINE TO TROUBLE

A Berkley Prime Crime Book / published by arrangement with the author

PUBLISHING HISTORY
Berkley Prime Crime mass-market edition / December 2012

Copyright © 2012 by Deb Baker.
Cover illustration by Trish Cramblet; *Honeycomb1* © Ihnatovich Maryia/Shutterstock;
Honeycomb2 © William Park/Shutterstock; *Bee* © vdLee/Shutterstock.
Cover design by Judith Lagerman.
Interior text design by Kristin del Rosario.

ISBN: 978-0-425-25180-5

BERKLEY® PRIME CRIME
Berkley Prime Crime Books are published by The Berkley Publishing Group,
a division of Penguin Group (USA) Inc.,
375 Hudson Street, New York, New York 10014.
BERKLEY® PRIME CRIME and the PRIME CRIME logo are trademarks of
Penguin Group (USA) Inc.

PRINTED IN THE UNITED STATES OF AMERICA

10 9 8 7 6 5 4 3 2 1

ALWAYS LEARNING   **PEARSON**

To the Cozy Chicks
for your loving support,
and to my readers who make my dreams come true.

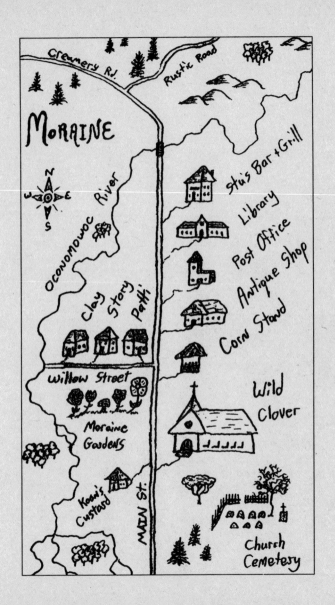

One

It took me and Hunter Wallace a long time to nail down the specifics of "living in sin" (as my mother is sure to call it the minute she finds out). We both did a whole lot of foot dragging. I was most surprised by my own heavy, cold feet, since at thirty-four I've also been experiencing that hormonal ticking clock thing, and Hunter is one fine man.

Still, when it came to the obvious next step in our relationship, the part where we made a commitment, the little voice in my head wouldn't shut up with all its insecurities. I suspect Hunter must have been experiencing the same thing, but if so, he kept it to himself.

The first issue was mine. I'd been (unhappily) married before and couldn't bear the thought of another scorching relationship, unless it involved love bites rather than burn scars. Second issue (okay, this one's mine, too): Hunter Wallace had lived a carefree single-guy existence, and I feared the idea of compromise and tolerance might be foreign to him. Based on the previous man in my life, I assumed that Hunter would be majorly set in his ways. But so far, I'm happy to report the toilet seat issue has been the only bump in the road. Still, as the pessimist side of me reminds the more optimistic part, Hunter and I are still in honeymoon mode.

Three blissful days and counting.

The last detail to be hammered out, the biggie that had held us up for the longest time, had finally been resolved. Sort of. The problem was that we both owned our own homes, and argued over which one we should live in. When Hunter first proposed our new arrangement, he said at the time, "I don't care where we live as long as we're together." But that romantic statement managed to slip his mind, because later we couldn't agree on where to live: his place, which was in a charming wooded setting but about the size of an outhouse built for two, or mine, which happened to be smack-dab in the center of town. I also have a thriving honeybee business due to a community of hives in my backyard, and my house is situated on the Oconomowoc River, not two blocks from The Wild Clover, the grocery store I own on Main Street here in Moraine, Wisconsin.

Guess who won that round? Me, that's who.

Besides, this was the Victorian where I'd been raised. I silently thanked my lucky stars that it was still in my family, that it was my home, and maybe, if Hunter and I had children, it would stay in the family for another generation.

Imagining the two of us with kids was so strange, but I kind of liked the idea. My biological clock ticked louder, trying to hurry me up, but I stopped the sound right there and then. I might have an impulsive streak—okay, I absolutely do—but rushing headlong into another marriage wasn't on my rash decisions list.

Hunter hasn't talked about putting his house up for sale yet or even suggested renting it out, which I guess is okay. We both have a little insecurity about this move, and I think we're both hanging on to what we had in the past. Just in case things go south.

But so far, so good. Fingers crossed.

At the moment, on a sunny Saturday morning in the first week of July, Hunter was watching me from a safe distance as I prepared to plunder my bees' overstocked honey pantry. And since honeybees have lots of eyes, I didn't stand a chance of sneaking up on them. Zillions of eyeballs were trained on me as I began suiting up in protective gear. Not only do my favorite flying insects have eyes on the sides of their heads, they also have three more tiny optics buried in body hair on their crowns.

I really hate wearing the bee suit and avoid it as much as possible, but since looters after their honey tend to tick off bees, I wasn't taking any chances.

I paused briefly in the midst of donning all my gear to rake my own eyes over the hot man I had decided to cohabitate with, a guy I'd known my entire life and had even dated all through high school. I regretted not having stayed with him after we graduated, and I definitely regretted tying the noose in my bad first marriage. But maybe Hunter and I had needed time to grow up, to take a shot at what else was out there, to come to the realization that the grass was greenest in our own backyards.

Hunter was about to head off for work at the Waukesha sheriff's department, but he doesn't look like your average cop. He wasn't dressed in a uniform (not that I would have had any complaints about that, since a man in uniform can be sexy as hell), but instead wore stylish undercover garb: a black T-shirt (with bulges where they should be), jeans (tight in all the right places), and Harley boots (which were cool, except that one of my fave male body parts are feet, and I like them best unshackled. Hunter, I should point out, has spectacular feet).

Next to Hunter, Ben sat watching me prepare, too. He came as part of the Hunter package when I said yes to our new living arrangement. Ben is Hunter's K-9 Belgian Malinois partner. He's smart, tough when he's asked to be, and gentle all the rest of the time. I breathe easier knowing Ben is watching Hunter's back, especially when they're out on Critical Incident Team business. C.I.T. handles the stuff that the local police aren't adequately prepared for, anything high risk, like escaped and dangerous criminals or hostage situations. It's our version of a tactical unit, not unlike a SWAT team.

Anyway, I'd barely zipped up my protective jacket when my sister Holly popped her head around the side of my house and whimpered, "Story, I have a big problem."

My sister usually looks like she just stepped off a catwalk. Tall, slender, perpetually tanned, expensively dressed, and impeccably groomed. But this morning her hair was as wild as her eyes.

"Anything that requires manly assistance?" Hunter asked, knowing full well that most of Holly's problems aren't much bigger than one of my honeybees. Then again, since Holly rarely makes any appearances before noon, and this was 6:00 a.m., I suspected her current problem might be a little more substantial than usual. If not to me, at least to her.

"No, thank you, Hunter," she said, barely giving him a glance. "I need Story."

Story Fischer. That's me. Daughter of Helen and Mike Fischer (dearly departed dad, who lost his life over five years ago to heart complications), older sister to Holly Paine (married to Max "The Money Machine" Paine), and granddaughter to Grams (who is sweeter than any honey I've ever tasted). When it comes to matriarchal families, we are one strong example of female-ruled hierarchy.

That might be why I love raising bees so much. Those girls run the show.

Not that the Fischer women are really bossing any men around at the moment. Mom and Grams are both widowed and live together in Grams's old farmhouse, and although Mom's in a new relationship with local antique-shop owner Tom Stocke, it's way too early to start ordering him around. Holly's husband is on the road most of the time, making him hard to pin down with orders. And Hunter and I are still in delusional mode. Real life hasn't intruded on us yet.

"In that case, since I'm not needed here, I'm off to go bring home some bacon," Hunter said, eyeing me up like I might be his BLT lunch.

"Working on the weekend?" Holly asked him.

"Have to," he answered. "Crime happens around the clock."

Hunter gave me a wink, then he and Ben hopped into his SUV and took off.

Holly hovered at the edge of my house. "No way am I coming into your backyard," she announced, "and you know it."

"Honestly," I sighed, unzipping the jacket. "You flip out over nothing." My sister has an unhealthy phobia when it comes to flying insects, in particular bees, even though she isn't allergic and she's never had a bad experience with them in the past. "Do they look like they care about you?" I asked, walking toward her. Unfortunately, some of the more curious honeybees must have been clinging to my jacket (which they tend to do), because as I approached Holly, she let out a bloodcurdling scream and ducked out of sight. I sighed again, in a combination of frustration and annoyance, removed the jacket, inspected the rest of me for miniature hitchhikers, brushed a few stragglers off, then found Holly on my front porch, sitting sullenly on the steps.

She started right in. "Max invited one of his company research and development teams to our house for this weekend. And I don't know what to do." The gathering surprised me, since her husband is a big honcho with an international company and spends what seems like three hundred and fifty days every year traveling. This had to be the first time he'd ever brought anybody from work home with him. "I really don't know what I'm going to do," she said again.

"You don't know what to do about what?" I asked, sitting down next to her. "It's not like you have to worry about taking care of the guests yourself." Which was true. A few months ago, Holly had hired Effie and Chance Anderson to be her live-in housekeeper and gardener/handyman.

Chance Anderson was our age, and had been born and raised in Moraine. All of us here had thought he'd eventually settle down with a local girl, but Chance had had his own ideas—he and Effie met through an online matchmaking service and had a long-distance courtship before they got married and Chance brought her home with him. When Holly found out they needed a place to live, she made them an offer they couldn't refuse, and they moved right into Max and Holly's "carriage house," as Holly insists on calling the guest suite above the garage. Apparently the original building was used to house horse-drawn carriages, and Holly likes the old-time reference. The apartment, like my sister's mansion, had been updated by the last owner and was a sweet little cozy den.

"But who's going to *feed* those people? I told Max I could do it, you know, play Martha Stewart for the weekend, but you and I both know I can't."

Unfortunately, she was right about that. My sister can't boil water, let alone an egg, so I could see her problem.

"How many are coming?" I asked.

"Three. And they're already here."

"They're at your house right now?"

Holly nodded and visibly slumped. "They came in last night in time for a sunset boat ride. They're all still sleeping. What am I going to do when they wake up? OMG, what if they're awake right now?" Holly, the acronym queen, just finished several months of therapy to control her nervous habit of using text-speak in place of plain English. She hasn't slipped up in a long time. Until now. And if she stopped right there, this would be only a minor setback. I couldn't help thinking that spitting out, "Oh! My! God!" instead of "OMG" would take the same amount of effort and be much more satisfying.

"Can't Effie handle it?" I asked.

Effie handles all Holly's housework. She's a few years younger than her new husband, in her late twenties, has a farm-girl frame, the strength of a mule, and should be perfectly capable in the kitchen.

"I asked her," Holly said. "Actually begged, but she said no, she doesn't cook."

Chance is a big guy, slightly overweight, which meant he likes his food. Maybe he was the cook in the family. But Holly shook her head when I suggested it. "Well, someone over there must know how to cook for a small group."

"Small!" Holly huffed. "We're talking *five* of us."

Like that was some humungous gathering. Good thing Max didn't suggest entertaining at their house more often. Ongoing dinner parties would send Holly deep into text-speak for sure.

I don't know much about what Max Paine does for a living other than he works for Savour Foods, and he's way up on their food chain, in more than one sense of the word. His company develops flavor enhancers, making things taste better—seasonings, sauces, that sort of thing. Which is ironic, really. Here's Max with a successful career in the food industry, and a wife who can't cook.

"Tell me, what does this visiting team actually work on?" I asked Holly.

"All I know is that they develop top-secret product lines," she said. "The reason I'm so stressed out is because they're food flavorists."

"So?"

"So," Holly said, "they know good food from bad food. They're *flavorists,* for God's sake!"

"I bet they're all a bunch of geeky chemists with slide rules in their pockets," I said. "Probably really dorky, and when they do take time to eat it's probably fast food. Relax."

To tell the truth, I didn't have a clue what a flavorist really was or whether they had gourmet taste buds. What I did know was that my sister Holly is a drama queen. Just because she's a few years younger than me shouldn't give her the right to act like a big baby and expect her older sister to take care of all her problems. We're talking about a woman who has been known to tackle shoplifters and wrestle them to the ground. What had happened to her all of a sudden?

"Hire a caterer," I said next, which seemed like a no-brainer for my wealthy sister.

"I tried," she responded. "Nobody can come on such short notice."

"What about Mom and Grams? They cook."

"Mom said you should do it. Grams can help make lunch. And Mom will take care of things at The Wild Clover while you help me out with tonight's menu."

Great. Just great. *Thanks a bunch, Mom.* "How hard can it be to throw together breakfast?" I said, realizing my fate was sealed. "Go pick up a dozen doughnuts and coffee, then take them out for lunch and dinner."

"I want to make Max happy. He's so proud of me, and now I'm going to be a huge disappointment to him. What am I going to do?" Now my sister shed a few tears for my benefit before saying, "I need you."

I groaned inwardly. I should be harvesting honey and getting ready to open the store. But what could I say? My sister had played the need card.

"Tell you what," I said, caving in. "Go home and freshen up. I'll bring over some bread, some hard-boiled eggs, a few jars of honey butter, and a little fruit. Would that help?"

Holly sniffed. "It's a start."

"What's tonight's menu?" I said, hating to ask.

"I don't know. What are you good at making? It has to be special, something that will impress everybody."

"Anything else I can do?" I put a little sarcasm into my tone, but it zinged right past my sister.

Holly dug a piece of paper out of her back pocket and scanned it. "Bring carrot juice," she said. "Make sure it's organic. One of them is a health nut and drinks it every day. And soy milk, too—another one is lactose intolerant. And no shellfish."

"Okay, I'll do what I can for today. Tomorrow you're on your own." Like that was actually going to happen.

"I'm hoping that they'll leave early Sunday morning for the airport, but that might be wishful thinking. Apparently the team isn't on the best terms with each other. Max says they've been arguing a lot. He thinks a nice relaxed weekend at our house, some boating and fishing, will revive their spirits and build camaraderie."

"So it isn't a business meeting?"

Holly shook her head. "Shop talk is off-limits the entire weekend."

"Okay then. Like I said, I'll figure out something."

And with her immediate worries taken care of, Holly bounced back to her old self, got up, and strolled back to her Jag.

"Let me guess," I said. "You aren't coming in to work for the next few days?"

She chose to ignore me and took off.

Several years ago, I'd purchased an abandoned church and turned it into The Wild Clover, a market where I sell Wisconsin products and produce, purchasing most of my stock locally. I'm immensely proud of my store, from the choir loft I converted into a gathering place for the community, to the honey displays front and center.

Unfortunately, The Wild Clover has been taken over by my family members. Yes, I own it—well, most of it anyway. At least I still have controlling interest. Holly had given me survival cash when I went through my divorce, which I'd thought was a no-interest, no-payment-for-eighteen-months type of loan. I should have read the contract her husband concocted, however, because in reality Holly had bought herself a chunk of my store. I didn't find the damaging clause (buried six feet under in ultra-fine print) until it was way too late.

Even though Holly denies my accusations, I suspect the brilliant idea to trick me out of full ownership came from Mom, who has been trying to worm her way into my business since its inception. In the meantime, I still control the business/financial end, while my family basically dumps the bad stuff on me and runs with the good.

Like what Holly's doing right now. Bailing on her responsibilities in more ways than one.

After first taking the time to hard-boil a dozen eggs, I hurried to the store and opened up. Usually, this is my favorite part of the day, taking a few quiet minutes before starting each new workday to survey my creation and relish the shop's kaleidoscope of colors and aromas. Today, though, I didn't have time to admire my handiwork, thanks to my sister's so-called crisis. I started down the aisles with a small basket.

I have to admit I'm not the world's greatest cook, either, not by a long shot, but owning the store and talking to customers about recipes has given me a quick and easy repertoire of simple, but scrumptious dishes. And as luck would have it, all the ingredients I needed were here at my fingertips. For now, I picked out strawberries, cantaloupe, blueberry muffins, crusty sourdough bread leftover from yesterday, a jar of pumpkin pie honey butter, and another jar of plain whipped butter and honey, and I was good to go.

Except I couldn't go, because Carrie Ann (my cousin and recently promoted store manager) hadn't arrived yet. A few customers came in as soon as I opened the door, and we caught up on news. Easy, because there wasn't any new news. Even the weather—consistently warm and sunny lately—refused to give us any reason to talk about it.

Pretty soon, my cousin came rushing in. Carrie Ann had a drinking problem in the past, but those days might actually be behind her. Hunter is her sponsor and he's doing a great job with her. He had his own problems with alcohol right after high school, when all of us were binging, only Hunter kept right on going until he found AA. He doesn't drink a drop now and has been a good role model for my cousin. She's even dating her ex-husband Gunnar again, and seeing their two kids on a regular basis. And she looks good—spiky, funky hair, a trim figure, and an outgoing personality that works well in our service-related business. That's why I made her manager on a probationary basis. If she can stay on the wagon through the twists and turns of life, the job is hers.

"Sorry I'm late," she said, her voice all rushed like the rest of her. "My alarm didn't go off."

"Everybody uses that exact same excuse," I said, searching my pockets for the truck keys and not finding them. "Now that you're a manager, you have to get more original."

"Ask Gunnar. It's true." Then Carrie Ann gave me a knowing smirk. "I see you and Hunter finally came up for air!" she said, referring to my mini-honeymoon with Hunter. I hadn't said a single thing about our new living arrangement to anybody except Holly, figuring it would leak out fast enough. Apparently it had. I felt a slight tremor shoot through my nervous system imagining what my mother would do to me when she heard.

My mother. What can I say about her? In the past, I've compared her to a rabid bulldog. She used to be stubborn as a mule, overly judgmental, and obsessively concerned with appearances, a façade-like world she built of sticks, and which I used to gleefully smash to pieces. I say she *used to be* all these things, however, because after being a widow for over five years, my mom has a new man in her life: Tom Stocke. I've never seen a woman's personality change overnight before, but now I find she's scary tolerant of me. At least she has been so far. But Mom never really liked Hunter, remembering his wild teenage years more clearly than the man he is today, so the living together news might push her back into mean mode.

"I have to take off," I said to Carrie Ann, refusing to think too hard about my mother's upcoming reaction. "Holly's having a crisis."

"Again?"

I nodded. "And can you call Milly and tell her I need help coming up with an easy but elegant dinner menu for a group of five?" Milly Hopticourt, looking for something fun to do after retiring, published The Wild Clover's monthly newsletter—and it turned out that the woman has a magic touch with recipe creation. I knew she'd come through for me.

"When do you need the menu by?"

"ASAP," I said, finally finding the keys behind the counter next to the register. "It's for tonight."

Right before I left, I remembered Holly's request for carrot juice and soy milk. I ran back to one of the coolers, pulled out the organic brands, and took off in my trusty blue pickup truck.

I like to think I'm a positive person. Or at least, I try to be.

As I drove along, the sun shining, songbirds singing, the air smelling of freshly mowed grass, I remember thinking it was going to be a great day.

Looking back, I should have just kept on truckin' right out of town.

Two

Holly and Max live in a small, exclusive community called Chenequa (pronounced Sha-ni-qua) about five miles from our hometown of Moraine. Wisconsin has a reputation for its tongue-twisting burgs. Some fun ones, those that tourists really mess up, are:

- Oconomowoc (Oh-con-uh-ma-walk)

- Waukesha (Walk-ee-shaw)

- Menomonee Falls (Men-ah-mo-knee falls)

- Mukwonago (Muk-wah-nuh-go)

- Ashwaubenon (Ash-wab-ah-non)

- Kaukauna (Ka-caw-nah)

And that's just a few.
Anyway, Chenequa surrounds Pine Lake, where lake

lots aren't your typical postage-stamp size—these average four acres each. The median home value is a cool $1.4 million. Holly's mansion is a gigantic historic home, completely renovated by the previous owner. Talk about overkill on Holly and Max's part. What childless couple needs six bedrooms and the same amount of full baths? But Max believes the bigger, the better.

Sometimes I wonder if he's compensating for . . . well . . . you know . . . an inadequacy. But that subject (spelled out S-E-X) is a topic my sister and I have always avoided discussing. Though now that Holly's been studying human nature since beginning her therapy sessions, I bet she'd have some insight into the reason behind Max's excessive material cravings.

I spotted Holly waiting for me at the bottom of her long driveway. Holly hopped into the truck, still whimpering a little as we drove around the side of her sprawling mansion and parked.

"They're awake!" she said, like it was some kind of shocking event.

"Don't worry, I've got everything for breakfast right here."

Holly grabbed one of the grocery bags and headed for a large patio table overlooking Pine Lake. She had been setting the table in advance, proving to me that she still could function on a primitive level. On second thought, that wasn't necessarily true, because Effie Anderson popped out through the kitchen patio door with an armload of plates.

"Hi, Effie," I said. "Thanks for helping."

"I keep telling her I won't cook, so don't even suggest it," Effie said before I could suggest it. How did all these people survive without cooking? I wondered. What did they eat? Canned and frozen goods? And didn't they have anything they could defrost for the guests?

"I should offer a basic cooking class at The Wild Clover," I said. "Everybody should know how to cook."

Neither Effie nor Holly let out shouts of joy at the prospect.

Effie seemed distracted and impatient, like she wanted to get back to her regular routine, so when she said to me, "Will you take over from here?" my immediate response was, "Sure thing."

"Oh, I almost forgot, Holly," Effie said, turning to my sister, "I discovered an enormous spider lurking in the rose garden. I almost put my hand right down on it when I was picking a bouquet for the table. Don't let your guests go out there. I'll tell Chance he has to deal with the problem right away."

"Ew. That's it for me," Holly said, turning a lighter shade of tan. "I'm outta the garden for good."

"Spiders are beneficial in a garden," I said to Effie, ignoring my sister's vow to make the garden off-limits. "They keep the pest population down. Spiders are good guys as long as they're left alone. Just like my honeybees, they'll only attack if they feel threatened."

"Except this was a brown recluse spider, I'm certain of it." A brown recluse's venom was powerful stuff, perfectly capable of killing a human.

"Is the thing still out there?" Holly almost shouted.

"Don't worry, I squashed it under my shoe. But there might be more, maybe a whole nest of them."

"I doubt it was a brown recluse," I said, trying to remember if I'd ever seen one of the poisonous spiders, although occasionally I've heard about someone getting bitten. "They're pretty rare in this area. And aren't they nocturnal?"

"I don't know anything about that, but it was big with really long legs. And brown. I'll send Chance to take care of any others," Effie said as she walked off in the direction of the carriage house.

"You're lucky to have her," I said, meaning otherwise Holly might have to actually kill her own spiders and deal with her own dishes.

"A real blessing, both Chance and Effie," she agreed. "Well, let's unpack."

Just as we'd gotten everything laid out, the patio door slid open and out stepped one of the guests I'd previously assumed would be a nerdy dork. She was anything but— tall, thin, and gorgeous, even in the jogging suit she wore. Long ebony hair gathered up in a band, perfectly arched eyebrows, full red-ruby lips, and classic femme fatale body language. She had everything a woman could possibly want in the way of male-enticing attributes.

So I instantly disliked her. Not that I have a history of good judgment regarding first impressions, but this kind of woman makes the rest of us feel small and insignificant. It didn't help that when she opened her mouth, she didn't even acknowledge my existence. I wasn't even worth a glance.

Holly put on a cheesy smile and her best manners (which she has plenty of when she decides to display them) and did the introductions. "Nova Campbell, this is Story Fischer, my sister."

"I don't eat breakfast," Nova said to Holly with a derisive expression, brushing off the introduction like I was a bothersome insect. She paused to take in the spread and found it lacking. I could tell that much by the upturned nose. "Especially this kind. Tell Max . . ." She hesitated over his name, putting some seriously possessive affection into it. ". . . I've gone for a quick run."

Her eyes scanned the table again and hovered over the jar of carrot juice. "And put my juice in the refrigerator. It should be chilled. And make sure no one else drinks any."

With that order, she trotted off.

"Did you see the way she treated me?" Holly said. "Like a servant."

"Please don't tell me she's really part of the team?" I said.

Holly nodded. "You should have seen Effie's reaction when Nova ordered her to carry her bag upstairs. And it's obvious the other members of the team can barely tolerate her. Thankfully, she went up to her room early with a headache, because she was about to give me a major one. I'm trying to stay calm and reserve judgment, but I see the way she looks at Max."

"Nothing to worry about," I said, hopefully. "You're a hard act to follow." That last part was perfectly true. Holly and I have a lot in common in the looks department—same eyes, height, etc.—but somehow she carries herself differently, more refined maybe, and is truly beautiful where I've always considered myself mildly pretty.

Soon after, Max elbowed his way through the door with a pot of coffee in one hand, a cup in the other.

Max Paine is passionate, intelligent, and has more than his fair share of dark hair, which I like on a man. Holly and Max stand almost head to head, and I've always suspected that one of the main reasons Max fell in love with my sister is because she's his equal in every way— strong, smart, and with a passion that matches his own. Except Max is all dark and swarthy and Holly is blond and fair. They started out their life together in classic post-college poverty, until they found out how good Max was at climbing ladders—corporate ones, especially.

Max's face lit up at the sight of his wife. He kissed her even before putting down the load in his hands. That put me more at ease regarding his houseguest's possible secret motives. My sister's husband better keep having eyes only for her, or he'd have me to answer to.

"Look at this beautiful table," he said, taking in the offerings with much more appreciation than Nova had. "Did you do all this yourself, gorgeous?"

Holly's eyes darted to me. She spotted my almost imperceptible nod of conspiratorial consent, so she went ahead and took the credit for breakfast. My sister was going to owe me big-time after this weekend.

"I better get going," I said. "It's going to be a busy day."

"I was hoping for a tour of your hives this afternoon," Max said to me. "My guests have expressed interest in your apiary."

"Really? They're interested?" I loved to show off my bees. It wasn't every day that someone came along and actually requested a tour. Usually, when they find out my backyard is a mini airport for flying insects, they run in the opposite direction. My bro-in-law had just scored major points with me.

"Absolutely. My flavorists are also naturalists," Max told me. "They excel in the natural sciences. Besides, they might find inspiration for a new flavor combination. Honey combined with something unique and exciting? Who knows? Anything is possible. Would later this morning work?"

"Perfect," I said, without thinking about the meal I had to prepare for them later.

"It's a plan then," Max said.

Holly followed me out to my truck. "You saved me this morning," she said. "But we still have a long way to go. Don't forget about dinner."

"Relax," I said, thinking, *Oops, too late*.

"What are you thinking of serving?" Holly was full of eager enthusiasm.

"A surprise," I said. Which was true. Whatever it was would be a surprise to me, too.

Three

On the way out, I saw Chance Anderson, Holly's gardener, trimming around a stand of day lilies near the entrance to the driveway. I stopped the truck, rolled down my window, and Chance's large frame straightened from his task. We spent a few minutes chatting about flowers, him leaning against my truck, me admiring his handwork.

"Everything looks great," I said. "You have a magic touch."

I could tell how proud he was.

"Just trying to keep up with the Joneses." He laughed. "Max's orders."

"That guy . . ." I said, shaking my head, letting the sentence die a natural death. Even the gardener recognized Max had an issue with size.

Chance Anderson is fun, relaxed, muscular, and perpetually tanned from working outdoors. Holly and I share the opinion that the sexiest men on the planet happen to be construction workers. I mean really? How many of us mind slowing down for road work? Not this girl. And Holly thinks Chance would have that same appeal if he'd lose a few pounds.

After silently agreeing with Holly's assessment of Chance, I said good-bye and drove off.

The road through Chenequa is one of the most beautiful I've ever traveled. It's a winding, charming pathway through towering hardwoods with brief glimpses of all those mansions along the lake. Wildflowers frame the sides of the road in magnificent displays of color from early spring to late fall.

When I spotted a four-wheeler stopped along the roadway just off one of our many trails, parked right next to a particularly rich patch of flora, I suspected what was going on even before seeing the coneflowers and columbine bunched in the woman's greedy garden-gloved hand.

"That's illegal," I shouted out the window, pulling over and throwing open the door, pounding over to the woman, who was wearing a safari hat with a strap under her chin and wielding a pair of shears. "You can't pick wildflowers here." This wasn't my first encounter with a violator. Wisconsin has an aggressive wildflower protection law. Not everybody knows that, so I've taken it upon myself to inform them when I bust the thoughtless buggers red-handed.

The woman had a narrow face and froglike protruding eyes, which she used to give me a hard stare. Then she said, "Who says I can't pick these?"

"The Department of Natural Resources," I answered, not really sure whose jurisdiction this particular crime fell under.

She actually had the nerve to bend over and snip off another flower, a beautifully formed purple coneflower.

I hate when people think they can take what doesn't belong to them, especially when they know better. And this woman was now properly informed. She slowly added the coneflower to her bouquet as though intentionally mocking my effort to stop her. I wanted to thump her for the smirk on her face.

"I'm reporting you." I was getting seriously ticked off. "What's your name?"

"Oh, give it up already. Get back in your piece of junk and drive on home." She did a brush-off wave with her hand.

While this wasn't the first time I'd gone out of my way to protect the natural world from human predators, usually when I explain the law to them, they become contrite and apologetic, not outright hostile like this piece-of-work. Where was local law enforcement when you needed it? Knowing our police chief and his motivations, probably hiding down some driveway, waiting to pounce on unsuspecting five-overers rather than actually doing some good for a change.

"Look," I said, with a tone that hopefully conveyed logic and reason, "take what you've already picked, but leave the rest alone, okay? I'm sure you didn't intend any harm."

Her gaze wandered over to a wild monkshood, one of our most valued and protected flowers. Believe me, as a beekeeper, I know my natives, and this one was not going to die at her hand.

"Don't even think it," I warned her, a big part of me wishing I'd breezed right past her without stopping. This day was *not* progressing on track.

She made her move.

I made mine.

Wearing flip-flops (my favorite footwear) during a

confrontation on unstable terrain isn't the best idea, but this wasn't exactly a well-laid plan.

I tripped and grabbed wildly for something to steady myself, which turned out to be the woman's hat. The strap around her chin stretched, and I heard her gurgle, the same sound my grandmother's dog Dinky makes when she yanks too hard at the end of her leash. A sort of gagging, strangling sound.

I really had been trying to stop the woman without getting aggressive. Really I had.

"Get away from me," she croaked when I quickly released the strap. She pushed me away from her and hurried for her ATV with the flowers still in a firm grip.

Because a woman can never be too careful, I thought, What if she has a gun in a storage compartment somewhere on the ATV? Or some other kind of weapon, like pepper spray?

But I decided I'd take my chances. Refusing to even think about consequences, I hustled to keep up, wishing my sister was with me. Where was Holly when I needed *her*? Not around, that's where.

"I'm sorry, I didn't mean to grab you like that," I said, moving faster than her, blocking access to the four-wheeler. "But I'm still reporting you. What's your name?"

"Get out of my way," she said, her buggy eyes almost popping out of their sockets. "And mind your own business. Do-gooders like you drive me nuts. Did you ever stop to consider that I might have a permit to pick these?" I could see the lie in her eyes. Before I had a chance to open my mouth, she continued, "No, of course you didn't. Self-righteous busybodies like you make me sick."

I decided to smirk right through the name-calling, realizing the absurdity of her claim. She went on, "Is this how you locals always treat visitors?"

I was about to blast her with my personal opinion of this particular visitor, but I was getting a really bad feeling in the pit of my stomach. Visitor? We have lots of visitors but still . . .

I groaned inwardly, because that would be just my kind of luck to have a run-in with one of the Paines' houseguests. Please tell me it isn't so.

"*Now* will you get out of my way?" she said, as though reading my mind.

I moved aside, momentarily speechless at the audacity of the woman.

She reached over and started the engine then turned back to me. "Oh, and here, if these are so important, you can have them." And she shoved the flowers right in my face before climbing onto the ATV.

It didn't help my growing concern when she tore off in the direction of my sister's house. And suddenly that particular four-wheeler seemed more than vaguely familiar to me. Maybe the clue was a "Queen Bee Honey" sticker on the back. Exactly like the one I'd stuck on Holly's machine last time I'd ridden it, right after I'd ordered a box of bumper stickers to promote my honey business.

Worse, the woman had left me holding the flowers, i.e. the bag, which was exactly when the police chief decided to pull up behind my truck, the tires of his car crunching on the gravel shoulder.

I have to admit, living in the same town I was born and raised in has its ups and downs.

One of the major downers got out of his vehicle, and glared at me with his hands on his hips. Or at least I suspected that Johnny Jay was glaring—hard to tell behind those mirrored sunglasses he always wore. Power and control were sport to him, and his reflective shades were just one of many props he used to exercise them.

I'd gone from kindergarten through high school with

Johnny Jay, and I didn't like him any better now than I did then. Usually I choose to ignore him when he comes strutting along. Unfortunately, *he* always chooses to badger me.

I pretended not to notice him, hard to do when he was right there in front of me, but I made the effort by refusing to establish eye contact.

"Picking wildflowers is illegal, Fischer," he said, scribbling something on a clipboard. "First I'm going to write out a citation. Them I'm confiscating the evidence."

"I didn't pick these," I said, sounding lame even to me. "Some woman on an ATV did."

He glanced up from the clipboard, "More lies from our *Story*," he said, putting special emphasis on my name. "When are you going to grow up?"

Then he ripped off a sheet of paper and handed it to me.

I couldn't believe the amount of the fine. "That's way overboard!" I complained.

"It costs more when the offender knows better."

While I was staring in sticker shock at the price for a medium-sized bouquet of flowers, I heard a click and looked up in time to see that he had taken a photograph of me with the incriminating wildflowers.

"Hand them over," he ordered.

"They better not show up on your dining room table," I said, reluctantly offering them up.

"You don't get a say."

"I'm not taking this lying down."

"Rumor has it, that's all you've been doing lately," he had the nerve to say. "With Hunter Wallace."

"I'll see you in court."

"It'll be my pleasure. But I tell you, I could use a break from dealing with you, so I'm heading up to the Boundary Waters."

The Boundary Waters, way up north, is as remote as

you can get. The fishing is good but everything has to be helicoptered in. There aren't even any toilets or any phone service, that's how isolated it is. Johnny Jay went at the same time every year and the whole town looks forward to the break. Ten days without the police chief was ten days in heaven.

"I'd be packed and gone right this minute," he said, "if I hadn't had to stop and handle another Fischer incident."

And with that, Moraine's unpopular police chief drove off, leaving me with an expensive problem to deal with.

Thanks to that woman.

Wait until I caught up with her again.

I used my cell phone to call Holly.

"Breakfast is yummy," my sister said, chewing into the phone. "Thanks for bringing it for us."

"Anytime. Listen, tell me, is one of your guests out trail-riding on one of your ATVs this morning?"

"That would be Camilla Bailey. She's one of Max's team members. Oh, here she is, just back from her ride. Why?"

"No reason," I said, hanging up and thinking that this was going to be a really long, stressful day. On one hand, I knew where to find the culprit, so I could make her pay the fine instead of me. On the other hand, her group was visiting my beeyard this afternoon and I'd have to be polite to her. And later I was actually preparing dinner for the Battle-Ax, and her teammate the Ice Queen.

I wished I hadn't gotten out of bed this morning.

Four

Some days, there isn't a thing you can do but try to get through them all in one piece without too much drama and disaster. This was definitely going to be one of them.

Johnny Jay's sneers, plus the pricey ticket he gave me for an act committed by someone else was just one more example of a sucky day happening no matter what I did to try and stop it.

In regards to his allusion—my real name is Melissa Fischer, but I've been called Story as long as I can remember. Mainly because I could look my elders straight in the eye and bald-face lie with such a sweet, angelic expression, it took a long time for them to finally catch on.

I admit it.

I used to make up stuff.

But Johnny Jay is wrong. I *have* grown up. Telling the truth is always the best path—I've learned the hard way—even when the consequences can be more painful than a bunch of angry honeybees defending their hive.

Nonetheless, in spite of my good intentions to tell the truth, the first thing I said to Patti Dwyre when I saw her in The Wild Clover later was, "Love your tattoo." I'd turned right around and lied mere seconds after mentally expounding on the benefits of truthfulness and priding myself on my changed ways.

But when it comes to paying compliments, dishonesty is still a gray area for me. How can I not lie sometimes? Pretending not to notice something as obvious as Patti's tattoo wouldn't work. Not wanting to cause hurt feelings should justify the occasional fib, right?

P.P. Patti, which stands for Pity-Party Patti (the reason becomes apparent quickly), is my next door neighbor and a cub reporter for the local newspaper. She might be inexperienced in investigative journalism, but she makes up for it with unconventional enthusiasm. She views herself through rose-colored glasses, in which she's a step above one of Charlie's angels. The rest of us see her more as a cross between Inspector Clouseau, Maxwell Smart, and a reincarnated medieval torturer.

Patti's mode of attire is always dark. "Shadow wear" she calls it. Today she wore an ebony halter top and a black ball cap, along with a homemade press pass around her neck that she'd made with items from an office supply store. Her pockets are always filled with techno-surveillance electronics, making her hips appear wider than they really are.

The tattoo I was faux admiring ran along her upper right arm.

Everybody in The Wild Clover drew closer to see what Patti had done to herself.

"A snake?" Milly Hopticourt asked after looking it over and breaking the silence. She'd just arrived with fresh bouquets of flowers from her garden to restock a bin near the entrance. In addition to being the one who would bail me out of the menu situation, Milly supplemented her retirement by growing flowers, and we shared the proceeds from the bouquets she sold at the store. "A cobra, I believe," Milly added with perfect confidence after another moment of study.

Patti rolled her eyes. "Noooo," she said. "It's a dragon. Like that woman in the book, the one who sticks it to everybody with her incredible technical skills. It doesn't look anything like a snake."

"I thought it was a lizard," Carrie Ann said, staring at it right along with the rest of us.

"That must have really hurt," I added.

"Drunk at the time, I bet," Carrie Ann, the recovering alcoholic, said, looking like she hoped it were true. My cousin seems to find unnatural delight in learning about other people's alcoholic missteps.

"Can't anybody say one nice thing about it?" Patti said, with a monster whine in her voice. "Story is the only nice one around here. I went through a lot to get it, almost passed out even. The least the rest of you could do is pretend to like it."

"Okay," Stanley Peck said, coming into the store just in time to join in. Stanley is a widower and the only other beekeeper in Moraine. "I'll say I do."

"It doesn't work if you tell me you're pretending," Patti said in a huff.

"Nobody's ever sticking needles in me," Milly said, wincing at the thought.

"It's not permanent," Patti said, and I could see the relief circling around the room. None of us wanted to have to look at that thing on a daily basis.

"Then why are you making such a big deal about fainting and all?" Carrie Ann said for all of us.

"The fumes," Patti said.

"Must have been one whopper-sized bubble gum," Stanley said, referring to those little tattoos we used to find inside gum wrappers.

"It's henna," Patti told us. "And you all can forget it. Forget I even showed it to you."

"We couldn't help seeing it," Milly said. "You didn't have to show us. It's right in our faces." Then she turned to me. "I was thinking an arugula and tomato salad for tonight, maybe some popovers with honey butter . . ."

"Let's go in the back," I interrupted, glad that Milly had started thinking about our dinner project, but hoping I was in time to do damage control, "and talk about it there."

But I was too late.

"What's going on?" Patti said, pouting. "You're planning a party, and you didn't invite me?" She gave me a hard look. "And I thought I was your best friend."

Patti's false assumption about our relationship was getting old. Sure we were friends, but at a distance . . . more like distant friends. Too bad she lived right next door, making the distance between us shorter than I was comfortable with.

I sighed when Milly moved away, leaving me to deal with Patti alone. "Holly and Max are the ones entertaining," I said, angling my way toward the front door. "Milly and I joined forces to prepare dinner for their guests."

"But you were going to invite me, right?"

"It's a business meeting," I lied again, breaking out into the sunshine. "With out-of-town guests."

"So am I invited or not?"

"Not." Sometimes the only way to handle Patti is to take a firm stand.

Her face crumpled. "You know how hard I'm working to keep my stories fresh. I'd like to see *you* find interesting news in a place like this. Lately, I've been covering kids' birthday parties. How pathetic is that?"

"Believe me, this dinner isn't news."

"With my ability to add spin, I could make it a head-liner."

That wasn't far from the truth. Patti definitely has a knack for bringing out the very worst in people. She also tended to create problems for anybody in close proximity to her. Which is usually me.

"You can't come," I said. "And that's final."

Patti, with a pout on her face, said, "Have you seen my water bottle? Is it in your office? I can't remember where I left it."

I glanced at the empty holster on her belt.

The latest addition to her arsenal was a personalized water bottle in a holster.

She'd ordered it online, with custom inscription that read "Stalkers Have Rights, Too" on one side and "I'm Watching You" on the other.

Who in their right mind supports stalking?

"You'd be surprised how dehydrated I can get when I'm following a story and a source," she'd said when the water bottle had first arrived. "This puppy goes in like this, and"—she'd strapped the holster around her waist, tucked in her new bottle, and put her arms in the air as if she had a gun aimed at her—"hands-free water!"

"Cool," I'd said at the time, one of those complimentary sort of fibs that I'm always struggling with, same as with the positive feedback I'd given her about the dragon tattoo.

"I haven't seen it," I told her now, thinking to myself that it could stay lost for all I cared.

Then I noticed the time. Max and his guests would be at my house very soon, wanting a tour of the beeyard.

"I have to run," I said.

"Where are you going?" Patti called out behind me. I pretended not to hear her.

A mistake, I know, because all she did was follow me, and popped up later where she shouldn't have popped up.

Five

Max called my cell phone to tell me they were running late, but that was after I'd already left the store for home. So I had extra time to go a few rounds with Lori Spandle, our local real estate agent and my archenemy. She was standing in the driveway of the house next to mine. Not Patti's driveway, but the one on the other side, where my ex-husband Clay used to live after we separated.

Technically, Clay still owns it, since by the time he gave up on the concept of "us" and left town, the housing bubble had burst. His house has lingered on the market ever since.

"What are you up to?" I asked Lori, hoping she had a decent buyer on the line.

Lori has a face like a pumpkin (round and orangish), and a personality like an invasive weed, i.e. obnoxious. She's been known to play around on her husband, our town chairman, a fact I learned when she slept with mine.

We've been butting heads since grade school, and she's less than thrilled that I know about her cheating ways. You would think she'd treat me with more respect considering what I know. I tell you, this town is barely big enough for both of us.

"Since I can't sell this place because of you and those damn bees," she said. "I'm going to have to rent it out."

"Again?"

Last time she'd done that there had been hell to pay. But that's a whole other story.

"This time I checked references," she said, snooty as ever.

Lori seemed way too pleased with herself. She was plotting something against me, that was for sure.

A casual observer, who doesn't know all the residents of this town as well as I do, might think I have an extreme case of people paranoia. But I know exactly what everybody in Moraine is capable of, and running the store has given me even more insight—some of it downright scary. One thing I've realized is this: Every single one of us has razor-sharp retractable claws. We go about our lives with them mostly sheathed. But it's only a matter of time before something happens to set one of us off, and we're ready to scratch somebody else's eyes out.

If Lori was grinning at me, she had just filed her nails into deadly daggers.

Before I could find out what she was up to, a car pulled up. I watched a tire scrape against the curb, bounce up onto it for a moment, then bang back down.

Grams.

My sweet grandmother was behind the wheel of her Cadillac Fleetwood. Even though she's becoming a minor menace to society, Grams still has a valid driver's license and isn't giving it up no matter what anybody says.

Besides, everybody in Moraine recognizes her car and gets out of her way when we see her coming.

"For cripes' sake," my mother said, getting out of the backseat. "See, Tom," she addressed her significant other, who was opening the passenger seat door with Grams's dog Dinky in his arms, "I told you. She shouldn't be allowed to drive anymore."

Oh, geez, Mom could be chairwoman of a new organization, Daughters Against Aging Relatives. Next she'd be passing a petition around town. Not that anyone would sign it. The residents of Moraine love my grandmother.

I've told Mom a zillion times to stop riding with Grams if she can't handle it, but my mother thinks she's somehow protecting Grams by being next to her. I have visions of Grams driving right for a big oak tree to get Mom to shut up, but that won't really happen. Grams is an angel when it comes to tolerating her lippy daughter.

"Hi, sweetie," Grams called to me, coming around the front of her car, looking as fresh as the mock orange blossom tucked in her gray bun.

"I wasn't expecting company," I said, a little confused by their appearance. Usually, I'd be at the store at this time of day, not home. "What's going on?"

"It's none of your concern," Lori said to me with a lot of snap in her tone.

"Still as peppy as ever, I see," Grams said to her. "But that's my granddaughter you're speaking to in that condescending tone of voice."

"Sorry, ma'am," Lori said.

Nobody messes with my grandmother. Not if they know what's good for them.

"Let's get a family picture," Grams said. "Helen and Tom, get right behind Story, and Tom, let Story hold Dinky. That's right. Helen, get in there."

Mom gave a big, loud, impatient sigh, but she did what she was told.

Dinky sure was happy to see me. I'd been her foster mom for a while, before I pawned her off on Grams. Dinky has her share of issues—peeing on people's feet and chewing up undergarments—but she's in obedience training with Hunter, so we'll see. If anybody can train her, it'll be Hunter.

"Well?" Lori said impatiently as soon as Grams was through with the photo shoot.

Shouldn't that woman be moving off by now, not hanging around us? And that comment she'd made, about it not being any of my business. What was that all about?

"What's going on?" I asked again while Grams took another picture, this time of Lori scowling.

"I'm looking at the house," Tom said, glancing sharply at my mom.

"To buy?" I asked.

"To rent. My place isn't very big."

That was certainly an understatement. Tom owned the antique store in town and lived in a tiny apartment in back of it. Small, yes, but fine for only one person . . . it wasn't half bad, unless . . .

I shot a look at my mother. She wouldn't meet my eyes.

"These two lovebirds," Grams announced, taking Dinky out of my arms, "are shacking up!"

At first I panicked, thinking she was talking about Hunter and me. Then I noticed that she was beaming at the *other* two lovebirds.

Okay, I didn't see that coming. My mom? And her boyfriend? Get out!

"But . . . but . . . ," I stammered. "You hardly know each other." I was barely used to the idea of my mother dating for the first time since my dad's death. Now she was moving in with the guy? And next door to me? This was too much, too fast.

"Sweetie pie," Grams said to me. "Don't be a prude."

I'm sure my mouth was wide open in total surprise. I took a good look back at my house, the one I'd grown up in with my mother and my father. How could Mom even think about living next door to it with another man?

"There must be other houses for rent," I said to Mom.

Lori butted in, "There aren't. This is the only one."

That was such a lie! I could see it in her evil little eyes.

"It's only for a little while," Mom said to me. "Until we find something more permanent, when we decide to make the next step."

"You have to sign the lease for a year," Lori told her.

"Six months is the most we'll consider," Tom said.

"Fine!" came the reply.

I turned to Grams. "Then you'll be alone, all alone." To Mom, "You can't abandon Grams."

Grams said, "I like living alone. Besides, Helen and I knew it was a temporary solution after your father died. We never thought it would last as long as it did. Your mother needs to spread her wings."

Like Mom was a teenager going out in the world for the first time!

"She should start slowly, with a place of her own first," I said, talking over Mom's head.

Tom, smart man that he was, kept out of it. He didn't say a word. Tom Stocke isn't a handsome man, not by a long shot, but he's a kind, considerate, easygoing guy, just what my mom needs to offset her sometimes anxious personality.

"You're living with Hunter," Mom pointed out. "Talk about calling the kettle black."

"She is?" Grams brightened even more, if that's possible. "That Hunter is a sex bomb."

"Mother!" my mom said to Grams. Tom was trying to hide his amusement but I saw it twitching at the corners of his mouth.

"Who told you we were living together?" I asked Mom. It sure hadn't taken long for news to travel out to the farm.

"Just about everybody, including that busybody neighbor of yours."

Patti has the biggest mouth.

"Are you ready yet?" Lori said to anybody who would listen. "I have a commercial showing in Stone Bank in an hour. Let's get started." Then she turned away and gave me an over-the-shoulder smirk.

With that, they left me standing between the two houses, alone, with my mouth hanging open in disbelief.

Not only did I have to absorb the disturbing fact that my mother was going to live with a man who was clearly not my father, worse, she was going to do it next door to me?

This day was beyond sucky.

It was an absolute killer.

Six

"Fascinating," Gil Green, the only male on Max's three-person flavorist team, said.

Gil had an excess of flab, blobbing up and over his belt and swelling all the way up to his jowls. But he made up for his fat with skinny, toothpick legs, making him look like a pregnant stork.

Max's employees were an odd-duck group, although not a single one of them had a pocket ruler as I'd expected.

Aside from his mismatched body, Gil had perfectly white, straight teeth that must have cost him a small fortune. And he had unsuccessfully tried to cover up his wedding ring tan with bottled bronze, which had turned it the color of rust. I didn't even want to think about what that move implied.

He also was a master gardener, he informed me when he feasted his eyes on all the flowers I'd planted for my honeybees. To show off his education, he insisted on

naming every single one of them in Latin *and* French.
Think "pompous ass."

Nova Campbell, I noted gleefully, didn't look as good
cleaned up as she had in the jogging suit. This morning
she'd had a fresh rosy complexion. Now she looked a little
green around her sharklike gills.

Max, Gil, Nova, and I were out in the apiary or, as I
informally call it, the beeyard. Holly was hugging the side
of the house to stay clear of the honeybees, and Camilla
had headed in the other direction as soon as they'd pulled
up without even glancing this way. Max said she needed to
get some fresh air.

She was going to need an oxygen tank when I got done
with her.

As I showed them around, I reveled in the fact that
Camilla still didn't know who she was dealing with. I
couldn't wait to see her face when she connected this tour
guide with the concerned citizen she'd treated so poorly.
I definitely had the home advantage.

Mom and entourage had finished up before the flavorists arrived. My mother had refused to discuss the
subject of the house with me even though I'd tried. Tom
maintained a poker face. Grams was busy taking photo-
graphs of just about everything when I attempted to quiz
her. But she said she didn't want to get between us, implying that Mom had warned her off. Lori had a stupid smirk
on her face, but that was her standard expression.

I had to find a moment soon to tell my sister what just
had happened with Mom and Tom, how they planned to
move in together right next door. But first the tour.

One of the aspects about beekeeping that fascinates people the most is when I work in my beeyard without protective gear, which I often do if I'm not harvesting honey. My
bees know me. They're used to me puttering around near
their hives, even opening them up and peeking in to see

what progress they've made. Beekeeping gear is cumbersome, too hot in the summer for comfort, and unnecessary unless I'm going in to steal their nectar (which I still needed to do since Holly had interrupted me early this morning).

Even those thick beekeeper's gloves are more of a burden than they're worth to prevent an occasional sting. My thumb gets nailed occasionally, but that's usually only if I'm careless and stick it on top of a bee while she's trying to go about her business.

The trick is to move slowly and stay alert.

Here are a few fun facts I shared with my audience after locating the queen inside one of the hives and pointing her out to them:

- Worker honeybees live only about four weeks, but the queen can live three or four years.

- During her once-in-her-lifetime lovemaking flight, she might mate with as many as fifteen or more drones.

- This tiny boss lady will then store all the sperm in a special body sac, because for her, once is enough.

- Worker bees feed her while she lays between five hundred and fifteen hundred eggs daily.

- She gets to choose the sex of each bee.

- If she fertilizes the egg, it's a girl. (She wants lots of girls because they wait on her hand and foot.)

- If she doesn't fertilize the egg, it's a boy. (And really, how many of those does she need, since they do nothing but lounge until that one and only mating flight?)

"That would be the life for me," Gil said, really enjoying the role of the drones. "All those females working, satisfying my every need."

"Well, at the end of the season," I added for his benefit, "the drones are kicked out to starve or freeze to death."

"Forget that," Gil said, changing his mind fast.

Just then, Camilla rounded the side of the house. Her bug eyes slid over the group in front of her and landed on me.

I grinned.

She didn't crack a smile, that's for sure. But I was really pleased to see her mouth pop open in surprise, just like mine had done when Mom and entourage informed me of Mom's future living arrangements.

Max tried to introduce us, but I stopped him. "We've met," I said, smug as a bug in a rug—or is it *snug*?

"This woman is your sister-in-law?" Camilla said to Max, forgetting her manners—if she even had any—with a bit of finger pointing. "She accosted me earlier."

Okay, that was rather extreme. "She was picking endangered native flowers," I shot back. "And you and I still need to have a little talk," I added, glaring at her.

"You're a menace," the flower stealer said. "I have witnesses this time, so hands off."

An uncomfortable silence ensued but didn't last long because Holly interrupted with a shrill scream. "One's on my arm!" she yelled.

Her husband rushed over to save her, accomplished the heroic feat, and rejoined us.

"Holly," Nova called out after assuming a possessive position next to Max, "you're missing out on all the fun." Then to Max, "Is she *always* like this?"

"Holly," I hollered, "you better get over here right now!"

"In a minute," she answered. As if.

My sister really needed to get with the program and defend her turf. I, in turn, would do my sisterly duty by keeping a watchful eye. Max, however, didn't seem to notice that Nova was making a play for him. Men can be so dense.

"If you're not interested, then why don't you run along home?" Nova called to Holly. "That staff of yours could use some watching over. They need someone who actually knows how to train them properly."

Well, wasn't that nasty!

"Nova!" Max said, a warning in his tone.

"I didn't mean that," Nova said to Holly, who was scowling, then to Max with a steamy smile, "I really didn't."

Then she went back to her preoccupation with hovering over Max, who was standing right beside me, fearless in the face of thousands of miniature insects. A few honeybees landed on Nova, too, but she didn't seem to mind, or else she was trying to impress Max. Or possibly she figured her stinger was more lethal than theirs.

Sting her good, I silently put out into the honeybee universe, hoping my little friends would get the message. Sadly, they didn't.

My backyard isn't very wide but it's long—perfect for plenty of hives—and it leads right down to the Oconomowoc River, where my kayak rests on the bank when I'm not out exploring river life. My favorite way to spend an evening is paddling along, taking in the calls of the wild and breathing fresh, fragrant air.

"What's that little place used for?" Max asked, pointing at my honey house, the small building where I process honey for packaging under the Queen Bee Honey label.

"Let me show you," I said, heading that way.

"I'm going down to the store," Holly called to us. "Meet me there later." And with that, before I had a chance to drag her into the group, she vanished around the side of the house.

My sister is denser than her husband when it comes to

handling dangerous women. But lucky for Holly, it turned out that Nova had other things on her mind at the moment.

"I'm not feeling well," Nova said to Max as I opened the honey house door and caught a whiff of that wonderful nectar. "I think I'll wait out here."

She *did* look flushed. I pointed out a bench down at the riverfront, and Nova walked toward it.

"Are you going to be okay?" Max called after her.

"I just need a minute," she said without turning. "A little nauseated, that's all."

The atmosphere became a few degrees lighter with her gone. Camilla and I weren't speaking directly to each other, though our eyes suggested continuing hostility, but even with that added stress, I was relieved that Nova wasn't inside with us. Everyone seemed to breathe easier (or was that just me?) while I showed them the equipment I used and let them sample some of my products, which included my latest experiment with adding rose petals to honey. A successful experiment I might add. It's delicious on scones.

We must have been in the honey house less than fifteen minutes, but when we came out, Nova wasn't in sight.

"Maybe she's waiting in the car," Gil suggested, heading for the driveway. "I'll go check."

Max gave me an appreciative smile. "Thank you for taking the time to show my associates your truly amazing apiary."

"The pleasure is mine," I told him and realized I meant it, even with Nova stalking Max and my issues with Camilla. I really loved showing off my work to people who appreciated it.

"Nova isn't in the car," Gil said, coming back.

"My kayak's still on shore, so she can't be out on the water," I said, walking toward the river, thinking she might have strolled farther up- or downstream on the bank.

As it turned out, I was sort of correct.

Nova wasn't on the water.

She was in it.

Arms spread, like she was doing a front float, face-down in the shallow water.

As I rushed toward her, I thought I saw a flash of movement on Patti Dwyre's part of the river frontage.

But when I looked again, nothing was there.

Except Nova was still in float position.

Max and Gil waded in right behind and overtook me. Camilla and I moved out of their way so that they could pull her out while I called 9-1-1 on my cell phone.

CPR turned out to be useless, even though the two men kept at it long after we all knew they couldn't save her. One hundred pumps per minute, more slowly as they realized the hopelessness of the situation. Not that it mattered. She wasn't responding to their efforts.

I couldn't help feeling guilty, because I'd gotten my careless wish.

Nova Campbell was gone for good.

Seven

We formed a tight circle around Nova, staring as if her eyes might flutter and she would sit up any second. While we waited for the emergency response I'd called in, Max and Gil continued to take turns trying to spark life. It must have been all of five minutes but it felt like five hours before sirens wailed. My numb brain realized I probably should have called Hunter to inform him of the dead body in his new backyard, but I still couldn't believe it was really happening.

Camilla and I weren't doing dagger eyes anymore. More important things had cropped up.

At some point Patti Dwyre appeared, and I noticed that the bottom half of her black sweatpants were soaking wet and her black sneakers squished with water, but I promptly put that information out of my mind, storing it for later.

"Who drowns in two feet of water?" Camilla wanted to know.

Who *does* drown in two feet of water?

"Suicide?" Patti suggested. "Was she unhappy enough to do this?"

Everybody shrugged, although that wasn't much of a possibility. I mean come on, would Nova really take her own life while all her colleagues were inside my honey house? While I hadn't liked her, she hadn't seemed either depressed or unbalanced enough for that to make sense.

Max had another idea, one that seemed more likely. "Maybe she had a brain aneurism and stroked out, falling face-first."

Everybody considered that.

The sirens were loud now, right out front.

"Or a heart attack," Gil added. "Those health nuts drop like flies."

Just then, Officer Sally Maylor pulled into the driveway and got out of her squad car. Sally is a good cop and a regular customer at the store. For a second or two, I expected Chief Johnny Jay to drive in right behind her. Then I remembered about his vacation. Thank God for small miracles. He would have ripped me up and down over what had just happened. This situation was definitely beyond my control, but he wouldn't have cared. He'd have been in my face so close I'd have been able to count his nose hairs.

"Back off, everybody," Sally said, and we cleared out to give her room.

An ambulance arrived right behind her. The emergency professionals took over, and the rest of us moved up to the house and watched the proceedings with heavy hearts and stilled voices.

Other cops started cordoning off the front yard to keep the gawkers under control.

Jackson Davis, the medical examiner, showed up in a white van. We're friendly, so he nodded to me in acknowledgment as he headed toward the ambulance crew.

Pretty soon, we saw a stretcher and empty body bag going past us toward the river. A few minutes later, it went the other way. The body bag wasn't empty this time. I felt sick to my stomach. It still seemed surreal.

Sally came over to us to get our statements, but first she pulled me aside and in a low voice asked, "Who are these people with Max?"

"Houseguests." I explained about the apiary tour. There wasn't much to tell.

"Looks like she drowned in water only up to her knees." Sally shook her head, as confused as the rest of us. "We'll know more after Jackson does an autopsy."

"How long will that take?"

"He's going to work on it immediately. We should have a preliminary report soon."

"She obviously must've had some sort of a serious medical condition and unfortunately had an attack of some kind at the river. Then she fell in and drowned."

"A medical explanation would make everything nice and clean," Sally said optimistically, before heading over to the others to do her job.

If only Nova had called out, I thought. If only we hadn't all been inside the honey house. If only . . .

At least my mother hadn't been standing right next door when it happened. Mom has a habit of showing up at the most inopportune moments, times that make me appear to be part of the problem, so it was a relief to have her out of the picture. Although she'd hear about it soon enough.

For once, Holly was going to be part of this particular equation, and she just might soften the blow. Then I realized that my sister hadn't actually been here when it happened. Like always, she was off the hook, leaving me to dangle alone.

Eight

I went over to The Wild Clover and found Holly in the back room finishing up a phone conversation with Max. She hung up.

"What a shock," she said, actually sounding sincere. "I mean, I didn't like her—I knew what Nova was up to, you know? She was making a run for my husband—but this is still terrible."

"It looked that way to me, too."

"I trust Max. Our relationship has been based on honesty and faith. It's especially important since he travels so much. Still, it bothered me."

"Well, she's gone now," I said, pretty shocked myself at what had happened right under my nose, at how quickly a living breathing human being can come to an end. But I barely knew the woman and what little I'd seen hadn't endeared her to me.

"I just wish this had happened someplace else," Holly said. "Another time, a place far away."

"I'm with you on that one. Max has to be major upset."

My sister nodded. "He took the others out for a late lunch," she told me. "He said I should stay here with you."

"I thought Grams was making lunch for them."

"Miscommunication. She thought Mom had taken the casserole out of the oven, and Mom thought Grams had. It burned up while they were out and about."

"Those two are like a comedy act." I took a deep breath, feeling weighed down by today's events. Which reminded me. "Mom's going to move in with Tom," I announced. "Can you believe it?"

"That's nice for Mom." Holly wasn't fazed one bit. "I'm happy for her."

"Am I the only one in the family who finds this disturbing?"

"Mom's moving forward with her life. You have to accept that."

"Are you psychoanalyzing me?"

Holly shrugged. "You're easy to read. Even though Dad's been gone over five years, you're still grieving for him, so you've created a world where Dad still exists on some level. Seeing Mom with another man is like the final nail in Dad's coffin."

"But they're going to move in right next to me! Lori has them all ready to sign papers. They were over there looking at it this morning. For all I know, they already *are* my neighbors."

"That," Holly agreed, "would be a total disaster."

"Mom's always been concerned about what the neighbors are going to say about everything. What happened this time?"

"Well, in this case she doesn't care, since you're her only neighbor."

"Very funny. You know what I mean."

"You'll adjust to the idea."

I changed the subject to discussing that night's dinner.

"How can you even think about food at a time like this?" Holly sighed. "Is anybody going to feel like eating anyway after what happened?"

"Are you kidding?" I said. "Why do you think a big meal is served right after every funeral?" Which was true. There's nothing like a big meal to ease some of the pain of loss. "Tonight's gathering will be like a wake. People also need to talk through their feelings."

"I suppose."

"Unless you want to do a carry-out or something."

Holly made a face.

"I have an idea. Max likes to barbecue," I said. "How about having him grill some steaks? And Milly said she's going to whip up a nice salad with vegetables from her garden, and popovers."

My sister glanced at me and frowned. "If Max is doing the entree and Milly's supplying the sides, then what's your role? Aren't you supposed to be handling the meal?"

"I am handling it. I'm the manager. You should try it sometime. Delegating really works." Suddenly I realized that Holly already knew how to delegate—she'd pawned everything off on me!

Right then someone tapped on the back room door, and after my shout to come in, Sally Maylor appeared in the doorway. She didn't look happy. "Story, Holly, there you are. I have a few more questions for both of you. Mind if I sit down?" She closed the door behind her.

"Sure," I said, popping up and unfolding an extra metal chair. "But I can't add any more to what I already told you."

"Maybe not, but Holly might be able to clear up a few things." She sat down and turned her attention to my sister. "Exactly how well did you know the deceased?"

Holly looked surprised at the question. "Not well at all. She worked for my husband, but I met her for the first time last night."

"And how did you two get along?"

Holly hesitated, then said, "Fine, I guess."

"Hold it!" I said a little louder than I expected. "Why the twenty questions? What do you care about Holly's relationship with one of her husband's employees?"

"It's standard procedure."

It certainly was not standard in the case of an accident. Were they thinking . . . murder?

Holly's cell phone rang. "I have to take this. I'll be right back," she said, hurrying out and leaving me alone with Sally.

"You might as well tell me what's going on," I said. "Or I'll call Jackson Davis myself." The medical examiner and I are good friends. He's shared details with me in the past, and I hoped he would this time, too.

Sally gave me a hard look.

Neither of us said the obvious, that I was also living with a cop who had inside connections. Between Hunter and Jackson, I'd get to the truth in no time flat.

"I won't tell a soul," I promised.

"We're just following up," Sally said, still dodging. "Looking at every angle. What was your opinion of Nova Campbell?"

"I didn't have one," I sort of fibbed. "I only just met her today. What do you think happened?"

"The ME has his suspicions, that's all I'm saying. More samples are going to the lab for testing."

"If she didn't drown, then what?"

"I really can't say."

"So she didn't drown? No heart condition?" I asked. "How about a brain clot?"

"I really have a few more questions for your sister. If

you think of anything to add to your own earlier statement, the smallest detail, let me know."

Geez, Sally was being difficult. And I'd given her discounts at the store, too.

She stood up, ready to track down Holly, and said, "This should be handled by the police chief. I tried to contact Chief Jay to tell him to turn around and come back, but he's out of contact range already. That's why he decided on the Boundary Waters in the first place, so he'd be incommunicado the whole time. Talk about poor timing."

"That's too bad," I lied. As far as I was concerned, Sally was wrong; the timing couldn't be any better.

"Until we can locate him, I've asked the Waukesha County Sheriff's Department for support. They'll assist with the investigation."

Suddenly, I grew wary. My premonition kicked in. "Who's been assigned to the case?" I asked.

"Not Hunter Wallace, if that's what you think," she said, reading my mind. "But he's looking for you, and he isn't happy."

Uh-oh. The honeymoon was definitely over.

Nine

"What the hell happened here?" Hunter demanded over the phone. He sounded just like Johnny Jay. As if this were my fault.

"She just keeled over dead while the rest of us were in the honey house," I said.

"Shouldn't I have been one of the first to know?"

"I wasn't thinking straight."

"Please don't tell me you gave her anything to eat or drink."

Okay, that was totally uncalled for! "What is that supposed to mean? Like my cooking is deadly?"

"Did you or did you not feed her anything?"

"I'm not even answering that." I was so mad at Hunter, I almost missed the implication of what he was saying. "Wait a sec, does this mean Nova was poisoned?"

"I don't know. Maybe. The ME suggested the possibil-

ity, but that's between you and me, okay?" A slight pause
then he said, "Say, 'Okay, Hunter, I promise.'"

"Okay, okay, I promise."

"So, did Nova Campbell eat anything?"

I could have mentioned the breakfast I'd taken over, but
I wasn't even sure she ate any of that, and I didn't appreciate Hunter right this minute, so I said instead, "And I still
resent that. Geez. You eat my food. Are you dead?"

Hunter had on his professional work voice and an attitude I didn't care for one bit. "Did anybody act suspicious?"
he asked.

I could have answered that Nova herself had been the
only one acting suspicious, but I figured that didn't count.
"Her death doesn't have to be murder, you know," I said.
"She was a health nut, probably ate something she found
outside, thinking she was Euell Gibbons. You remember,
that outdoor guy who said a pine tree was edible and
actually gnawed on the bark to prove it?"

Hunter sighed as though he had a massive headache.
"Homicide can't be ruled out until the department has more
information and determines otherwise. That's standard
procedure. I want to get over to Holly's house, and offer my
assistance. They have a team going through there right now.
Nobody can go back inside until they're satisfied."

"Where are Holly and her guests supposed to go?"

"That's their problem. I have my own."

"What are they looking for over at Holly's house anyway? It's not like Nova died there."

"When they're done, they're going to comb the riverbank," he said, dodging my question. "They probably
won't find anything after all the tromping around. Sally
should have been more careful. She just assumed it was
natural causes and didn't take precautions. Like I said, I
have my own problems."

"What exactly *are* your problems?" I was starting to get even more testy. *I'm* the one who'd had to deal with finding a dead body.

"It happened right in my backyard," he said. "That makes me involved on a personal level. I should be heading up this investigation, but how can I when the death occurred right where I live?"

"So you excused yourself from the case?" I didn't know if cops did that, but attorneys did when they had conflicts of interest. I knew that much.

"I had to, and I had to tell the captain why. This is a huge conflict of interest." I could sense Hunter was squirming a little. I also sensed he wasn't telling me something. "What?" I said.

"The captain didn't know that I . . . eh . . . we . . . lived together until this happened."

"So now was when you got around to telling her?" I heard the anger in my voice. "When you had to?"

I'd met Hunter's superior once. She was a formidable human being, tough as nails, probably chewed them for breakfast, but still . . . I was beyond testy now, just thinking about Hunter's commitment issues.

"You were hiding me," I said, "like a dog in a no-pets-allowed apartment building." He didn't have to say it, because I'm good at filling in the blanks. He hadn't planned to publically announce our arrangement in case it didn't work out! In which case, he thought he'd just slip out the back door and nobody would be the wiser. I fumed, letting some of my divorce damage influence my thinking.

"That's not true," Hunter insisted. "It's just that I don't like mixing my personal life with my professional life, that's all. Not that I've ever had one to share before. Story, I'm learning as I go, and I'm sorry I disappointed you."

I sniffed.

Hunter sighed again and said, "The best answer, the

most logical, is to find Johnny Jay and get him back here to do his job. But until the chopper he took to the Boundary Waters gets back to civilization, nobody even knows where he went."

I really wanted my man back, the earlier version who had eyed me up with a promising smirk and a twinkle in his eye. This new guy wasn't nearly as likeable. For a very brief second or two I actually toyed with going into the Boundary Waters myself and dragging the police chief home.

Even if it meant my butt on the hot seat. Which it would, knowing Johnny Jay. He would suspect me of wrongdoing just for being in the vicinity of a dead person, and this time it had happened right in my yard. Handcuffs and jail, for sure.

I cursed the day that man had become our police chief. I've had a target on my back ever since.

I sent a silent message to the police chief, threw it up in the air, and wished it Godspeed.

Run, Johnny. Run!

Ten

"Arugula, tomatoes . . ." Milly ticked off a list of supplies she needed for the meal. I was already sick and tired of the whole affair, and we had hardly started. "Red onions. . . ." She had a shopping basket over her arm and added items as she went. "Dijon mustard . . ."

"I have arugula in my garden," I told her. "I'll go get some in a few minutes."

"No hurry. You can bring it to Holly's when you come."

Then off she went down aisle four while I picked through the bone-in rib eyes, doing a mental head count and adding a few more steaks for good measure. That way we'd be prepared in case someone unexpected showed up or Max overcooked one. Lots of reasons for spares, especially when your rich sister is paying.

Holly had decided to take charge of dessert, which meant she was pondering which of the local cheesecakes in the frozen food aisle to defrost. We've got a rainbow of flavors, so she was good there.

Right then, Patti Dwyre crept up behind me—a bad habit of hers—and said, "I'm starting to think you're jinxed."

"Oh, come on, that isn't fair."

"The value of my house is going to drop like a rock."

"Save that sort of talk for Lori and her next rampage. She tells me that all the time." I almost opened my mouth to ask Patti about the state of her attire at the time of Nova's death, but decided I had other things on my mind at the moment. Patti could wait.

I set aside the steaks, and debated which potatoes to get. Red or fingerling? I decided on red.

Patti didn't miss the clues leading up to tonight's event as she followed me around in produce. "You're getting ready for that 'big' dinner that I'm not invited to?" she asked, using finger quotes.

"You got it."

"You're a hard person to stay friends with."

"Look who's talking."

We locked eyes. "What is that supposed to mean?" she said, narrowing hers.

"I really am busy right now."

"No, really, I insist." Now the Pity-Party face arranged itself, getting ready to whine.

I shouldn't have opened my big mouth. Now I was stuck. So I said what had been on my mind ever since we scooped Nova out of the river. "Your pants and shoes were soaking wet when you joined us on the riverbank," I said. "You have some explaining to do."

"I didn't hold that woman under water, if that's what you think."

Patti had a smug look on her face, like she knew something and was about to gloat. She also was hiding something. I was sure of it.

I put my basket down next to the potato bin and grabbed Patti's arm, heading for the back room where we'd have more privacy.

"She didn't drown," Patti said, "And we both know it."

I really wanted to share what I knew with somebody. My sister was too involved and would freak out. But Patti was the town's official gossip, an overzealous reporter, and if the verdict came back murder one, Patti was at the top of my suspect list, based on her mysterious whereabouts at the time of death. Still, most of me totally believed Patti didn't do it. After all, what would be her motive? Besides, Patti was really wound up. If she'd been the one who offed Nova, she would have stayed in the background, which she does all the time, and she's really good at it.

"Whatever we're about to discuss about cause of death," I warned her, "has to stay between me and you. Holly can't know."

"You're kidding right? I'm a reporter now. I've learned to keep information tight to my chest."

"You don't keep anything confidential. That's your job. To blab."

"Besides," she said as if I hadn't spoken, "I already know exactly what really happened without any input from you. Nova Campbell was poisoned."

Okay, now Patti had my full attention. "Who told you that?" I asked her, trying to appear surprised instead of suspicious.

"Nobody. I guessed."

"That was more than a good guess. Can you please explain how you came to that conclusion ahead of all of us, including even before the medical examiner?"

"I bet Jackson knew the minute he saw her. Because she didn't have a drowned expression on her face."

"Which is?"

Patti demonstrated with a lax, calm, openmouthed,

sightless expression, making me wonder for the ump-teenth time if she had all her marbles.

"That's drowned," she said. "Here's poisoned."

This time she screwed up her face, sticking her tongue way out and bulging her eyes.

I had to admit, that was the exact look on Nova's dead face, that second one.

"What killed her off?" Patti wanted to know once she put her features back in place. "Strychnine? Cyanide? So many perfect poisons to choose from!"

"It doesn't have to be murder," I pointed out. "She could have eaten something that . . ."

". . . gave her fatal indigestion?" Patti finished for me, the hint of sarcasm telling me she didn't believe it for one second.

"What about mushrooms? What if she picked and ate poisonous mushrooms?" I did a mental checklist of toxic possibilities—fungi and plants from our area:

- Little brown mushrooms—a person has to assume all brown ones are bad since they all look alike.

- Lilies of the Valley—even the water in a glass they've been kept in is poisonous.

- Rhododendrons—don't use the flowers to make tea if you want to see tomorrow.

- Yew trees—American or Japanese, same thing, don't steep the leaves.

- Rhubarb—the vegetable is tasty, but the leaves can kill you.

"She could have ingested a whole host of different things," Patti agreed. "Ammonia, mothballs, kerosene, insect repellent."

I took a moment to stare at Patti, then said, "Yes, but I was thinking more along the lines of accidental ingestion. Who would eat anything from your list unless they wanted to commit suicide the hard way? And none of those items make effective murder weapons. Can you imagine trying to slip mothballs into someone's food without them knowing? Impossible."

"True, but someone could have given her LSD. Maybe she was hallucinating and thought she was a fish."

"I have work to do," I said, realizing this conversation was getting more ridiculous by the minute. I went back out to the produce section and finished selecting potatoes. Patti was still my shadow.

"Let me help you," she said.

"Milly and I have tonight's dinner handled, but thanks for the offer."

"Not the meal, silly, the investigation."

"I'm not investigating a single thing and don't get me started on the many reasons why." Patti knew perfectly well that we'd been in some really scary hot spots in the past, and I wasn't about to go there again. "After tomorrow," I told her, "I'm going back to business as usual. In the meantime, I'm not getting involved."

"But it happened right in your backyard!"

"Doesn't matter."

"Ha! That boyfriend of yours gave you orders, didn't he?"

"Hunter doesn't own me."

"We'll see about that." Patti's eyes shined with excitement. "To prove he doesn't control every move you make, you have to help me get inside the inner circle for this story. Tell Holly's husband that the local newspaper wants to cover the dinner, which is completely true, and I won't write a thing about the dead body until you say so."

"The local newspaper doesn't care about a dinner party."

"Are you kidding? Dinner with a bunch of suspects!"

I could tell that last comment was a slip because Patti's eyes did a shifty thing. The woman was not to be trusted. Not one bit. "I don't have to prove anything to you regarding my relationship with Hunter," I told her. "In fact, you need to explain to me why you were in the water at the same time Nova plopped in."

"There's nothing to tell. Come on, invite me along."

I didn't know what to think, my mind was going a million miles an hour. My radar said this would come back murder, and my brain had an issue with Patti. My intuition literally quivered with warning bells. Patti had an agenda, but what exactly was it?

While I worked my brain over for a really good excuse why Patti couldn't come along, one she'd accept, Holly came into the back room holding a cheesecake. "I've been worried about what might have really happened to Nova," she said to us in a whispery voice. "What if she didn't have a medical condition after all? What if her death was . . . suspicious?"

I slid an eyeball from her to Patti, a signal to Patti to shut up about poison. Thinking Nova had died of poisoning wasn't going to make my sister feel better, probably worse. And then she'd flip out about that.

Patti caught my warning. Thankfully, my sister missed it.

"You wondered how she could drown in two feet of water, right?" Holly went on. "What if somebody held her under? Sally Maylor asked me some pretty strange questions." Then my sister did a theatrical gasp. "What if she was murdered, and I'm a suspect? And I wasn't in the honey house with the rest of you, so that's even worse. OMG, I'm going to faint."

"You better sit down," I said, taking the cheesecake from her and placing it on my desk.

"The police questioned you?" Patti said, smelling a

story. She produced a notebook and flipped to a fresh page. "Tell me about that."

Ever since Officer Maylor had left to track down Holly with more questions, I'd been too busy to get Holly alone and ask her about their exchange. And now here Patti was, right in the thick of things, actually thinking she would take notes.

I grabbed the notebook from her. "This whole conversation is off the record," I said. "You aren't writing a single thing down, now or later. Agree or forget it."

We locked eyes again. I won. She nodded.

"The cops will put me at the top of their suspect list," my sister said. "Sally asked me if we got along. That's bad, isn't it?"

"Nonsense," I said. "Nobody knew how you really felt." Except me. And now Patti, I could have said. Which wasn't really a good thing, so I added, "And it wasn't that you didn't like her. How could you, barely having met her?"

"That's right," Holly said, visibly relaxing. "I bet Sally asked everybody that same question."

"She asked me the same thing," I said, seeing even more relief. "Sally told me she was going to look for you. Did she find you?"

Holly nodded. "She wanted to know every single detail about the morning and why I didn't stick around for the tour. See, this is like a real murder investigation."

"They're still just speculating about how Nova even died. They don't have any proof of anything. We don't, either. Unless you've heard something I haven't."

"No," Holly sniffed. "I haven't heard anything more."

"Then you have absolutely nothing to worry about," I said as Holly's cell phone rang. My sister answered it and listened, growing visibly paler under her usual perfect tan. When she hung up, she told me what I'd already heard from Hunter. "That was Max," she said. "The police are at our house. Searching it." Her bottom lip quivered.

Patti addressed Holly. Instead of her whiny, poor-me voice, she sounded strong and competent. Her new job was working wonders for her personal growth. "I can help you out," she said. "I even have a press pass."

"What does your press pass have to do with anything?" Holly glanced at the homemade pass dangling from Patti's neck.

"It gives me more free rein than an ordinary citizen. If you're worried that Nova Campbell was murdered, I can circulate and ask questions while I'm covering the dinner. People will talk to me. People like to see their quotes in the paper. I'll ask each of them where they were when the victim died and what went through their minds when they realized she was dead. Then if she *was* murdered, we'll be a step up on who did it."

"I can tell you exactly where everybody was," I said, thinking Patti could be overly dense when it came to espionage. "They were all in my backyard. And you're going to control yourself until the ME rules one way or the other. What part of 'off the record' didn't you understand?"

"Just because she died there doesn't mean . . ." Patti remembered our pact about keeping the poison secret because of Holly's stressed out condition.

"I'm really hoping she had health-related issues," Holly said to Patti. "Let's try not to make a big deal of it yet. And I don't want you writing anything that isn't true."

"Then you better let me at the truth. It might totally clear you."

"That's a thought," Holly said, not giving it any thought at all.

"What kind of cheesecake did you pick?" I asked Holly to change the subject.

"A mix of wedges—New York, chocolate caramel and pecan, chocolate Amaretto, Black Forest cherry."

Then I remembered something Holly had mentioned earlier, when she asked for help with her guests. Besides Nova's carrot juice, one of the others had some kind of dietary restriction. "Remember your list," I said. "Someone can't have cheesecake. Lactose intolerant."

Holly sighed. "Thank you. I totally forgot. Camilla can't eat any cheesecake."

Patti grinned and went after her gig from another angle. "Let me come tonight," she said to Holly, "and I'll bring another dessert, one that's lactose-free. I'll even serve. You won't have to lift a finger."

"Fine," my dizzy sister said.

A few minutes later, from the back room doorway, I watched them wander off, heads together, suddenly best buds. That's when my mother showed up and she didn't look one bit happy.

"I need to talk to you," she barked. "Right now."

Eleven

It's no secret that my mother and I have issues. Calling our relationship "complex" would be a huge understatement.

Unlike some parents, Mom never wanted to be my best friend. Which is fine—I've seen moms like that, and it's not easy on the kids when Mom wants to wear their clothes. Or hang out with them. Or insist on knowing every single detail regarding their daughter's boyfriends or social circle as though the parent is one of the kid's best friends.

But it would be nice if Mom liked me a little more for the person I am, instead of always wanting me to change into some other version of me. Which isn't even realistic. That person doesn't exist.

Our whole relationship has been like one big roller coaster ride: sometimes nonstop crazy, sometimes starting out gentle and fun, then becoming so scary I want to jump off. Only I'm trapped in the restraints and can't move.

In the past, I've been passive-aggressive with my mom, thinking that was the best way to get by. Not that I realized there was a professional term for my condition until my sister, the wannabe psychologist, clued me in. I'd let Mom throw zingers at me left and right while I'd barely defend myself in a simpering sort of way (that's the passive part). Then I'd do even more to make her crazy mad, the whole time subconsciously enjoying her discomfort (the aggressive part). Passive-aggressive. That's me. Or was.

That's what Holly says anyway. I really don't think I ever had such deeply repressed motives. I'm pretty sure if Mom and I lived across the country from each other, our relationship would improve tremendously. Living in a small town and working with my family members has been . . . challenging at best. Another understatement.

But ever since Mom hooked up with Tom Stocke, she'd mellowed out and actually seemed to enjoy my company. A new mom had emerged.

Right this minute, however, judging by the flames shooting from her eyes and ears, the old Mom was back for a visit. I just hoped it wasn't going to be an extended stay.

My sister had counseled me on what to do in case of such a situation. I knew exactly how to react. Holly and I had role-played until I got the hang of it. I was about to set some boundaries. No more passive-aggressive behavior.

Mom looked me up and down. "Don't tell me you're working here at the store in those clothes." My standard outfit of capris, T-shirt, and flip-flops has been an ongoing source of argument for years. "How unprofessional. Haven't we discussed this before?"

"Mother, what I wear is my choice. And please stop

saying such hurtful things to me." There, I said it. Holly would be so proud.

I saw Mom's surprise. She recovered quickly, though. "What's this I hear about your sister's houseguest keeling over dead in your backyard?"

"It's true." This wasn't so hard. In the past, I would have either denied the obvious or apologized profusely.

"What will people say?"

I shrugged. "That a woman died in my backyard."

"Stop being flippant." Mom was getting hot. "It's one thing after another with you. Poor Holly, a guest dying like that." Did I mention that Holly is Mom's favorite? Hands down. (As if it isn't obvious.)

"I thought you'd have some concern for the dead woman."

"You know how this town gossips," Mom said.

"I had no control over what happened to Nova Campbell." Oh, no, was that a roundabout apology? It was. "And it's been hard on me, too. A little compassion on your part would be nice."

Mom gaped.

I switched to the subject that really had me upset. "And another thing"—I was really on a roll now—"while we're having this little chat, you are NOT moving into the house next door to me."

"Someone needs to keep an eye on you."

"I'm an adult," I sort of shouted, losing a little composure. "I can keep an eye on myself just fine."

"Is that right? Really?" Mom said and started ticking off on her fingers. "You've allowed an alcoholic to move into your house," that was a low blow—we've often discussed how Hunter hasn't had a drink in years, "you've promoted another problem drinker to the position of store manager," Hunter was an alcoholic but Carrie Ann was a "problem drinker"? And again, both were sober, "you have so alienated the police chief that he actually looks for reasons to torment you. How many times has Grams had to pick you up at the police station?" (A few).

I let her keep going, in order to get it out of her system.

"And those bees!" Mom continued, waving a finger in my face. "How much conflict have they caused in our community? That crazy neighbor of yours has been a bad influence on you, too. I bet she was right there hovering over the body like a buzzard." (So true.) Mom paused to give me an evil eye. "Aren't you going to say anything in your defense?"

I let the silence hang for a beat or two, then I said from the script I'd memorized: "You and I need to limit our contact for a while. I love you very much, but I just can't deal with your constant criticism. You need to go."

"Wh-what? That's all you have to say?"

Then I went off script. "You need to leave the store and not come back for an indefinite amount of time."

"You're *firing* your own mother?" All kinds of emotions had crossed Mom's face during our little "chat"—first self-righteousness and calculated disapproval, now outright disbelief and astonishment that I was handling this confrontation so differently than in the past. The latest flicker was a dawning realization that I meant what I said.

"Yes. Yes, I *am* firing you."

"But we're family. You can't."

"Yet I am."

Mom stared at me for what seemed like forever. I held her gaze. Then she turned and walked out.

I felt worse than if I'd just shut up and put up.

But I immediately forgot about our latest tensions when I went back out on the floor and Carrie Ann told me that the town was abuzz with gossip that my sister's husband had been having an affair with the dead woman.

"Max was *not* having an affair with Nova Campbell," I said when she told me the rumor.

"I know that," my cousin said. "But I thought you should have a heads-up about what's being said."

"Who's spreading the rumor?"

"Take one guess."

"Lori!"

Carrie Ann nodded. "I'm pretty sure she was the source." Then she said, "Your mom just blew out of here. I thought she was on the schedule to work right now. What's up with that?"

"I fired her."

"What?" Carrie Ann stuck a pencil behind her ear and frowned. "We're pretty short staffed. Holly's preoccupied with her dinner party and hasn't lifted a finger to do anything other than pick out dessert, which she didn't even pay for. You're helping her with that dinner, so you aren't going to stay here long. Only one of the twins is available. And now you fired Aunt Helen right before her shift?"

Trent and Brent Craig were college students who helped out at The Wild Clover around their school schedules. They'd been with the store since its inception.

Carrie Ann had a point. I hadn't thought of the predicament I'd left her to handle. "You're the manager," I said. "Can't you fix this?"

"Not when you go over my head and randomly fire employees when they try to clock in."

"I'm sorry," I said, accepting responsibility and feeling an uncontrollable need to apologize to someone. "I'm sorry. But she went too far, and I lost it."

"Milly would do in a pinch, but she'll be with you at Holly's."

"How about Stanley Peck? He owes me a favor for all the beekeeping help I've given him. He could bag for you at least. And answer phones."

"I'll call him. But we need to solve this more permanently." Carrie Ann gave me a frustrated look, the same exact one I've worn myself many times in the past.

"Whatever you decide works for me," I said, grateful to have someone else doing a little worrying about business. You know what they say about misery loving company.

Twelve

"They've almost finished collecting samples at the Paine residence," Hunter told me over the phone. "Then the samples will go to the crime lab for examination. Max and his guests are already back. They're being questioned right now. Where's your sister? They need to talk to her, too."

"Why? Sally already did."

"Well, they're going to do it again."

"She was here a while ago then took off with Patti."

"If you see her, let her know. Can you meet me at home?"

Before answering I paused briefly to consider tonight's event and the amount of prep work involved. Milly would take care of most of it. I'd bring over the steaks and potatoes, so I was in good shape. Besides, maybe Hunter wanted to apologize for his rotten attitude earlier.

"I'll be there," I said.

Only, when I showed up, Hunter acted like he didn't even remember about his bad behavior. And he and Ben weren't alone. A forensic team was waiting at the bank of the Oconomowoc River.

"I thought you weren't on this case," I said to him, keeping my voice low as we approached the bank.

"I'm not, officially. But these are my guys. Professional courtesy and all that. They need you to walk them around, explain what transpired. Since I wasn't here at the time."

Okay then, another little dig about not calling him immediately after it happened. "Right here," I said to his forensics team, pointing down into the calm, shallow water. "This is where we found her." I walked them through the tour I'd given the others before Nova died, starting with Holly cringing by the house, the rest of us meandering through the beeyard, Nova saying she didn't feel well and deciding to stay outside while the rest of us went into the honey house, then coming out to find her facedown in the river, the whole horrible effort to revive her.

I left out a few things. For one, the tension between Camilla and me, since that had nothing to do with anything. I'd thought long and hard about mentioning Patti's weird behavior between the time we went inside the honey house and the moment we realized we couldn't bring Nova back. I'd seen movement out of the corner of my eye at the riverbank, and my neighbor's wet pants and shoes proved she'd been in the water.

Patti acts suspicious on an ongoing basis; she's hard to read and impossible to understand even on a good day when she's willing to share her convoluted logic. But I hated the thought of siccing Hunter on her by relating those observations. In her own time and her own way, I trusted that Patti would explain what the heck had been going on.

Besides, Hunter was still being a crab-ass.

I also skipped over Nova's snide behavior toward my sister, how she'd disparaged Holly's fear of bees, then had gone on to criticize her household-management skills. I wasn't about to give the cops a reason to look any more closely at my sister. I was in serious protection mode.

After I finished talking, they asked me to go over the whole thing again.

Some of the members of the team were tinkering with tools, siphoning up water samples, kneeling down near the spot I indicated, all very absorbed in their specific jobs.

When Hunter took a phone call and wandered off with Ben at his side, the canine as intent, alert, and serious as his partner, I went into the garden and picked a bunch of arugula for tonight's salad. While I was in the kitchen washing it, I saw Hunter come inside alone. I considered turning around, running out the door, and sprinting back to the store. Instead, I decided to wear my big girl pants. I waited where I was.

He started right in. "If you had asked me if I thought I'd ever have to submit to an investigation involving a death in my own backyard, I never would have believed it was possible."

I controlled my eyeballs. Instead of rolling them, I met his flashing ones. I could have reminded him that I *was* sort of used to situations like this (my short, dead-end block had become a real dead-end for a few other poor souls in the past). But saying that wouldn't have defused the situation one bit, so as hard as it was, I kept quiet.

My heart thumped, though. Was he about to bail on our relationship already? I chewed my lower lip waiting for the shoe, or rather for his Harley boot, to drop.

"If you want to move back to your house until this is resolved," I said, keeping my voice neutral, "I'll understand." Which was a whopper of a lie, but I was giving him an out. Though if he took it, I'd never speak to him again.

Suddenly Hunter's features softened. "I'm not that easy to get rid of, sweet thing," he said, coming over and pulling me close. "We'll work through this. It's only a bump in the road."

Wait until he found out about the next "bump," the one where my mother moved in next door. Even though I'd strongly asserted myself by demanding that Mom not move in there, odds favored her doing exactly as she pleased. Which usually was exactly the opposite of what *I* pleased. Mom didn't let my feelings slow her down. And I suspected once Hunter found out, that teeny little bump would become a serious-sized mountain.

Then I remembered a really important question I'd forgotten to ask Hunter earlier. "What were the samples you said were collected over at Holly's?"

"For one, they found a half-empty sport water bottle in the victim's room."

"You mean half full," I corrected him, staying positive.

Hunter paused, then chuckled, giving me a glimpse of the man I love. "Half full then." He changed the subject, his eyes traveling the length of my body. "How about later tonight we start over with half naked?"

That sounded fine to me, but I knew Hunter better than he knew himself. Once that man gets on a trail (hot or cold, whether officially working it or not), he stays on it until the bitter end. How else would he have been promoted to detective so fast? But at least he was making a token effort to acknowledge there was an "us."

"What was in the water bottle?" I said, snuggling into his arms.

"Carrot juice," he said. "We also found a bottle of it in the refrigerator. Both are in toxicology testing right now."

My carrot juice? Could something in it have killed Nova Campbell? My palms started to sweat, my mouth went dry, and my heart was misfiring, the beat too fast. Instead of admitting that I was the source of the questionable carrot juice like I should have, I froze up. My mouth refused to open, and my brain said we were going to wait and see what Jackson found. That was the choice I made on the spot, more than likely unwisely. But Hunter was so wrapped up in the case, he didn't notice my reaction. After that revelation, he went back out to the river to work with the forensic team.

Believe me, I wanted to tell him. But by the time I had an argument with all the different voices in my head, weighing the pros and cons, Hunter was gone. *And what if nothing came of it?* I rationalized. I'd just saved myself from another one of Hunter's little temper tantrums.

It took me some time to recover from the latest bit of shocking news. I trudged up the stairs, fell spread-eagled on my bed, stared into space for an indeterminate amount of time, and wondered if the universe was out to clobber my new relationship before it had barely started.

When I could function again, I realized it was time to go over to Holly's house. I changed into a yellow sheath dress and dressier flip-flops. Then I walked to The Wild Clover and removed every carrot juice container from the cooler, placing them in a box in the back room with a note that warned, "Do Not Use!" Just in case the entire batch was contaminated. Just in case I was indirectly responsible for Nova Campbell's death. Just thinking about it made me nauseated.

But the last thing I wanted was to panic everybody about possible poisonous ingredients in the food at Holly's house right before Milly and I served dinner over there. Holly and Max had enough to worry about without considering that the source of a guest's early departure from this world might possibly have come from their very own kitchen.

All this was pure speculation on my part anyway, of course. If Hunter had really been concerned, he would have warned them. Part of me wished I didn't have as much information as I had. My imagination was firing on all cylinders.

The most logical solution (in spite of my overly active imagination) was that Nova Campbell had eaten something she shouldn't have. End of story.

But I planned to keep my eyes open and my ears to the ground.

After packing last-minute supplies into my truck, I drove to the Paines' and joined Holly and Milly in my sister's expansive, state-of-the-art kitchen—the one she never uses. Her kitchen would have made the country's leading chefs want to move right in. It was full of cool features: a Sub-Zero fridge, two ovens, high-quality pots and pans all hanging within reach, razor-sharp knives capable of slicing right through the thinnest paper.

Just to be on the safe side, I opened the refrigerator and perused the contents. No visible carrot juice at least. The police had presumably taken it with them.

Working quickly, I sliced the baby red potatoes, dusted them with sea salt and rosemary, and popped them in the oven for a slow roast.

"I'll watch those for you," Milly said. "Go on and see the others."

Holly and I left Milly in the kitchen, preparing the arugula salad. She was actually whistling while she worked. Outside, Chance Anderson was setting up to serve drinks. He wore a bow tie and looked like a high-class bartender, a role he played well.

Moving away from listening ears, I brought Holly up to speed on my relationship concerns.

"Hunter's going to leave me," I told her. "I just know it."

My sister studied me, then said, "You have serious abandonment issues."

"I do not."

"You do. Though I'm not exactly sure why, since nobody has ever actually deserted you. I mean, with Clay, you're the one who ended the marriage, not him. Are you afraid of being left alone?"

"I can handle alone." And I could. As if I was ever really by myself anyway, with so much family in town. Still, I really did like my alone time.

"Are you clingy with him?" the junior psychoanalyst asked.

"Of course not."

"Complacent?"

I thought about that one. "No, but maybe I *have* been kind of passive-aggressively encouraging him to go back to his house."

"So you want to do the rejecting first, in case he has intentions of leaving."

I thought again. "Maybe. Geez, what's wrong with me?"

"Nothing that can't be fixed. You've had some losses— Dad dying, then your marriage failing. You should talk to Hunter. Tell him how you feel."

"Oh, right, sure."

"I know you can talk to him about anything. You're just being difficult."

I love my sister. When she's not cowering around honeybees, or sucking up to Mom, or brooding because Max is away so much, she's the best sister a girl could have.

Thinking of our mother reminded me, though. "Mom came into the store foaming at the mouth," I said. "Just like the old days before Tom arrived on the scene. And I did just what you told me to do. I stood up for myself."

"Good girl. And what happened next?"

"I fired her, then she left."

Holly stared at me. Her mouth even dropped slightly open. "Please tell me you're joking."

"You told me to set boundaries, so I did. The store is off-limits to her."

"We didn't role-play anything about you kicking her out!"

I gave my sister a weak smile. "I know. I made it up as I went."

Holly tried to smile back. "Well, we'll work through this, and you have good friends to see you through your trials and tribulations." Then she laughed out loud because just as she said "good friends," Patti Dwyer arrived. My neighbor wasn't exactly a shining example of love and support.

A minute later, Max and his guests began wandering out onto the patio.

Cocktail hour had begun.

Thirteen

Talk was all about Nova, of course. Things like:

- What a shock
- Never suspected she had health issues
- And so young
- Odd that the police searched the house
- Though probably routine, of course
- Had her family been notified

Family? I hadn't even thought about Nova having a family, or how they would feel when they found out.

"She was divorced," Max told us, standing with his two remaining team members, each with wineglasses in their hands. "The ugliest kind, according to her. No love lost there. No children from the marriage. And both her parents are dead."

"No siblings, either," Camilla added. She had on a shapeless, brown pantsuit from a bygone era. Not once had she glanced my way.

Gil, on the other hand, couldn't take his eyes off his coworker, which reminded me of the wedding-ring tan on his finger. Was he a widower? Or divorced? Or a cheater like my roving ex had been? I decided it wasn't any of my business, though my cynical side suspected the worst.

"I'm sure the police will track down a relative," Max added. "However distant."

Patti had actually cleaned up for the event. She still had her all-black thing going on, but this time she wore a sleeveless shift (the first time I'd ever seen her in a dress) and flats, and she'd left her ball cap at home. Unfortunately, the first thing you noticed was the awful flaming dragon tattoo on her arm. That thing was impossible to miss.

"I brought a three-berry pie," she said, holding it out in her hands.

The pie looked tasty. "You made that?" I asked.

"Don't sound so surprised. I can bake."

We went into the kitchen together and Patti left the pie on the counter with Milly.

"I'm going to mingle," Patti said to me when we had a moment alone, "and get the lowdown on those two visiting characters. If this comes back murder one, I'm all over it like flies on—"

I cut her off. "That's a good idea—mingle—but don't upset anybody with any accusations or wild speculations. Try to blend in."

Sure, right.

"Don't eat or drink anything," Patti whispered to me on her way out.

How could I avoid that at a dinner party? I couldn't help noticing that everybody around me was drinking something. Soon they would be eating everything in sight. Still, knowing about the poisoning wasn't doing my taste buds any good.

My imagination has always been hard to control, and this time it was going all out. I kept reminding myself that Nova had been the one and only victim. Either it had been an accident or not, but the rest of us were perfectly safe. Probably.

In the kitchen, the steaks were ready for the grill and heavenly aromas were wafting from the ovens, a combination of rosemary potatoes and Milly's popovers.

Though she wasn't helping with the food prep, Effie Anderson had arrived to help keep the kitchen clean, an act of kindness that Milly found particularly wonderful; the two women had really hit it off. I took a moment to imagine myself with house help and the hefty bank balance to pay a staff. It sounded wonderful in theory, but realistically, Holly wasn't any better off happy-wise or health-wise or any-other-wise than me. In fact, I liked my life just the way it was. Especially assuming Hunter and I worked things out.

I served as gopher, helping out where I could. While I worked, I started creeping out over how easy it would be to slip a little poison into practically anything. Then I thought of how many toxins were out in nature and how many were manufactured and how much evil exists, and those thoughts got me even more nervous.

What did I know about Holly's weekend company? Nothing, that's what.

Just then, Camilla walked past the kitchen. I scurried after the flower thief.

"What did I do to offend you this time?" Camilla said when she saw me bearing down on her in the hall.

"I hate to bring this up but . . ." I began, skidding to a halt.

She sniped, "Then don't."

"I really have to. You'll be leaving tomorrow and there's something I need to discuss with you before you go." I told her what had happened with the wildflowers, how Johnny Jay thought I'd picked them and how he gave me a hefty fine. "Obviously, you should be the one to pay it, not me," I said, finishing.

All the while I was talking, Camilla had her standard scowl, but as I wrapped it up, something changed. First she made a noise that sounded like an oink. Then she sputtered. My first thought was, oh, no, she's been poisoned, too. But then she let loose, laughing out loud, rather derisively I thought, definitely not in a nice laughing-with-you kind of way.

"You're laughing at me?" I said.

"Damn straight," she said. "You really deserve what you got."

"For what? For caring about our earth?"

"Oh, give me a break."

"You owe me for the ticket."

"Okay, look, I'll pay the fine."

"Unless you want to wave your special *permit* in the police chief's face. Maybe then he'll tear up the ticket." Okay, that was unnecessarily sassy of me. After all, the woman had just agreed to pay the fine. With a bad attitude, yes, but that was no reason for me to get all sarcastic.

Camilla's nostrils flared as she dug through an oversized purse, pulled out a checkbook, wrote out a check, filling in all but my name, since she hadn't bothered to learn it. She handed the check over, and stomped off to join the others outside.

"And you'll tell the police chief what really happened,

right?" I called after her, knowing there wasn't a fat chance of that happening. For one, Camilla and Gil would be gone before Johnny Jay returned from his fishing trip. For two, Camilla couldn't stand me. The fact that she'd written the check at all was miraculous enough.

I folded the check and tucked it away. In the background, I spotted Patti slipping upstairs to the second floor. That woman would stop at absolutely nothing.

I sighed and went back to the kitchen.

The evening had all the ingredients that make an event spectacular. Too bad Nova's death had put a damper on things. A perfect view as the sun passed over the lake, soft candles illuminating the warm summer night, plenty of alcoholic beverages, and flowing conversation, thanks to Max's gift for entertaining. Not that he had much experience on the home front, since his job kept him away so often, but I imagined he did a lot of fine dining with clients during his travels. He smoothly turned the topic away from Nova and on to more pleasant subjects. There was a general sense of relief when we went into small-talk mode. We all needed and welcomed the respite.

Max, a cocktail in one hand, tongs in the other, hovered over the grill like the old pro he was. "You and Milly will eat with us, of course," he said to me when I stopped to admire his expertise.

"Of course," I said. "It smells delicious."

"Milly says no, but we'll convince her."

"She's a stubborn woman," I said, knowing it to be true. Milly was a sweetheart, but once she made up her mind, it was set in concrete. "And I don't think she eats much meat."

"But what will we do with the extras? I know, why don't you invite Hunter to join us?"

Now, that was a wonderful idea! My man is a certified, official carnivore. Give him a cut of beef and he purrs like a Bengal tiger after a successful hunt. I was starting to relax with my second glass of red wine. The ridiculous thought that someone would try to poison any of us began to fade from my mind. What an absurd idea anyway. The steaks had gone right from the store onto the hot grill. The popovers and salad came from Milly's own kitchen and my garden, the potatoes had been in my care. Patti had brought the pie. She was just being neurotic with her dire warnings. What else was new?

"Where are you?" Hunter answered his cell phone on the first ring.

"Where are *you*?"

"Home." It took a moment for me to connect his home with mine. We had an "us" house now.

"I'm at Holly's," I told him. "She needed help with tonight's dinner."

Silence. Then, "When did you decide we weren't having dinner together?"

What was this? An interrogation? "This morning. That was Holly's big problem she was so freaked about."

"When were you going to tell me?"

Had I forgotten to mention it to him? Now that I thought about it, I had. "I'm sorry, things have been a little off today, what with someone dying in the backyard and all. It slipped my mind."

I'd had a trying day. I was a bit crabby, too. Where had our total bliss gone? Was I supposed to tell him every little move I made? And apologize for every little thing that bugged him? Okay, I had to calm down. Right this minute, I couldn't stand being around myself. Time to readjust my attitude.

"Come over. We're having steaks," I said, shaking off my mood.

"Steak?" he said. I could hear his tone lightening already.

"And Milly's making popovers. They'll be hot out of the oven soon."

"I'll be right there then." Which reassured me. If Hunter wasn't worried about poisoned food, I wasn't going to worry, either.

I hung up and turned to find myself almost nose to nose with Patti.

"I found out all about the 'big secret' they're working on," she stage whispered, finger quoting the big secret part.

"Tell me, what is it? Did you find secret papers upstairs?"

"No, I found out from that guy Gil. He's drinking some million-year-old Scotch, and it's really loosening his lips. You aren't going to believe this."

Patti went on to describe what she'd gotten out of the drunk flavorist. Apparently, the team had stumbled upon something amazing during their mixing and matching.

"What they discovered was on the lines of miracle fruit," Patti said. "Those little red berries that make sour things taste sweet? Vinegar, pickles, stuff like that, they actually taste sweet when they're combined with the berries. Gil said protein binds with taste buds and acts as a sweetness inducer when it comes into contact with acids. It tricks the tongue."

"I've never heard of such a thing."

"It's true. Look it up on the Internet. Search for miracle fruit and it comes right up."

"Okay, so? That's already been discovered."

"Yes, but get this." Patti's eyes were shining orbs. "This group has figured out how to make vegetables taste like candy!"

I contemplated what I'd just been told. "Wow," I said.

Patti's head bounced up and down, reminding me of a bobble doll. "Just imagine kids begging for more broccoli. It could taste just like chocolate or cake frosting."

Could chocolate veggies tie in with Nova Campbell's death? "Maybe a taste test did in Nova," I suggested. "What if she whipped up a combination and tried it out on herself?"

"It's possible," Patti said.

Yes! That would mean the carrot juice from my store had nothing to do with her death. Nothing at all. Unless she used it in her experiment, but that wouldn't count, because it would've been her actions, not mine. I really liked this theory best so far.

"Or," Patti said, "the competition could have murdered her."

"What competition?"

Patti's eyes slid left, then right, like we were high-powered corporate spies. Next, she'd be talking out of the corner of her mouth. "You know," she said, "all the big corporations are cutting each other's throats to end up on top. If word got out that the team was on the verge of a big discovery, someone might be eliminating them one by one."

I hated that idea. "But then wouldn't Max have been the important target?" I reasoned. "He's higher up. Not only that, do you see any strangers around here? I mean other than the team members? Anybody hiding in the bushes?"

Luckily, just then I heard the familiar sound of Hunter's Harley coming up the drive. Patti slunk away to do God only knew what.

I watched with admiration as Hunter parked and approached. He looked great in a cotton button-down, chinos, a navy blue blazer and brown loafers. And he was all mine! It still hadn't totally sunk in.

The rest of the evening seemed to fly by. The food was fabulous—Milly's popovers were crispy on the outside, custardy on the inside, the arugula salad rocked, and my rosemary potatoes turned out perfect. I sampled every single flavor of cheesecake, and had a small piece of Patti's three-berry pie. I could tell that Hunter had his ears and eyes open, that part of him couldn't help being on the job, surrounded as he was by potential murder suspects.

The other part of him thought the steak was the best he'd ever had.

Fourteen

Next morning, I woke up feeling all warm and cozy after a night of . . . well . . . never mind. Moving serenely through my coffee ritual, I let Ben out in the yard to do his thing, harvested the honey from my happy bees, who had already started their busy day, showered, poured another big cup of coffee, left still-sleeping Hunter a love note, and went to The Wild Clover to open up.

What a beautiful day. The big dinner was over, no one had ingested any toxic substances, and Gil and Camilla would soon depart, taking with them any other residual stress and tension that seemed to have accompanied them on their trip. The truth about Nova's death would emerge, and turn out to be something we could all live with. No murder, no suspects, no worries. A night of love can change this girl's entire perspective on life.

Even my personal life was back on track. Yes, Hunter and I had made up. Plus my mother was persona non grata and even Johnny Jay wasn't around to harass me. Inside The Wild Clover, I raised my eyes to the overhead windows where stained glass from the building's previous life as a church still cast rays of streaked sunlight into the interior. I smiled again, feeling excited and happy about the new day.

Life was good.

Then Lori Spandle walked into the store.

"Find any more dead bodies in your backyard?" she said with a smirk.

I could think of one particular body I wouldn't mind adding to the compost heap. Or dropping off in the deepest part of the river with lead weights around her ankles.

Lori kept going. "Your mother is just about ready to sign on the dotted line. We're setting up the meeting. Want to witness the transaction?"

"Lori, don't you have a broom to catch?"

"Who else but another Fischer would live next door to that swarm of dangerous bees? Your mother is used to creepy-crawly things. She has you."

I punched a finger into Lori's rib cage, directly between her big boobs. "I'm in the process of eliminating riffraff from my life." I poked again. "If you aren't here to buy my products, your name will move to the very top of the list of poor contributors to my general well-being. I'm cleaning house, so shop or get lost."

"Ewwww. Aren't we testy today?"

Just then, Stanley Peck showed up and ended the standoff. "Carrie Ann said I should come by to learn how to open up the store," he said to me, ignoring Lori. "Care to show me how?"

That cousin of mine was turning out to be a top-notch organizer. Who knew that once she came out of her drunken stupor she'd have real people skills? The store looked shiny clean, the displays twinkled, and she was positioning new hires for the future. If she kept it up, I wouldn't have to worry about Holly's no-shows or my mother's too-many-shows. Because they wouldn't be on the schedule at all.

"What are you standing around for?" Stanley said to Lori, knowing our history. He shoved a shopping basket at her. "Get cracking."

Stanley has always been a close friend and our shared interest in beekeeping has now sealed our bond forever. He has his drawbacks as a customer service representative, though, which is only one of the hats my staff has to wear. First of all, he doesn't tolerate BS, which we get a lot of at the store. Second of all, his method of communicating his disapproval typically involves waving a firearm around and threatening to use it. I didn't want holes in the store's ceiling.

I made a mental note to look into banning guns from the store, now that Wisconsin has made it legal to carry concealed weapons. I doubt that Stanley has a carry permit anyway, though. He doesn't believe that the government has any business telling him what he can and can't do.

After Lori left in a huff, some of our more agreeable customers wandered through. Stu from Stu's Bar and Grill stopped in to pick up his newspaper, which had only just arrived. Usually they are here long before now.

Stu is such a hunk! He has the best bedroom eyes in the world.

"They're betting Nova Campbell was murdered," Stu said, sharing comments from his bar clientele. "Actually placing bets on who did it."

"And?"

"Holly's in the lead. People know that your sister didn't like the dead woman. And I can see why, if what they say is true about her husband and his employee."

"That rumor isn't true," I informed him. "If you'd met the dead woman when she was alive you'd see why Holly didn't like her. I didn't like her, either, right from the very beginning."

Stu paused to scan the front page of our local newspaper, the *Reporter*, which I referred to as the *Distorter* for obvious reasons. For one, Patti worked for it and I knew how she operated. For another, the paper didn't usually have anything worth reporting, so it tried to stir the pot by printing a lot of opinion pieces, which bordered on libel.

"She was pretty," Stu said, holding up the paper so I could see the photograph of Nova Campbell right on the front page.

"Is that all you guys care about?"

"Pretty much." And with that Stu was off, but not before he gave me a wink to let me know he was messing with me.

Milly stopped by to replenish her flower bouquets. I picked up a newspaper from the stack and showed her Nova's picture. "I wonder where they got a photograph so quickly."

"Driver's license," Milly said. "That's what they usually do. That's a good-looking photo. You should see mine. I look like a convict."

"I was just about to read the article about her," I said, noticing Patti's name below the byline. I sighed before delving into the body of the piece.

Here's what I read:

Nova Campbell died suddenly during a tour of a local honeybee apiary owned and operated by Story Fischer, who also owns The Wild Clover. Her store has been the gathering place for some of Moraine's most speculative observations and innuendos, and this current tragedy has added fuel to the fire surrounding one of the oldest and certainly most colorful families in the area—the Fischers.

Is it possible Campbell's death could be related to the environment she so innocently entered? Was she set upon by a swarm of killer bees? And what about the younger Fischer sister, Holly Paine (nee Fischer), who is married to mega-millionaire Max Paine, the deceased's boss? According to several sources, the deceased's relationship with this family member's husband during Campbell's brief visit to our usually quiet town of Moraine is under scrutiny.

Did jealousy drive Holly Fischer over the edge?

Or was a certain husband's secret affair(s) in jeopardy of discovery?

And what about adding more flavoring to the suspect list in the form of two of Nova Campbell's team members? Was someone eliminating the competition from within?

Or did Nova Campbell take her own life?

All this is pure speculation, of course, because two law enforcement agencies working side by side have failed to cooperate by answering questions the public deserves to know. Investigators working the case actually demanded a gag order pending more autopsy details, but intimidation can't stop this reporter from giving you all the news, all the time.

Stay tuned as the "Story" develops.

"I'm going to kill her," I said out loud, before realizing the stack of papers had attracted a small crowd. Some smart aleck in the back of the bunch wanted to know who it was I was planning to kill next, in a kidding sort of way (I think). Anyway, we sold out of papers within the next fifteen minutes. Some customers bought two, one for themselves, one for a friend.

"How could the paper's editor run this garbage?" Carrie Ann said when she read the piece. "Isn't there some kind of law against smearing your character in public?"

"Yes, there is. It's called libel."

I dug out my phone and called Hunter. Real life had intruded on our fairy-tale happiness.

Again.

Fifteen

Before noon, Sally Maylor had a warrant to bring Patti Dwyre into the police station for questioning. She asked Hunter for assistance. According to the acting chief, either Patti had made up a pack of nasty insinuations, or she knew something that needed to be shared. That hadn't been exactly what I'd hoped for. The last thing I wanted was a thorough investigation into my family members' lives. I'd really thought they'd just throw Patti in a jail cell and leave her there.

I spent my lunch break planted out in front of her house, wanting a ring-side seat as she was taken into police custody. I hoped for some graphic police brutality to go with my peanut butter and honey sandwich.

I was still flaming mad. Of all the nerve! Hadn't I befriended that woman? Grudgingly, okay, but I'd made an effort way beyond what I had to. When she finally came into view now, it was all I could do not to rush over and throttle her.

"I'll never reveal my sources," Patti said from the top step of her porch right before Hunter and Sally steered her toward Sally's squad car. "You can't arrest me. I'm with the media. And besides, you're hurting my arm. Ouchee."

Hunter didn't seem to hear her. I could tell he was angry, too, judging from the steam rising from his collar.

"Patti," I called out. "When I get my hands on you, I'm going to hurt more than your arm!"

"Story, is that you? Help!" she said, too dense to realize we were on opposing sides this time. "Don't let your boyfriend torture me," then to him, "I'll hold out until the bitter end. My lips are cemented shut."

Speaking of cement, I wanted to bury her under six feet of it.

"You made a promise, Patti," I said, getting close enough that only Sally and Hunter could hear. "Off the record, you promised, remember? And talk about embellishing!"

"I found another source," she said, talking low, too. "Not you. Someone else came forward."

So what did that mean? It was okay to break my confidence since someone else told her the same thing? That certainly sounded like Patti logic. As for the other source, I'd bet my best pair of flip-flops it was Lori Spandle.

Watching them drive off, I imagined a few effective torture techniques I'd like to use on Patti—boiling in oil, toilet dunking, de-nailing those stubs she calls fingernails. Not that she could ever give up any real information, because she didn't have a real source. She'd made the entire thing up.

Within another two hours, the *Reporter* had issued a statement retracting the entire article, claiming a disgruntled employee had sabotaged the printing process, and ended by saying that said worker's employment had been terminated effective immediately.

But the damage had been done. That one stupid article would have serious consequences.

In the meantime, business at the store had never been better. I've never seen so many customers run out of milk before.

I silenced my cell phone because it was ringing off the hook and caller ID told me there was only one determined caller—Mom, the last person I wanted to talk to. Hopefully, Holly was too busy with her remaining guests to read the paper or pay attention to incoming calls from Mom. The longer Holly didn't know, the better.

One of Stu's Bar and Grill regulars came in to let me know that Stu's canoe and kayak rentals had gone way up since somebody at the bar suggested that gawkers could tour the actual location of the latest town crime scene.

That particular spot being the riverbank in my backyard.

"Don't you think everybody is being ridiculously outrageous?" I said at one point.

But people love drama. They don't care if it's true or not, and our small town in particular seems to thrive on digesting, regurgitating, and spewing the stuff back out.

Mid-afternoon, the twins arrived to take over for me, a very good thing, since I couldn't take one more sideways glance or barely concealed outright stare. Pretending nothing is wrong when everything is going down the tube isn't easy.

I took off for my street, and the one chance I might have to do a little digging of my own. And it wasn't going to be in my backyard, even though I had ideas about where to place a Patti-sized shallow grave.

I wanted to creep around to the back, but one of the

gawkers in a canoe happened to be passing as I peeked around. Instead, I decided to be bold.

I walked right in Patti's front door.

Just the kind of luck I like (but don't find too often), Patti had forgotten to lock up in all the excitement of her arrest.

Why, I asked myself, had my neighbor been in the river at the exact same time that Nova Campbell keeled over dead? And why was she hiding that fact, refusing to answer when I confronted her? Now she had gone out of her way to misdirect attention toward Holly and me, making us appear responsible for Nova's murder when she knew we weren't.

Patti Dwyre had to be after more than a killer story. And mad as I was at her, I knew she wasn't a dummy, either; she had to realize what she'd written would put her in big trouble with her boss. And with the cops. And with me.

So she must've been operating out of desperation. I was going to find out why.

I'd been in Patti's house before but never upstairs. Now I headed right up the steps, toward the room where she snooped with her telescope. She had a brand-new one, judging by the shininess of the scope and all the cardboard packaging scattered on the floor.

My neighbor is a true minimalist, nothing nonessential anywhere, which made my mission that much easier. Or it would have, if I knew exactly what my job here was or what I was looking for. But I told myself I'd know it when I saw it.

I took in the contents of the room—the telescope, the bare closet, unadorned walls, a few pieces of electronic equipment (a camera, video camera, high-powered binoculars)—all on the top of a desk.

Inside the desk, I found a stack of letters. They looked

old; even the rubber band binding them together had seen better days. It broke when I tugged on it. The letters were all addressed to a Patricia Bruno at a Chicago, Illinois, address. And the return address came from the Southwestern Illinois Correctional Center.

"What are you doing?" I heard behind me. A voice out of nowhere. The letters went flying to the floor, scattering, while my heart skipped a row of very important beats.

I whipped around.

"Patti! What are you doing here?" I tried to look nonchalant, a failed attempt on my part due to the setting and circumstances.

She bent and gathered up the letters. "We should be real honest-to-goodness partners," she said. "You're better at snooping than you think."

"Thanks," I managed to mumble, wishing Hunter had had the foresight to inform me when they let Patti go.

"But you know too much," she continued, moving closer, eyes narrowed, suggestion in her tone. "Now I'll have to kill you."

I'm sure all the blood drained out of my face.

Then Patti said brightly, "Just kidding. Boy, are you touchy."

I started counting, sure that ten numbers (no matter how slowly I counted) weren't going to help this time, they never did when it came to my neighbor. Maybe a thousand would work but even that was doubtful.

"Come downstairs," she said, putting the letters back into the drawer. "And I'll explain everything. This is all my fault. I underestimated your snoopiness."

Look who was talking!

Just to be on the safe side, I made her go downstairs first.

"My married name was Patricia Bruno," she said,

plopping into a chair. "In that life, which seems like a bad dream, I made a big mistake and married a guy who wasn't who I thought he was."

Patti? Married? Wow! I never would have guessed.

"Okay," I squeaked, sitting down, too, and clearing my voice before saying, "I can understand that." The whole town knew that my ex-husband had turned out to be a creep and a total womanizer.

"Your jerk wasn't in the same league as mine. The guy was older than me and he'd been in prison more than once, but I only found that out later. Which wasn't the worst of it. The minute we were married he started mistreating me. You don't need the details, but it was ugly. Right away, I'd had enough and tried to leave. He told me he'd kill me if I did."

"That's awful," I said. "But obviously, you got away."

"The next time he landed in jail, I made my escape. Divorced him, moved here." Patti leaned forward in the chair. "You might have heard of him. His name is Harry Bruno."

I actually *had* heard of the guy. "The Chicago mobster?"

"That's the one."

For the second time in a matter of minutes, I was speechless. First, when Patti had threatened to kill me. Now, after hearing that the woman sitting across from me had been married—and to the mob at that.

"Does he know where you are?" I asked, thinking he must not since he hadn't killed Patti yet.

Patti gave me a weak grin. "I'm sure he does. He's in organized crime. He can find anybody, eventually. Besides, we actually talk on the phone now and again. Anyway, I made sure I kept tabs on his actions when he got out of jail, and I got really lucky. Because he met somebody else right away and married her."

"That must have been a relief," I said.

"You bet it was."

I felt for Patti. I really did. But she still had some explaining to do. "I'm really glad you confided in me," I said, "but your personal problems don't explain why you wrote that horrible article about my family. That doesn't have anything to do with your past."

"I'm so sorry that happened. I panicked," she said, "and felt I had to divert attention away from myself. I wish I'd never followed you home yesterday and never went into the water to try to save Nova Campbell. If this gets out, I'll be put away for life. Once you hear me out, you'll understand."

Oh, yeah, right. "This better be really good, because I'm totally out of patience with you."

"Oh, it is good." Patti sank back. "I was Harry Bruno's first wife. Nova Campbell was his second."

That hit me like a ton of bricks. I hadn't seen it coming at all. I blurted without thinking, "So did you kill her?"

Patti jumped up, clearly upset. "See, even you think I did! What would everybody else say? The same thing. But I didn't even know she was in town until I saw her in your backyard and recognized her from their wedding pictures I'd seen online. When she doubled over and fell into the water, I should have turned and run away."

She had that right. She should have. "Instead you went to see if you could help."

Patti nodded. "She was already stone-cold dead."

"Okay," I said. "This isn't the end of the world. Just because you found her first, doesn't mean you killed her."

Patti snorted. "Yeah, right."

Then I thought of something else. "Won't Harry Bruno show up for retribution once he hears about her death? They might have been divorced, too, but from what I've heard these families protect their own."

"What do you think this is, *The Godfather*? He hated the woman."

"How do you know?"

"I told you, we still talk once in a while. He's asked me to come back to him, but no way is that going to happen." I saw worry cloud her face. "I hope he finds somebody else quickly again, because I don't want him around here bothering me."

"I just wish you hadn't dragged my family through the mud." I got up and headed for the door, not sure that her story and her point of view justified what she had done. Although I did feel a little sorry for her.

Patti's whole situation haunted me as I walked down the street.

Unfortunately, when I got back to the store, a new rumor was making the circuit.

The carrot juice in Nova Campbell's water bottle had been loaded with poison.

Sixteen

"Water hemlock," Hunter said from a metal chair in the back room of my store. Ben and I were in the process of completing our standard greeting. Me, rubbing the top of his head. Him, giving me several warm love licks. Hunter and I had already greeted each other in a more traditional way, though my skin still tingled from his touch. "I don't know how this news got out on the street so fast."

The latest tidbit really was spreading faster than a flash flood.

"Water hemlock is common around these parts," my man continued. "The stuff grows in wet open areas, along shorelines for example. It could be growing along the river behind your house for all we know."

I noticed it was now "my" house, not "our" house.

"It's the most toxic plant in the United States," Hunter kept going. "Just rubbing up against it, getting any on your skin, can cause seizures or even death."

If it grew around here and was that deadly, how could I have no idea what the plant even looked like? I needed to look up a picture of this killer plant and eradicate it from my property if I found any. Hunter waited while I used my computer to search for water hemlock. An image popped up of a tall delicate plant with wispy greenish white flowers in the shape of umbrellas.

"That's it," he said. "Like I said, poisoning can even occur through contact with your skin. Also, the plant has a hollow stem. Kids have been poisoned from blowing whistles with the reeds. That's how deadly it is."

"Geez," I added, amazed that water hemlock had never been on my radar. Poison ivy, yes. Hemlock, never.

"And get this," he said, "according to the ME, the plant smells just like a carrot! Probably tastes like one, too, although I'm not about to test that out."

I cringed. Spiked carrot juice was the worst of all the available possibilities. How could this have happened?

"Please tell me the rumors about it being in her carrot juice are wrong," I said. "That she really died from touching it, or from blowing on it, or something?"

"Nope, apparently the roots were pureed and added to the juice in the refrigerator."

I must have given some kind of clue to the emotion swirling around inside me, because Hunter said, "What's wrong? You don't look so good."

"I've had better days."

"So whoever supplied that juice is the one I need to find."

I gulped.

Hunter gazed at me, his expression patient. "Anything you'd care to add at this point?" he asked.

I've known Hunter Wallace long enough to read him. Not that he's exactly an open book. More like a classic with a hidden theme that you have to dig deep to discover. But I knew that look, the one he was giving me.

Hunter already had my name stamped on the juice.

I didn't have much of a choice. "Fine," I admitted. "The carrot juice came from The Wild Clover. I've already taken the rest of that shipment off the shelf." I pointed to a box in the corner with my hand-scribbled warning label. "Take the whole box and test every single one. I won't be surprised if the whole batch is contaminated." I brightened a little. "That would be good, right? That would mean no one we know is responsible."

"I'll have it checked out."

My man was in interrogation mode. "So why'd you bring carrot juice over to the Paines' in the first place anyway?"

See, this was the part I didn't want to tell him. I was used to being in the middle of controversy, having an uncanny knack of showing up in the worst possible place at the worst possible time, but I hated that my sister was the one in Hunter's scope. "Holly asked me to," I said reluctantly, but quickly added, "but Nova asked for it in the first place. Holly was only accommodating her guest."

"That doesn't look good for her. You know that, right?"

"Holly doesn't know a thing about plants," I reasoned. "Unless it's a dozen roses. And she isn't devious. She wouldn't have plotted something out in advance like that." Which was true. My sister never planned ahead for anything. This whole carrot-flavored toxic plant mixed with carrot juice was way beyond her range of abilities.

"I tend to agree with you," Hunter said. "But that's only my personal opinion and doesn't count."

At least he'd made that admission.

"What else aren't you telling me?" Hunter asked next.

I thought about that question. Honestly, I couldn't think

of another secret . . . oh, wait, time to come completely clean. Besides, anything to get him off my sister's trail. "Patti was wading in the river when Nova died." There! Let him go after crazy Patti Dwyre instead.

Hunter leaned back and studied me. My eyes wanted to dart away, but I forced myself to maintain eye contact. "Let's hear it," he said.

I told him the story—leaving out the part about snooping in her house. I have to hang on to what little pride I have left. About Patti's past marriage, and how Nova was wife number two, and how Patti said she went into the river to try to save her. Finally, I repeated the lame reason she gave for writing the damaging article, which was to divert attention away from herself. I finished with, "Patti's trouble."

"That's what I keep telling you," Hunter agreed.

"So I suppose you're going to say you told me so."

"I told you so." Hunter stood up. "You'll have to tell Sally what you know about Patti's past, since she never said a word about her connection when we took her in."

"Can't you tell Sally?"

"It better come for you. Want me to come along?"

"No, I'll finish up here then stop down at the station."

Right after Hunter and Ben left with the box of carrot juice jars, Patti called my cell phone.

"I'm taking a little vacation," she said, "until this blows over."

"It's not going to blow over until you tell the cops the truth. I just told Hunter."

"They aren't my biggest worry at the moment. I did some serious thinking about Harry. He might actually come looking for me, and I don't want to be found by him. The man turns ugly on a dime."

She hung up before I could reply.

A little while later, Holly pounded into the back room.

"Where is that evil witch?" my sister shouted, too upset to care that the door was still open and our customers couldn't help but overhear her at that pitch and volume.

Patti couldn't have picked a better time for a little R&R. If she thought her mobster ex-husband was scary, she hadn't gone up against my sister.

I jumped up and closed the door. "Relax," I said, ignoring my own advice.

Holly proceeded to rattle off a string of text acronyms. I caught some of them, mostly the ones that had an *F* in them. After that, she popped back into regular speech again. "Where *is* Patti?"

"Gone," I told her. "She can't do any more damage."

"There isn't any more to do!" she exclaimed. "And now the police are saying that Nova was poisoned! With carrot juice from *my* refrigerator. Max is totally ticked off. He's calling his attorney, and we're suing that stupid paper *and* Patti Dwyre."

I heard voices and commotion in the main part of the store. "Stay back here until you calm down," I told her. "I have to go see what's happening out front."

Holly slumped into my chair. I left her there.

The store was hopping busy. And my banished mother had materialized behind the cash register.

I tried not to march on my way over.

"We have to stick together," she said to me before I could open my mouth. "It's time for damage control after that slanderous article hit the paper. You and I should have a nice chat soon about the other things that are on your mind, okay? But right now we have to unite." She didn't wait for my response, just went on checking out the next customer as though nothing was amiss between us.

I saw Mom had put out a tip jar next to the register.

"Patti Dwyre had a mental breakdown," she brightly informed each customer. "We're taking donations to help with her recovery costs." There were several bills poking out of the top of the jar. "Did you see that crazy article? Patti clearly wasn't herself when she wrote it." Several customers added more dollar bills and change to the jar in just the few minutes I was there.

I ducked outside to arrange my scattered thoughts and plan my next move regarding Mom. Most of the females in my life share the same traits:

- Assertive . . . no . . . change that to aggressive

- Overly confident in their own abilities

- Competitive

- Controlling

I could go on, but I was distracted by the one female I knew who was the exact opposite of most of the other women in my world: Grams, who was sitting outside on the bench with Dinky. Grams is patient, loving and not afraid to show it, accepting of others just the way they are, and totally easygoing. I hope I've inherited at least a few of my grandmother's good genes.

"Your mother is sorry," my grandmother said.

"Then why doesn't she just say so?" I plopped down beside her. Dinky crawled into my lap and up to my chin and we played dodge the stinky tongue.

"Your mother has apologized in her own way. By coming here today, she's showing her love for you and her commitment to our family."

"A simple 'I'm sorry I've been so mean' would have done it."

"She can't, sweetie. Helen just doesn't have it in her to verbalize an apology."

I conceded that Grams was probably right about Mom,

and we sat together for a long time, chatting up neighbors and customers as they came past, Grams spreading the story Mom had concocted about Patti's breakdown. I figured that mental part really wasn't too far from the truth.

After a while Holly came out and nestled next to Grams. My sister and I gave each other a look over our grandmother's head that said we were in this together and we would stay strong. My sister was back from the brink.

Then Holly actually went back in to help Mom at the register, Grams wandered away, snapping pictures, and I settled back into my office to catch up on paperwork. Except my mind kept straying.

Known facts (according to my wandering mind):

- Nova Campbell had been intentionally poisoned with water hemlock.

- I had delivered the catalyst (carrot juice) that turned out to be part of the murder weapon.

- Holly was the one who had asked me to bring the carrot juice.

- She knew Nova was making a play for her husband.

- Holly was the perfect suspect—motive, opportunity, means.

Only my sister wouldn't know a toxic weed from a prize flower. She couldn't tell the difference between a black cat and a skunk. She thought nature was something you viewed through paned windows, or at least from behind screens and shutters so that creepy critters couldn't attack you. And if she *had* ventured into the great outdoors with the sole purpose of procuring a poisonous plant, something as innocuous as a squirrel would've sent her screaming. I knew that for a fact.

In short, if Holly had really wanted to poison Nova, her MO was more likely to have been dissolving a load of sleeping pills into a wineglass and then offering it to her. But poison really wasn't Holly's style—rather than such a desperate option, my sister would have taken her opponent to the mat, both verbally and physically. Then she would have sent her packing.

Holly wasn't a sneaky little wimp.

But our murderer was.

So, who was he or she?

If I discounted my family members (which was a given) and Patti Dwyre (who was crazy, but I didn't really think she was a killer), I was left with only two very viable suspects: Gil Green and Camilla Bailey. Could they be any more obvious? Two flavorists. Talk about people who knew how to mix and match and come up with a deadly floral dose.

Nova's death must have had something to do with that project they were all working on, that thing about turning vegetables into some kind of candy. And judging by my own first (and second) impressions, Nova Campbell couldn't have been a pleasant coworker. So the only real question was, which one of the two had done the deed?

I called Hunter. "Have Max's guests left town yet?" I asked, hoping I could grill them before takeoff.

"They aren't going anywhere. Not with one of their coworkers murdered. They've been ordered to stay put."

So, the police weren't putting all their eggs in the Holly basket, either. "Perfect!" I said. "I mean . . . uh . . ."

"You're so transparent," Hunter said, amusement in his tone for a change. "You want to protect your family. I understand that. But you really need to stay away from the case, Story."

"Don't make me lie to you about not getting involved. You know I already am."

After all, this was my family we were talking about. My sister, her husband, me, all of us. Hunter is a great investigator and I'm sure his team is, too, and I have all the faith in the world in Sally Maylor. But still, I couldn't just sit back and watch.

"You're impossible," Hunter said.

"So are you."

"I'll make sure you're locked up."

"Promise?" I replied, putting some suggestiveness in my tone.

We disconnected.

I went out to the front of the store, where Milly Hopticourt arrived with her wagon full of flower bouquets. By now, late in the afternoon when people were thinking about evening meals, we were extra busy. And for once, we were fully staffed—the twins, Carrie Ann, Mom, Stanley, me, and even Holly, although she rarely counted as a full staff person.

"I stopped off at your house," Milly said to Holly, "to drop off a few things for your guests that I whipped up."

"Thank you, Milly," my sister said with a ton of gratitude.

"You're the best," I told Milly, having pretty much forgotten about feeding guests rather than interrogating them.

"That Effie is so sweet," Milly said. "What's happened is such a shame. It's upset the entire household. Imagine! Poisoned!"

"Speaking of poison, tell me more about water hemlock," I said, while we worked together to arrange the bouquets.

"It's a member of the carrot family," Milly said. That made sense, since Hunter had already told me it smelled like carrots.

"The roots are the most toxic part of the plant," she

went on to a growing audience as customers overheard the topic and joined us. Even Stanley Peck sidled over to listen. "*Cicuta*, or water hemlock, is also called cowbane, because if it's allowed to grow in pastures, cattle will chew it, and that's the end of them."

"If water hemlock is deadly enough to kill something the size of a cow," Stanley said, "imagine what happens to a human!"

We all thought about that for a few seconds.

"Does it grow around here?" Holly wanted to know. I could actually read her mind. If it did, she wasn't venturing out into the wild ever again. She sure was a big baby when it came to the natural world.

Milly nodded, confirming another factoid already in my knowledge base, thanks to Hunter. "Yes it does. In fact, I can show you where some is growing right now."

"We need to eradicate it," someone in the group said. "Let's go now!"

Just then, Lori Spandle showed up, heard that last comment, and assumed we were talking about my bees. "About time everybody wised up," she said. "Story Fischer's bees are aggressive. And you all read the *Reporter*. They might be responsible for killing that poor woman."

"Stuff it, Lori," Stanley said. "That's hogwash and you know it."

I noticed that Lori had a file folder with her. If those were rental papers for my mother to sign . . . well . . . they better not be. I hadn't even had time to prepare Hunter yet.

"Mom," I said to my mother, who still had control of the cash register. "We're going with Milly to identify water hemlock."

"I'll stay here and mind the store," she said.

"No." I had to get her away from the paperwork in Lori's clutches. "The twins can watch the store. Besides, most of our customers are coming along with us, right guys?" A bunch of them nodded.

"We can handle things here," Trent agreed.

"Well, I'm definitely *not* going," Holly said. "I'll help Trent and Brent."

"See," I said to Mom. "Plenty of volunteers to stay. Let's go."

"But we have business to conduct," Lori said to my mother.

"It'll have to wait," Mom told her. "Story's right, I need to know what this dangerous stuff looks like. Some of our neighbors raise cows. They will want to know if it's growing where it shouldn't."

"Then I'm coming along, too." The real estate agent in Lori wasn't letting go.

"Where's Grams?" Mom said, her neck swiveling in all directions. "She should come along and take pictures of it."

"Here I am!" We saw an arm shoot up in the air from the back of the room. My little grandmother had to be delighted—usually Mom exhibited extreme impatience with Grams's photography, yet now here she was, endorsing it.

A whole pack of us headed down the street, Milly in the lead.

Hunter happened to be driving south on Main at the same time we were traveling north. He pulled over, rolled down his window, and called out to me, "You haven't organized a lynch mob, have you?"

Without slowing down, Mom said, "Hello, Hunter. We're about to get a lesson in poisonous hemlock."

At that, Hunter parked his truck and jumped out, released Ben from the back, clipped on a leash, and joined us as we marched past Stu's Bar and Grill. Some of the bar patrons joined us, too.

Milly led the way down to the left side of the bridge, where we edged along the Oconomowoc riverbank. She had quite an entourage by the time we cut through the brush and followed the river. "None of this along here is it," she told a few of the more hesitant souls who were reluctant to touch anything remotely green and growing, just in case it happened to be water hemlock.

Hunter, Ben, and I brought up the rear of the party. Hunter took my hand as we stepped over rocks.

I had to admit to myself that it wasn't the same without Patti tagging along. She was usually the first in line when it came to adventure. She would have loved this outing. I told myself I didn't really miss her. It just wasn't the same. I was only saying that Patti would have been in the thick of things if she'd been around. In her element.

Where, I stopped to think, *was Patti now?*

I've wondered a lot about my neighbor's secretive past. Turns out, she really did have some skeletons in her closet. But if she had family to stay with, I didn't know where they lived or who they were. Before she caught me in her house, Patti had never shared a single private piece of information, always redirecting personal questions away from herself.

Up ahead, Milly continued into a marshy area where cattails grew tall and muck squished between my flip-flopped toes. Milly hadn't said anything about our having to plow through mud.

She came to a halt. "There it is. Make absolutely sure you don't touch it!" she warned us. "Just look."

Mom was up front and center, with Lori leeched on to her like the blood sucker she was. We made a path for Grams and her camera, and the group took turns moving forward and viewing the pretty plant that had played the major part in killing Nova Campbell. In its natural set-ting, it looked harmless, with whispery, lanky, delicate flowers and leaves. No one would ever suspect it of such toxic potential.

Except maybe a flavorist.

"Has Sally thoroughly questioned Holly's house-guests?" I whispered into Hunter's ear. "And confirmed their whereabouts that morning?"

"You mean she should?" We made eye contact. His were dancing.

"Am I interfering again?"

"Just a little."

"Sorry."

On the way back, Lori and I accidentally bumped into each other, and she slipped and fell into the river. Her file folder and paperwork sank with her.

Oops.

Seventeen

Lori Spandle and I have been getting in each other's face since first grade when she started our ongoing war by throwing me off the school's play equipment. I'd broken my arm.

So her little dip in the river was nothing compared to some of our earlier skirmishes.

She came up out of the murky water sputtering and spitting, her round face beet red, which was really nothing new. It was a pleasure to watch as the rental papers scattered in the water, sinking slowly, the ink running in unreadable streaks.

Others stepped forward to help Lori out of the water. I could hear her swearing like a truck driver, showing the world the real Lori Spandle. I immediately stepped back, happy that my small role hadn't been obvious to the rest of the group. Hunter, however, was on to me immediately.

"Did you really just push Lori into the river?" he

whispered, the lightness of his tone cluing me in that he was enjoying the moment almost as much as I was. He'd seen Lori in action and didn't like what he saw, either. As part of her quest to undermine me, Lori had actually hit on Hunter back in high school, and then again after we reconnected as adults. Wasn't she supposed to be married? Such a pity our poor cuckolded town chairman, Grant, was stuck with her as a wife! Although her husband wasn't a great prize himself.

"You're going to appreciate it even more," I said to Hunter, leading him away as quickly as possible, "once you hear what she's up to now."

I hurried Hunter over to Stu's, to an outdoor table behind the bar and grill, out of sight, but definitely not out of Lori's mind, based on my name, which was being taken in a whole lot of vain. I'd have to watch my back with her, but what else was new?

Hunter released Ben from the leash, and he plopped down at our feet, licking his paws.

"Have you told Sally about the Patti connection yet?" Hunter wanted to know.

"I will. Right after we leave here." At the moment my mind was on Lori and my mother. "Brace yourself," I warned Hunter. "This is not pleasant news."

He sighed, one of those really tired kinds of sighs—deep and long, implying he wasn't prepared for what I had to offer, but was resigned to whatever it turned out to be.

"My mother and Tom Stocke are moving in together," I told him. Hunter's eyebrows shot up in surprise. "I know," I said. "Who would have thought? Aren't they way too old for that sort of thing?"

Hunter pondered my announcement for a few minutes then decided to say, "Good for them. I like Tom. He's good people."

What? Was I the only one who could see how wrong this was? Holly approved. So did Grams. Now Hunter, too?

I cleared my throat. "There is just one tiny issue that goes along with their decision. One small problem we need to discuss."

"I'm braced," he said.

"Mom and Tom are moving in next door to us, into my ex's vacant house."

To the casual observer, nothing about Hunter changed much. You'd have to know him as well as I do to see the signs. They were subtle—jaw and lips a little tighter, nostrils slightly twitching (one at a time), Adam's apple quivering, eyes planted on the river as though deep in thought.

As I waited for him to say something, I tried not to revert to the same old pessimism I'd been struggling with. I wanted to believe in the power of us. He wasn't going to leave me over this, was he? My mother had never been kind to him. Hunter didn't deserve what she was about to dish out. In fact, he shouldn't have to go through any of what my whole family was dragging him into. A body in his new yard, his live-in lover (that's me) the bearer of poisoned carrot juice, my mother spying from next door, like a vulture, watching and waiting.

If I was Hunter, I might run like hell.

I waited some more.

Eventually, he rubbed his chin. He scanned the river. What was he thinking? Was I turning out to be a liability he couldn't afford? After what seemed like forever, Hunter finally spoke. "I'm going back to the house for something to relieve the headache I feel coming on."

The house. During the honeymoon phase, it had been "our" house; then when things got dicey it turned into "my" house; now it was "the" house. Not a good sign.

"Are you okay?" I had to know. *Please say yes.*

"Probably," Hunter replied.

Right then, we were interrupted by a very unpleasant piece of news delivered without a single gossipy bit of advance warning. Someone from the top of the bridge, right above us, said, "Well, look what we have here."

I didn't have to look up to know that smug, arrogant voice.

Johnny Jay! He was back. And the timing couldn't be worse.

I should have immediately found Sally when I had the chance and given her the information about Patti. Now the chief was back in town which meant that Sally was back to being just a regular cop. Darn. Well, at least Hunter was here to support me.

Hunter went into professional mode and greeted the chief as he walked down from the bridge to join us. Then Hunter said, "We have a few more pieces of the murder puzzle. Why don't you sit down with us and we'll fill you in?"

"I don't need Fischer's twisted interpretation of the truth," Johnny said. "Or anything from her boyfriend, either. You aren't on this case, Wallace."

"I know that," Hunter said. "But you'll want to hear what we know."

Johnny Jay pulled a phone from his belt and punched in numbers. Hunter rubbed his forehead.

"I'm trying to explain to Hunter Wallace that he isn't needed here," Johnny said after identifying himself.

Hunter closed his eyes and rubbed his head some more.

"Your captain wants to speak to you," the chief said snidely, handing the phone to Hunter. Johnny Jay's territorialism has been broadcast far and wide and nobody challenges his authority unless they want a long battle. It just isn't worth it to most other law enforcement agencies.

Hunter listened, then disconnected and handed the phone back to the chief. "I need to get going," he said. I suspected he was being called off to preserve the peace. Hunter and Johnny Jay have gone a few rounds in the past and this had the potential of escalating into one of those manly pushing and shoving and in-your-face situations. His captain was probably doing a smart thing.

"You'll be okay?" Hunter asked me.

"I can handle myself," I half truthed, then watched him take off with Ben.

The chief eyed me with a scowl. "You and your sister stay put. Don't attempt to leave town."

"When have I ever run away from a fight with you?" I replied, playing tough. "I live for these moments."

"Fischer, I'm going to keep reading my legal book until the time is right, and then I'm going to throw it at you."

"Bring it on," I said.

"And where is that nosy neighbor of yours?" he asked. "I'd like a word or two with her."

"You're on your own there."

I went back to the store, tired from a very long day. After making sure everything was stocked properly and running smoothly for the evening with the twins on duty, I went home.

Later, when Hunter and Ben came home, we sat on the front porch, eating Chinese carryout right from the boxes. We didn't really have much to say to each other.

Patti's house was dark.

So was Mom's future home.

Male bullfrogs called into the night, trying to attract females. The river hummed with awakening nocturnal life.

When Hunter went inside, I decided to push my kayak out onto the river and spent the next few hours paddling around, clearing my mind of all thoughts.

When I returned, Hunter and Ben were back outside, waiting for me on the bank. Hunter wrapped his arm around my shoulders and we walked into the house, which still seemed to be waiting for the right possessive noun to make it special.

Eighteen

Bright and early Monday morning I tended to my bees, greeting them as they came out on their little hive porches and flew off to forage. The summer months are carefree in the apiary, since honeybees are able to find so many flowering plants. Some of my bees landed on me before taking off, up close and personal with all those little eyes. I wasn't wearing my bee suit but I'd taken the standard precautions, most of which are plain common sense. As I tell visitors in advance:

- Don't wear perfumes or strongly scented shaving creams. Either the bees will mistake you for a flower, or they will take a strong dislike to your smell and let you know how they feel. Either way, you might get stung.

- Wear light colors (whites and beiges). The very worst would be a bright floral pattern. Same reason. Don't look like a flower.

- Since honeybees are naturally curious, they will crawl inside loose-fitting clothing, get trapped, and start stinging. Sweat pants with elastic cuffs and rubber bands to keep them out of tight places are a beekeeper's best friends.

- Don't go barefoot, especially in a yard like mine where I encourage clover and dandelions to sprout freely. Little critters can't see giant feet descending until it's too late for both of you.

See? All common sense.

After my bee hello, I had to deal with a canoe on the river. I don't usually pay any attention to traffic on the river, but these two guys were taking pictures of my backyard from one of Stu's rental canoes. I threw a stone or two and they took off. The nerve!

Then I tossed a Frisbee for Ben until I was exhausted (he could have played forever), packed my man off with a kiss, and walked down Main Street to open the store. Milly Hopincourt showed up first. Thankfully, everything seemed back to normal, the way it should be, the way I needed it to be.

"I'm handling all the meals for the Paines' guests," she informed me.

"You shouldn't have to do that."

"Max is paying me very well. The extra cash will come in handy. Besides, I'm enjoying it so much I'm considering opening a catering business." With that, she headed down the aisles to stock up on supplies for her next round of meals.

Carrie Ann came in next, saying, "Sure has been a lot of action around here." I noticed how fresh-eyed she was. As her cousin and friend, I pay attention to things like that. We can't let her dive back into the bottom of a bottle of beer, or vodka, or whatever she used to drink, which was just about anything she could get her hands on.

"The police chief is back in town," I told her.

"Oh, no. I'm so sorry," she said. "That man has one big vendetta against you."

"Tell me about it."

My cousin settled in behind the cash register while I straightened my Queen Bee Honey display and considered Johnny Jay's prejudiced attitude and fat-skulled head. Not listening to the information Hunter and I had was downright unprofessional on his part. By now Sally must have run a background check on Nova, and the chief should already know that Nova and Patti had been married to the same man. Even the most incompetent investigator should've been able to track down that info. The part about Patti wading into the river, though, was an important detail only known by Hunter and me.

So, since Johnny had gotten all snarky and cut us off, did we have any further obligation to keep trying? What had he said about me, that he didn't need my twisted interpretation of the truth? Fine then. Johnny Jay could take a flying leap, that's what.

I was beginning to understand how Patti could have written that awful article to redirect the investigation away from herself. Because my whole family could profit from a little redirecting right back at her with the news that she had been the last one to see Nova alive. Murder, I'm finding out, brings out the finer pointing in people.

But even Hunter had fallen silent on the subject, at least for now. Knowing him, he would decide he had a professional obligation to report what I'd told him about Patti, but it wouldn't begin or end with the chief. Hunter would backdoor it through his own department.

Then Johnny Jay would come looking for me. I couldn't shake that man no matter what.

Right before lunch, my mother showed up, but I'd known she was coming. Without talking to me first, Carrie Ann had put her back on the schedule. Which should've made me mad, but it was a good decision on Carrie Ann's part. Mom and I exchanged pleasantries, making me think she'd decided to give me at least the same courtesy she extended to people she didn't know. Progress—I think.

Then I took off for Holly's house.

When I pulled up, Johnny Jay was just leaving.

"The noose is tightening," he said. "I have an entire jail block in reserve for your family." He smirked before driving off. Johnny Jay needed serious counseling to get past whatever he had against me. It was clouding his judgment. The guy has always been a bully and a jerk, everybody in town knows that, but the excess attention he spends on trying to bring me down isn't healthy. For either of us.

Holly, Max, Gil, and Camilla were all congregated around an outside table covered with delectable dishes, thanks to Milly. I saw Effie out in the rose garden, wearing some kind of netting all over her body.

"Chance must not have eliminated the spider threat," I said to my sister.

"No!" she said. "Effie says they're still all over the place. Chance doesn't want to spray chemicals, so they have to handpick the spiders wearing thick gloves or try to squash them underfoot, and now more are hatching." Holly shivered at the thought of creepy-crawly critters.

"What was the police chief up to?" I asked after pulling her aside. Camilla hadn't even acknowledged my existence, but Gil gave me a big smile and wave.

"Asking a whole lot of questions, the same ones everybody already answered, but this time around a few more details came out."

Darn! If only I'd been a little earlier, I might have

learned a lot more from Gil and Camilla's official statements. "Anything revealing?"

"Well, it's no secret that Gil and Camilla had a hard time putting up with Nova, but that's sort of beside the point."

"Why's that?"

"They both have ironclad alibis for the entire period of time the chief asked about."

That certainly surprised me.

"Go on," I said.

Holly leaned in and whispered, "They were together. In Gil's room. And they weren't one bit embarrassed about it, blurted it out right in front of Max and me when they could have kept it private between them and the chief."

Now that she mentioned it, I remembered Gil and Camilla looking a bit cozy together during dinner at Holly's. Except . . . "Camilla was out on one of your ATVs that morning," I said. "I saw her myself. Has everybody forgotten that?"

"That was earlier in the morning. The chief only asked about our whereabouts between eleven a.m. and leaving together for your house."

"And those two were in bed together then?!"

"Actually they have much better alibis than I do," Holly said grimly. "Nobody can back me up. Or Max. We both were off alone. Max was in his office and I was hiding out in my own room."

"Somebody's lying. I think Camilla did it."

Holly shook her head. "The chief seemed satisfied with their story."

"So neither of them had an opportunity to add poison to the juice?"

"Apparently."

Rats! There went my pet theory. I sighed and thought about the new information. And came up with another idea—Camilla and Gil were in on it together! They could've been in bed together in more ways than one. Camilla could have been out selecting the perfect poison while Gil arranged their alibis.

All I had to do was prove it. I'd keep it to myself for the time being.

Holly clutched my arm. "Johnny Jay told me his noose is tightening around my neck. I can actually feel it. He wasn't at all nice to me. What am I going to do?"

"Relax," I told her. "He threatened me with the same noose. In the end, justice will prevail." Which I didn't believe for one second. I've been on a jury during a trial and seen firsthand how random "justice" actually works. But I had to say something to reassure her.

My sister forgot all about her own problems when I told her about the Harry Bruno, Nova, and Patti triangle.

"Nova and Patti, married to the same guy? That Patti is such a mystery woman," Holly said when I finished. "Do you believe her?"

"She said Nova was dead by the time she got to her. If Nova had drowned, Patti would be suspect number one. But poison? That was premeditated, and Patti claims she didn't identify Nova as Harry's second wife until she showed up in my yard. Patti didn't have time to arrange to murder her with poison."

"Passion is a strong motive."

"She didn't do it," I said, firmly.

I sure hoped I was right.

Nineteen

When we rejoined the others, talk around the lunch table had to do with the police chief's visit, their orders not to leave town, and whether Johnny Jay really suspected any of them.

I slid into a chair next to Max and kept quiet as a mouse, but listened like an owl.

This whole thing was starting to remind me of one of my favorite board games, Clue.

Holly and Max's house is a lot like the layout of the original board. A millionaire's mansion with a library, billiard room, conservatory, the works. Except we already had a pretty good idea where it happened (or at least began)—in the bedroom, on the nightstand where the juice glass had been found, then on into my backyard. And the murder weapon wasn't a lead pipe or candlestick. It wasn't even a revolver. It was poison, which I didn't remember being an option in the game.

The only question left was who did it? Ms. Scarlett (aka Camilla)? Or Colonel Mustard (Gil)? Or both of them working as a team?

As much as I'd enjoyed the game, though, I really hadn't been very good at it, always focusing on one suspect from the very beginning instead of spreading out my suspicions. Food for thought, I decided. I didn't want to fall into the same old losing strategy.

My game-playing fantasy was interrupted by Gil. "This certainly has been awkward." He glanced at me. "Story might as well know, everybody else does."

Camilla saw me glance at her and actually had the decency to show some discomfort. I tried not to smirk and thought I did a pretty good job of refraining. I made a mental note to find out if she really did have special permission to pick wildflowers. I doubted it, but wanted to confirm that she'd lied to me.

"I heard about your alibis," I said to Gil, keeping my voice neutral, thinking these two sure seemed overly blabby about their personal affair.

Gil went on, "Nothing like having your dirty laundry exposed."

His lady love shot him dagger eyes. He noticed and tried to backpedal. "Not that I'm calling you dirty laundry."

Camilla got up and left the table.

"You certainly stuck your foot in your mouth this time," Max said to him, filling a cup with coffee from a carafe and handing it to me. I smiled my thanks. Max was a true gentleman. Holly had chosen well.

Max frowned at Gil. "Both of you know that Savour Foods discourages this kind of involvement between employees."

"It's not like one of us is the other's supervisor," Gil argued. "Based on how little we liked or respected the woman, it's lucky we even have alibis, or we'd be the primary suspects. I really wish I hadn't ever handled that juice jar."

I came to full attention after that remark. "Your fingerprints were on the jar?"

Max answered, "Gil wrote a note on the jar with magic marker: *Don't drink. This belongs to Nova.*"

"I was trying to be helpful," he said to me. "Nova got all possessive and combative over every little thing."

"That must have looked to Johnny Jay like you were warning away others, so the correct person would be poisoned," I said, wondering why Gil wasn't in custody.

"This is ridiculous."

He got up and went inside.

Max apologized to me for his employees.

"Not necessary," I said. "You aren't responsible for their actions."

"Those three never worked well together. I should have split them up long ago. Although I guess two of them worked together too well!"

"What was the main problem?"

"They were in such competition with each other. A little competitiveness is healthy, but theirs bordered on cutthroat, each of them taking credit for successes they hadn't earned, backstabbing each other, forgetting what it means to be a working team."

Holly overheard her husband and joined us. "Poor Max," she said, standing behind him and rubbing his shoulders and neck. "They fought like children."

"I could never get through this without your support," Max said to her, then to me, "It's not easy being away so much."

At that I thought more about Max and my sister, how they rarely shared this aspect of their marriage with me, the struggles and their unity. Sure, Holly was the first one to gripe when Max was on the road too long, letting me know she loved and missed him, but this was my first insight into her role as a supportive wife.

And I'd thought she only cared about her looks and avoiding work. My sister actually had more depth than I gave her credit for.

"Was the new discovery contentious?" I asked.

"More so than any other. Each of them wanted to take all the credit."

Holly kissed the top of Max's head and sat down.

A few minutes later, Chance drove up and parked near the carriage house. Effie rose from a kneeling position beside a red rosebush, pulled off the netting protecting her from the big bad spiders, and went over to join her husband. From their body language I got the distinct impression they were arguing. Effie had her finger in his face and her posture screamed anger even though she wasn't raising her voice. I couldn't hear a word as much as I tried.

Chance folded his arms across his chest in defensive resistance and his feet and body were angled slightly away from his wife.

"Looks like the honeymoon is over for them," I observed. Even an online matchmaking service couldn't guarantee a match made in heaven.

"Relationships," Max observed, "are never easy."

I certainly had to agree.

Twenty

"Any leads yet?" I asked Sally Maylor when she popped into The Wild Clover to buy a soda, leaving her squad car idling outside, as usual.

"A few loose threads to follow up on, but not much. I'd like to slap cuffs on those two guests, though," she whispered to me. "Something smells to high heaven. What a relief to turn this whole investigation over where it belongs, in the chief's lap."

"Johnny Jay is after Holly, you know. He's overfocusing in the wrong place."

"Anything you want to share about Camilla Bailey and Gil Green? Something that I might not know yet? Something I can use to help your sister get out from under the microscope?"

Sally has a heart of gold, almost making up for the heart Johnny Jay is lacking. "They didn't get along with Nova," I told her.

"Check," Sally said, and I assumed that meant she already had that info on her radar.

"Both of them have the background to concoct a lethal poison."

"Check."

"The two surviving coworkers were comingling."

That earned a snicker from Sally before she said, "Check."

"Camilla went out on an ATV that morning."

"And you're implying . . . what?"

So I told her about our confrontation. "She could have been searching for hemlock."

"Is that all you have?"

"What about that warning note Gil put on the jar?"

"I know about that, too."

"Convenient that they both alibied each other."

"Cops don't always believe alibis, you know," she said, popping open the soda and glancing out the window at her vehicle.

"I didn't know that!" And I didn't.

"You watch too much television," Sally said, shaking her head in mock disbelief. "You have to stop believing those cop shows. The real world works differently."

"I don't have time for the luxury of sitting in front of the TV."

"Hunter keeping you too busy for that?"

"Don't you have anything better to do?" I said with a laugh.

Soon after that Johnny Jay arrived to do his smoke and mirrors act. "I have three major suspects," he said from a metal chair next to me in the back room, where he was tilting the chair onto its back legs. I had to fight the urge to give him a shove backward.

"Nobody invited you into this room," I said.

"Where's that list of mine?" He pretended to check his

breast pocket and came up empty. "I don't need it anyway. Your sister's on it, for one. The jealous type, isn't she? Doesn't tolerate other women getting too close to that husband of hers."

"Now who would tell you a dumb thing like that?" Obviously he wasn't going to take the blatant hint to leave.

"A reliable source."

"Reliable? That fraudulent news article, right? The one written by Patti Dwyre? You should be out hunting for her instead of lounging in my store."

He kept going, "Then there's the husband. Max Paine. Smooth guy, friendly type, but he has an agenda. Maybe Campbell was putting a kink in his style, or she was about to tell the Mrs. a thing or two."

"Pure fiction."

"Then there's the sister-in-law." It took me a minute to realize he was talking about me. "Little sister needs help eliminating some competition, threatening to disrupt her fancy lifestyle. So big sister decides to handle the problem once and for all. Brings over some poisoned juice. End of problem."

"You've been watching too many cop shows," I said, using Sally's line. "I want you to leave my store right now."

"Want to come with me and make a full confession?"

"Johnny," I said, leaning in close, "you don't like me very much, do you?"

"Doesn't matter. I don't let personal feelings affect my work." He glared at me, and I'm happy to report he was the first one to look away.

He'd answered the question all right, the creep. "It doesn't affect your work? Really? What a crock," I told him. "You blame me for everything that happens in Moraine. Your obsession with nailing me for some kind of serious jail-time offense is affecting your work in a big way."

Johnny stood up and said, "I'm done with you for the time being, but I'll be back."

After he left, I called Hunter. "How does a person file harassment charges against a cop?" I asked.

"What did I do now? Can't we just talk it through?" I heard the amusement in his tone.

"Not you. I have more interesting ways to handle you. Seriously, how?"

"Document injuries, take photos, name witnesses."

Okay, then. I didn't have any injuries to take pictures of. And now that I thought about it, Johnny Jay was very careful when he hassled me. Hardly any witnesses, ever, except maybe Patti once or twice.

Hunter read my mind over the phone and said, "Lay off Johnny Jay."

"What? The guy just left my store. He came here and accused me of killing Nova Campbell."

Hunter sighed into the receiver, loud and deep. "Do you and the chief have to go through this every single time something happens in town? Just stay away from him."

"He's the one showing up on my turf."

Then I went on to complain about Holly's houseguests and how nobody seemed to be trying to gather evidence against them, which I didn't get because in my book this was an open-and-shut case and maybe I should just investigate myself since if I didn't, a certain vindictive police chief would make life living hell for me and my sister.

"Besides, if I was going to kill anybody," I said, finishing my rant. "It wouldn't be a weekend visitor. The dead body would belong to Johnny Jay."

"Are you done?" Hunter asked.

"Not quite. What about the box of carrot juices from my store?"

"I haven't heard back yet, but I'm expecting those to be fine."

"In a perfect world, the entire box would be contaminated. But, of course, it would be the only one from the distributor that was, so nobody else would get hurt. That would clear all of us."

"I like your world, but it isn't very realistic, although stranger things have happened. I'll bring home pizza."

"At least something's going right today."

Next up, I had a meeting with Milly to go over the store's monthly newsletter.

"Your arugula and tomato salad was fantastic," I told her. "And the popovers with honey butter were heaven. Let's put them in the newsletter."

Milly beamed like she'd found the golden egg, which was the way she reacted every time I praised her recipes. "We still need to add a few honey-based sweet treats," she said. "I've got several ideas."

All of us at The Wild Clover looked forward to sampling her "ideas."

"To think of all the times you've used ingredients from the wild," I said. "Like watercress and morel mushrooms. But now with this whole hemlock thing, maybe we should stick to store-bought items in the future."

Milly didn't agree. "You and I know the difference between an edible plant and an unknown," she said. "We might not be able to identify everything out there, but we aren't careless."

Which was true. In our area, we have some of nature's tastiest plants growing on our doorsteps (well, almost on our doorsteps). Besides watercress and morels, we have:

- Ramps—these taste like a cross between onions and garlic

- Asparagus—under the electrical wires along roadsides where birds drop seeds

• Puffballs—white mushrooms the size of basketballs

• Chanterelles—mushrooms with a peachy flavor

• Hickory nuts—a real delicacy

I sure would hate to give up all of those beauties.

"Milly," I said. "Water hemlock is really creeping me out. I admit it. You told us not to touch it, right?"

"Yes, but now that you've seen it, you know to stay clear of it."

"But it would be okay if I wore gloves?"

"That would be the only way to handle it safely."

"Interesting."

"What are you up to?"

"Just curious."

While Milly sat at the computer in the back room creating the framework for the next newsletter, I helped the twins unload cases of award-winning Door County wines—cherry (both sweet and dry), panacea peach, cranberry, plum, and Peninsula dinner reds and whites.

"How come you're always around to help with wine shipments?" Trent said, laughing. The twins had recently celebrated their twenty-first birthdays and were now officially of drinking age.

"We really can handle it without you," his twin brother said with an ear-to-ear grin.

"I haven't tried this one yet," I said, pulling out a bottle of Razzle Dazzle Raspberry.

We bantered back and forth, but at some point I stopped listening, because the pieces were connecting in my mind. Camilla had been wearing gloves when we had our little tiff over wildflowers. If I could get my hands on those gloves and have Jackson Davis test them for trace evidence, it's possible he might find a nice sample of a certain poisonous plant.

That would nail her to the wall for good.

I spent some time trying to picture the scene, focusing on the gloves Camilla had been wearing, but I must have been too angry to have paid much attention. All I knew for sure is that they weren't colorful or flowery, so they must have been a nondescript neutral color.

After making sure everything was operating smoothly at the store, I drove over to Holly's house again.

Twenty-one

"You want to take out a four-wheeler?" Holly said, standing barefoot on her patio, wearing short-shorts and a halter top.

"You sound surprised."

"Where are you planning to go?" she asked.

"Just riding around." I dodged. "It's a nice day, thought I'd explore a bit, feel the wind in my hair."

"I'll come along," my sister said. "Max took Gil and Camilla up to Holy Hill."

Holy Hill is a nearby basilica, and one of our most spectacular landmarks, not too far from where Hunter had lived. People make pilgrimages year-round to the National Shrine of Mary and its tower with a breathtaking panorama of the Kettle Moraine area. Max and guests could be gone for hours.

Effie walked toward us from the carriage house. "I

heard you say something about an ATV," she said. "If you plan on riding, I have to warn you, it's going to rain."

We all looked up at the sky. Sure enough, black clouds were rolling in fast.

"A short ride then," I said.

"I'll put my shoes on," Holly said, heading for the house.

"And I need to borrow a pair of gardening gloves," I added to her retreating back, not ready to elaborate, not wanting her to know of my suspicions until I had more concrete proof. But Effie cocked her head to the left, watching me, and I felt more of an explanation was necessary. "In case, I, uh, find, uh, an injured animal or something. That happened once. I came across a cooper's hawk with a broken wing. If I hadn't had a pair of gloves along, I wouldn't have been able to rescue it."

Which was a true story, so my cover had the ring of credibility to it.

"I think there are a few pairs of gloves out there on the worktable," Effie offered. "Help yourself, but don't forget that some animals around here are rabid. If you spot a normally nocturnal animal, like bats or foxes, during the day, stay away."

Holly bounced out then, and we went to the outbuilding where she and Max store all their toys. Besides several four-wheelers, they also own a Jeep for all-terrain fun, commercial-grade lawn and garden equipment, and two snowmobiles.

While my sister fired up one of the ATVs, I spotted several pairs of gloves on the worktable where Effie had said they'd be, and decided that once we returned from our ride I'd confiscate every glove on the premises. I had tucked a plastic bag in my pocket exclusively for that roundup job and was pretty excited about turning my find over to Jackson for analysis.

That was the beauty of being an average citizen instead of law enforcement. Hunter would have to go through all kinds of red tape to get his hands on somebody else's gloves that might have been used in a murder. But me, since I have no authority, I also have no responsibility. I can do exactly as I please without ramifications. Well, almost as I please.

With me in the driver's seat and Holly sitting behind me, we roared down a path that connected to a trail which in turn led through the countryside. It was the same trail Camilla had followed the day we'd met under those far from ideal circumstances. To think she'd probably gathered her poison right after that meeting, or even before! The thought made my skin crawl. That flower bouquet in her fist must have been a distraction for anybody wondering what she was really up to.

At first, the air smelled of freshly mown grass. We waved to Chance out on a riding lawn mower. Then the air blowing in my face changed to fragrant pine as we entered a copse of evergreens. The trail had been recently groomed, thanks to volunteers who worked together, claiming sections to patrol and manage.

"I smell mock orange," I called out as the heady aroma of orange and jasmine assailed my senses, reminding me of the white mock orange flower my grandmother had worn in her hair.

Much too quickly we arrived at the scene of the Camilla/Story conflict. I turned off the engine, waited for Holly to swing off, then walked her over to the spot. I decided to tell her all about our first meeting, all the details as I remembered them, gloves and all. Earlier, I hadn't wanted to stress her out any more than she already was (which was plenty), but now it seemed like the appropriate time to clue her in.

"I have a strong hunch that Camilla murdered Nova,"

I said, finishing up. "After all, it fits." I ticked off my bullet points for her. "Means: with her flavorist background, she should know her plants, including poisonous ones. Motive: Max told us about the growing conflict within the group. And opportunity . . . well, I'm still working on it now that Gil and Camilla gave alibis for each other. But Camilla certainly could have had the opportunity to pick water hemlock."

"Camilla *is* kind of strange," Holly agreed. "They both are. But your motive and means could apply to Gil just as easily as they do to her."

"It has to be one of them. We know *we* didn't murder Nova. And Max certainly didn't. Who's left besides those two?"

"Patti."

"She didn't do it," I said, not for the first time. "I'm placing my bet on Camilla Bailey. Here's my plan—since the only way to handle hemlock is with gloves, and Camilla was wearing a pair when I first met her, I'm taking all the gloves at your place to Jackson Davis for an analysis."

Thunder rumbled in the distance.

"We better get going," Holly said, looking up at dark clouds forming in the sky.

I scanned the growth. "No water hemlock here. Let's go back to the house, but slower. You drive so I can keep my eyes peeled."

"Ick, I don't even know what water hemlock looks like, and I don't want to know."

About a quarter mile down the road, I asked Holly to pull over near a marshy area. She waited on the ATV while I made my way down to the water, carefully inspecting the flora. The last thing I wanted to do was accidentally brush against the stuff. All the years I'd been so carefree, but now paranoia had set in.

And with good reason: I spotted the water hemlock

almost instantly, lacy flowers waving gently in the increasing breeze.

I hurried back to the ATV and announced my discovery to Holly. "She must have picked it right over there," I decided. "Too bad Johnny Jay refuses to hear a word I have to say."

"I'd like to wrestle that guy to the ground and get him in a scorpion death lock for what he's doing to our family."

I took a moment to savor the image of Johnny trapped in my sister's vise grip.

I felt a drop of rain, then two. Overhead dark clouds grew angrier.

"Hurry up," Holly said, "and get on."

"Let's go collect some gloves." I swung up behind my sister and we were off as the rain came beating down on us.

By the time we pulled into the outbuilding, we were soaking wet.

Twenty-two

"I've decided you can't have them," Holly said, taking one of her formidable wrestling stances right in front of the table with the gloves in the outbuilding.

"What's wrong with you?" I asked her, surprised that she was directing all that aggression toward me.

"Think this through," Holly said, water droplets dripping from her hair, her top plastered to her chest. "What if Jackson finds something with the gloves?"

I gaped at her, just as wet. "That would be awesome!"

"Okay, what would be the next step?"

"Um, I guess at that point, Hunter could advise us," I suggested. It was a good thing Patti wasn't here. She hated asking for help from any male in one of our investigations. According to her, it was wimpy, sexist, clinging, subservient . . . the list went on and on, and none of it was complimentary.

I used to wonder about P.P. Patti's backstory, why she

was so fiercely independent almost to the point of care-
lessness, and why she didn't date. For a while, I figured
that maybe she found women more attractive, since she
had such a dislike for the males of our species. Now I
knew the truth. She'd had to get super tough to survive and
escape her abusive ex-husband.

No wonder she'd dissed me every time I suggested
including Hunter in any decision making.

"And then, what happens after?" Holly prodded me.
"What will Hunter and Jackson tell you to do once it's
established that a pair of gloves has residue from water
hemlock?"

I wrinkled my nose in disgust, because I hated saying
it. "They'd insist that I take it to the police chief. Can you
please come to the point?"

Holly hadn't relaxed her challenging physical position.
Maybe because she could tell that I was still looking for
an opening to snag the gloves. I should know better—I've
never gotten past her when she went in pin-down mode,
not once. "Then what?" she demanded. "What would the
chief do?"

I beamed. "He'd arrest Camilla Bailey for murder
one."

"Really? That's how you see it?"

"Well . . ."

I'm not completely dense all the time. I finally figured
out where this was going. "And how do *you* see the next
scene?" I asked rather weakly.

"Johnny Jay would pull me in for questioning." In case
I didn't know who "me" was, Holly jammed a thumb
toward her own chest. "Or Max. Or both of us. Because
all the gloves around here belong to us, not Camilla. He
might even arrest you as an accessory to murder, claiming you were trying to implicate a guest while covering
for me."

That *did* sound just like Johnny Jay. What had I been *thinking*? My word against Camilla's, with Johnny Jay as judge? He'd never believe that I'd really seen Camilla wearing gloves the same day Nova was murdered.

"Let's take a breather and figure out how to get around this little glitch," I said. "In the meantime, I'm going to make a phone call. Camilla told me she had a permit to pick wildflowers. If she lied about that, maybe she'd lie about her alibi, too."

We made a mad dash through the rain for the house and, after toweling off, sat down in the kitchen.

I called the DNR and was redirected thirteen times (Holly actually counted) before a computer-generated voice advised me to use the state's website. My sister hauled out her laptop.

"I doubt Camilla actually had permission," I said, scanning one link after another within the spiderweb of a website. "It says here that nobody can pick wildflowers, especially on public land, without an endangered-species permit."

"Maybe she has one."

"Issued by Wisconsin?"

"Probably not. She hasn't been here long enough."

"That's the only route to the permit here. Every state is different. And look at this—intentionally violating that law means a big fat fine and as much as nine months in jail. Or both. Actually, Johnny went easy on me."

Holly read the screen when I turned it toward her. "That's what it says, all right."

"She's busted for lie number one," I announced, pretty pleased with our progress so far. We'd found a bunch of water hemlock on the path Camilla had taken; she'd picked flowers as a cover while wearing a suspicious pair of gardening gloves (I'd bet my store that one of Holly's pairs of gloves would turn up with hemlock residue all over them); then lied about having a special picking permit.

Still, it was all circumstantial, and since Holly refused to give up any gloves, the only really important thing I could do was destroy Camilla's alibi. Because if I couldn't break that, she'd get away with murder.

Max and the others soon arrived back at the house, having been rained out of their tour of Holy Hill. I'd really hoped for more time so I could rummage around in Camilla's bedroom, but that would have to wait. I remembered that Patti had snuck up there the night of the dinner. Had she discovered anything? Probably not, or she would have told me.

At some point, I found myself alone in the kitchen with Gil. I decided to ask him about his work. "Tell me about the whole 'making vegetables taste like candy' thing you're working on," I said to him.

He sat down at the table. "What would you like to know?"

"Is it ready for market?"

Now he gave me a huff. "These things take significant time. They need to be perfected, then pass rigid inspection before appearing on the open market. We have a long way to go."

"Can you and Camilla continue your research without Nova? Wasn't her knowledge important to the project?" I suspected that Gil was the type of pompous ass who wouldn't appreciate anyone else getting more credit than he.

Another huff, and he proved me right. "She was a big nothing as far as the project is concerned. We'll make more headway without her and her self-serving ways. She spent more time taking credit for *my* work and trying to get into the boss's pants than actually producing anything."

Well, wasn't that a harsh attitude considering she was

a coworker and a dead one at that. Gil didn't even try to hide his bad feelings toward her.

"Any more contact with the police chief?" I asked.

"Contact? Not really. We gave statements, he called a few times for clarification of a few facts, but other than that, he seems to be preoccupied with chasing down more realistic suspects in the case."

I arched a brow. "More realistic suspects," I said. "Really?"

"Everybody knows where I was during the time in question," Gil said smugly.

I looked into his confident eyes and thought, *You certainly made sure of that, didn't you?*

Twenty-three

For the rest of the afternoon I stayed busy at the store planning new ways to create appealing displays and socializing with my customers. Being an integral part of the community is important to a business owner—caring about each and every person who steps through the entry-way is one of the keys to a successful enterprise. So I encourage all my staff to chat.

To a degree, of course. Carrie Ann has been known to abuse the privilege.

At five o'clock, I turned things over to the twins and walked home.

A Mercedes-Benz was parked outside Patti's house. Or not exactly in front of her house, more like between mine and hers. It was black with heavily tinted windows, and it had an Illinois license plate. I didn't have to be a good guesser to know who owned the car: Patti's ex, the Chicago mobster Harry Bruno, that's who.

Instantly I came up with a scenario. Harry Bruno found out wife number two had been murdered. And he'd assumed that wife number one had killed her. Not a stretch considering Nova had pretty much died at Patti's back door. How incriminating must that look? My brain said he was here for retribution.

I made a snap decision that either Hunter was coming home right now with his sidearm, or I was calling Stanley Peck for some firepower. I imagined the trunk of that Mercedes was filled with automatic and semi-automatic armory.

Even without the plates and insider information about Harry Bruno, I'd have known the car wasn't from around here. Moraine is a truck and SUV town with an occasional oddball like the Cadillac Fleetwood Grams drives. But a Mercedes? Never.

Speaking of Grams's Caddie, just then I saw it come creeping around the corner from Main Street. I had a front-row view at the curb when Grams attempted to park in front of the expensive car by nosing in. She almost made it. But then she clipped its front side panel with her nice and sturdy back bumper. As soon as she felt the impact, she slammed on the brakes and rolled down her window. I saw Dinky in the passenger's seat take a header onto the floor, but he bounced right back up like he was used to doing summersaults.

"What happened this time?" Grams asked me. "I thought I had plenty of space." Which she did. Plenty of room in front (like a mile), zero in back.

"Just a minor graze," I lied, eyeing some significant damage to the Mercedes. As usual when Grams misjudges, I couldn't see any damage to her car, not a scratch. The Caddie was like an armored vehicle.

I glanced around. Nobody was rushing us. "I suggest you swing hard to the left but go very slowly, then pull into my driveway and tuck up close to the house." Where the owner of said vehicle might not spot her right away and put two-and-two together. In which case he might show up wielding a two-by-four. Or sporting a forty-four.

Ignoring my directions, my grandmother rolled up her window, hit the gas, bounced up onto the curb, ran over my lawn and, after a lot of arm waving and pointing from me, ended up right where I'd told her to park.

As soon as she got out, I hustled Grams and Dinky into my house and ran to peer out one of my windows facing Patti's house.

"What are you looking for, sweetie?" Grams wanted to know, practically breathing down my neck.

"The owner of that Mercedes."

"There was some kind of animal crawling around behind the car," Grams pointed out. "It came out of the bushes on the opposite side of Patti's house. I think it's a bear."

"We don't have bears around here." I swung my head and caught motion behind the Mercedes, but couldn't make out anything more.

"Sure we do," Grams insisted. "Once in a while one gets lost and shows up. I'll go throw stones at it before it gets into your garbage can."

I grabbed Grams. "Stay here where you're safe." Then I looked out again. "Where did it go? Is it still there?"

For a minute, neither of us said anything or saw anything. Then I called Hunter on my cell phone. "Time to come home," I told him.

"I love how you miss me."

"Are you almost here?"

"And I love that breathy voice, it's really sexy." I assumed he was talking about my panicked breathing. Wasn't a cop supposed to be able to tell the difference between lusty desire and abject fear?

"Please tell me you just turned off Main Street with Ben."

"Not even close. I took a call right before my shift ended. I'm way on the other side of Waukesha . . . Boy you sure are acting smoking hot. Next time can you give me a heads-up?"

"Gotta go," I said, disconnecting and speed dialing Stanley.

"Well, I'll be," Grams said from beside me while I prayed that he would answer. "The bear went right under the car, just flattened and scooted underneath!"

I swung my head in that direction but missed the action again. As soon as I heard Stanley's familiar voice I said, "Something's going down over at Patti's house. How fast can you get here?"

"I'm on my way."

No need to tell him to come bearing arms. That was Stanley's standard mode of operation. How he's managed to stay out of jail this long is a miracle, and one I hope continues.

"We should call 9-1-1," Grams said.

"That means Johnny Jay."

"Oh, Lordy, forget it then. I have a better idea, I'll take pictures from the window, you go investigate."

I spotted movement inside the living room window next door. "Someone's inside Patti's house. See there?"

Grams squinted where my index finger pointed. "The light's not too good. Why don't I go over and knock on the door? See who answers." She had her point-and-shoot camera clutched in her hand.

"What about the bear?" I asked.

"I was only playing with you," Grams answered. "I'm pretty sure that's just Patti Dwyre, acting suspicious. All dressed in dark clothes and sneaking around like some kind of ninja."

"Who's in her house if Patti's under the Mercedes?"

"Can't be a good thing," Grams observed, understating the obvious.

Right then, Stanley came running in through my back door, his eyes almost as shiny with excitement as crazy Patti's can get. Grams, who was really getting into the spy act, said to him, "I'll knock on Patti's door. You cover me."

And before I could blink, she had scooped up Dinky and was gone, with Stanley right behind her. I ran out after them and swung my head toward the car on the curb, watching them with one eye as they headed for Patti's front door.

Before I knew what happened, I heard something loud, a big *kaboom*.

And the Mercedes at the curb actually blew to pieces!

Deafening noise, shooting flames, the works.

I let out a scream, realizing that Patti (or whoever) might have still been under the car when it exploded.

Everything after that seemed to play out in slow motion.

Me, with my hand over my mouth, rooted to the spot.

Grams with Dinky and Stanley on Patti's porch, staring out at the street.

The front door wrenching open, and a man rushing out, almost bowling Grams over. So this must be Harry Bruno. He didn't live up to the stereotypical Italian mobster persona. He was all around medium: medium height, medium brown hair, medium weight (no big plates of pasta for this guy), casually dressed rather than wearing an expensive suit. He wasn't even wearing a Rolex. But most important, was he armed?

Stanley waved his weapon, which had appeared out of nowhere.

The guy's face twisted in disbelief and rage when he got a look at what was left of his car. He turned back and pulled out a gun even bigger than Stanley's. Nobody breathed while Harry and Stanley played chicken with their pieces.

Out of the cover of my eye, I was relieved to see a big black blob disappear around the other side of Patti's house. Presumably Patti herself, which meant she was okay.

I also realized how lucky my grandmother was, safe from mob retribution for winging the Mercedes since the front end wasn't recognizable any longer. At least somebody might live through this.

A tire rim actually rolled down the street, just like in the movies.

Stanley yelled at the guy to explain himself, then put his own weapon down on the ground and his hands in midair in a white-flag gesture.

The guy slung the ugliest foul language I'd ever heard at my friend, and Grams threatened to wash his mouth out with soap.

"We didn't do it," I yelled, thinking he probably thought we had.

At that point, the guy turned tail and hustled to the corner before disappearing down Main Street with sirens screaming in the distance.

Grams had been right.

Nothing good could come of any of this.

Twenty-four

"What do you mean, nobody saw anything?" Johnny Jay said, acting tough and belligerent. "The three of you just happened to be standing around when a car exploded, but nobody saw a thing?" He kicked a piece of metal. "Start from the beginning again."

"How many times are we going to have to repeat what we already told you?" Grams said, taking picture after picture of all the details—metal hunks, police squad, all the players involved.

Dinky sniffed at Johnny's pant cuff before squatting and peeing on his shoe.

"That means she likes you," Grams informed him.

Johnny Jay glared at her, as he tried to wipe the top of his shoe off in the grass.

"We were around back of the house looking at Story's beehives," Stanley said for the umpteenth time. "We didn't see a thing but sure we heard the explosion."

The three of us had been quick on our feet, deciding in a unanimous vote to lie up a storm. I had used my effective bullet points to rapid fire information at Grams and Stanley. I said:

- Mafia!

- Hunting for Patti!

- Bad guy!

- Deserved it!

That's all the information they needed to rally around and follow my lead.

No way did we want the police chief targeting any of us. Secondly, if we told the truth and nothing but the truth, Stanley would get busted for having an illegal weapon.

With siren's wailing ever closer, Stanley had confirmed that he didn't have a license to carry. Worse, the gun wasn't even registered. We threw it in the window well behind the house and covered it with leaves.

Nor did we want Johnny Jay to go after Patti, the actual perpetrator. I didn't want her to get in trouble for protecting herself. She had enough problems. I briefly wondered where she learned how to make the explosive device, and where she'd gotten the supplies. Knowing Patti, she'd been stashing them, preparing in advance for this day to arrive.

From what I'd just observed, the ex-husband had a worthy opponent in my neighbor. My bet was on Patti. She'd just won the first battle. The war was a slam-dunk, if this move was any indication. Plus, with her ability in the stealth department, she had the advantage of surprise on her side.

Anyway, back to the present situation, Johnny Jay

continued to threaten and bully, but we'd been through worse with him.

"I bet it was terrorists," Grams suggested helpfully after his blustering wound down. "Al-Qaeda. Or Taliban."

Johnny gave up and sat in his car writing up a report while a tow truck loaded the bombed-out Mercedes to move it to the station where experts would go over it with a fine-toothed comb.

It wasn't until Hunter pulled up that I realized the ramifications of our group lie. Now I would have to either include Hunter in the deception, which he wouldn't be happy about, or lie to him like we'd lied to Johnny Jay. Which he *really* wouldn't appreciate.

I felt guilty for all the deception, but honestly, I couldn't see a way around it.

"Al-Qaeda," I said to Hunter, forgetting in the heat of the moment that I'd told Hunter about Patti's past.

"Let me see . . ." Hunter said, studying the remains of the Mercedes on the tow truck's flatbed. Ben sniffed around in the wreckage. "Black, expensive Mercedes, Illinois title, car bomb, bet if we ran the plates the registration would belong to . . . oh . . . let me guess . . . Harold Bruno?"

With that slick deduction, he beamed in on me with "the look."

"I didn't do anything," I said. "Ask Grams. Or Stanley."

"We have an obligation to inform Johnny Jay of Patti Dwyer's situation," he said, not even bothering to try to get more information from me. "Whether he wants to hear it or not."

"Fine. Good," I said. "Let the chief go after Bruno, make him explain what he was doing inside Patti's house."

A manly eyebrow went up, and I realized my mistake. But I was a pro.

"Just an educated guess." I covered. "He wasn't in the

car, and if it really belongs to him, parked right in front of his ex-wife's house, what would you think? He has to be stalking Patti, right?"

"Probably." Hunter looked around. "Where did your cohorts go?"

Stanley, I noticed, had disappeared, hustling out of there at the first opportunity. I guessed that my window well would be empty when I looked.

Grams had vanished, too, but she reappeared, backing out of my driveway in her Caddie. Normally, I let her hit the chief's SUV all she wants, but only when he isn't around to witness it. Hunter must have read my about-to-panic mind because he raced over to guide her out of the drive and point her straight down the street.

Johnny Jay watched with a frown as Grams slowly made her way to the stop sign. At least he didn't see her put on her right directional before turning left. Thank God.

Then we had the talk. The chief let us get started at least. First, Hunter and I told Johnny Jay about Patti's connection to Nova Campbell.

"I know that already," the chief said. "What's wrong with you two that you just can't stay out of my face? Do I have to make another phone call?"

Hunter's face went all dark and closed up, a sure sign that he was getting really angry.

"Maybe you should go in the house," I advised him. "I'll finish up here."

Hunter gave Johnny a glare that I hope I never get and stomped off. Which was exactly what I'd hoped for. Now I didn't have to put Patti on the spot by telling the chief about her role in finding Nova. And Hunter would just assume I had.

"You're really a piece of work," I told Johnny.

"Fischer, I'm warning you. Keep your nose out of

police business. You'll be on my receiving end when the time is right. Until then, stay out!"

I stomped off, too.

I felt like Hunter and I had been doomed as a couple from the second he'd moved into my house. Nothing was going right. Somebody was poisoned in our backyard, and my whole family was implicated in the murder. Mom was about to move in next door. Patti was quickly bringing down real estate values with car bombs going off . . . what else? As if that wasn't enough!

Choices presented themselves:

I could continue ruining Hunter's life.

Or I could set him free.

I plopped down in a chair on the porch. Ben trotted over and gave me a lick. I returned the affection with a few ear scratches.

Johnny pulled out, did a U-turn, and turned right on Main toward the police station, driving after the tow truck.

Hunter came out and joined me. We sat silently for a few minutes, then he said, "I need a beer."

So I got him one. And one for me, too. It was the least I could do.

We took big draws. "The pizza is in my car," he said. "I'll get it in a minute."

Then I said, "I've decided to cut you loose."

Hunter sputtered a mouthful of beer. "This sounds serious. I'll be right back," he said, getting up and going inside.

While he was gone, I watched darkness creep up slowly, just enough to tell me another day was almost done. Patti's house was dark. So was the house my mother would occupy.

Ben left the porch to water a tree.

Hunter came back out wearing shorts. And he was

barefoot. I stared at his feet as he sat back down. I've always loved his feet more than any other man's. His are perfectly formed, not too flat, not too wide, lean enough that I can trace the fragile bones, with dark hair on his bronzed toes, and well-groomed nails. Super sensual.

But he knew exactly what I thought of his feet. Was he using my fetish against me?

"I'm cutting you loose," I repeated.

"Like a fish on a hook?" Why didn't Hunter seem worried? Was he glad? Relieved?

"You deserve better," I said.

"But I love you, babe."

"Nothing bad happened to you when we had separate homes."

"Really?"

I thought about that. "Nothing like this. Every day when you come home from handling really bad situations, I've got more problems for you."

He took another drink from the bottle.

I started giving him reasons to leave me. "There was a murder in the backyard."

"You couldn't foresee what would happen."

"And look at this," I waved an arm toward the street. "You come home to relax and instead here I am, surrounded by burnt car parts."

"Wasn't your fault."

"I tell myself that every time something bad happens to me. It's not my fault, I say. But some people just have bad luck their whole lives. They're always in the wrong place at the wrong time, and that's me. Jinxed!"

Hunter squeezed my knee. "Come on. It isn't that bad."

"And now we have my mother moving in next door. It's bad enough we work together, but this?"

Between Patti's snooping and my mother's interfering ways, Hunter and I were a thing of the past for sure.

"Where do you expect me to go?" Hunter said, and even though this had been my idea, my heart sank with a thud.

He was so close and so sexy and this was the hardest thing to do. "Home," I said. "To put things back the way they were before."

Hunter put an arm around my shoulders. "I'm sorry," he said. "I can't do that."

"Why not?"

"Because I accepted an offer on my house today."

I jerked far enough away to look straight into his eyes. They weren't messing with me. He'd really sold his home. "Why didn't you tell me?"

"I thought I'd surprise you. It just happened a few hours ago. I didn't know you had such little faith in us or I would have held off."

"It's not us I'm so worried about. It's me. I'm the problem."

Tears were threatening to burst. One got away, and I swept at it with my fingers.

"Don't you want to know the details of the sale?"

"It doesn't matter."

"Don't you even want to know who bought it?"

Listen to him. Our whole future was ruined and all he wanted to talk about was a stupid house sale! "Sure," I said, not meaning it.

"I sold it to Tom Stocke."

My mother's boyfriend?! "I thought they wanted to rent," I sputtered.

He smiled. "Tom fell in love with it at first sight and changed his mind about renting," he said. "I figured this was the best solution all around. Are you upset with me?"

He was kidding, right? Suddenly our future seemed so much brighter.

"I could always look for a place to rent," he said.

"Come here." I pulled him toward me. "And let me thank you properly. Give me those sexy feet."

It was a good thing it was dark and private on my dead-end block.

Twenty-five

Tuesday dawned gray and damp. Through the night, it had rained hard and the wind carried in a cold front. That meant my honeybees would be hunkering down in their hives. I spent half an hour tidying up in the honey house, cleaning equipment and watching rain fall in the garden, thinking all the vegetable plants were really perking up under the deluge. Their caregiver (me) hadn't been very attentive to their needs lately.

Hunter and I had made up. Again. And I had promised not to blindside him with any more insecurities. With Tom buying his house, Hunter had committed to us. Now it was my turn to go the extra mile. I vowed to uphold my end, and we agreed to weather whatever storms came our way.

But although my man and I were back on track, plans to resolve my family's role in the investigation had derailed.

I hadn't been able to think of a single way to catch

Camilla and Gil lying about their whereabouts. I didn't
have a single other person as a suspect, either. Discounting
Patti, Nova hadn't been in Moraine long enough to make
any new enemies. The trail ended at my sister's house,
where my persons-of-my-interest hunkered down just like
my honeybees, waiting for their own storm to pass and
the sun to shine once again.

We needed to find us a killer. Since I wasn't keen on
the idea of my sister or her husband taking the rap, and I
wasn't about to let Johnny Jay pin it on me, I had to get a
break soon.

Call me crazy, but I missed Patti more than ever. She
might be useful in solving the case. If nothing else, she
would be able to tick off the killer enough to make an
attempt on her life, and we could take it from there.

After walking down to The Wild Clover and opening
up, I decided to give my overtaxed brain a rest from the
murder and dive right into the community's latest drama—
our very own car bomb explosion, of which I had eye-
witness inside information.

"What happened?" Carrie Ann asked me.

"Patti's ex-husband was foolish enough to show up."

"A woman's wrath is a powerful thing. Trust me on
that." Carrie Ann didn't even blink an eye about Patti
having been married in the past. She just took it in stride
and didn't ask for any of the more soap-opera-ish details.

I studied my cousin. At the moment, Carrie Ann was
my most normal friend. She'd taken the long way getting
to that point, but along with her ongoing recovery from
alcoholism, Carrie Ann has established herself as a caring person with a good head on her shoulders.

So I filled her in on Patti's real situation, confiding in
her all the details.

"Harry Bruno is after Patti. I'm concerned for her
safety," I finished. "I really wonder where he went after

he headed toward Main Street. If he left Moraine, how did he get out of town? It's not like he could just call a cab or catch a bus."

"It'll be hard for him from here on out without wheels. And Patti knows how to blend into the woodwork," Carrie Ann said reassuringly.

For the rest of the morning, we passed around the word—keep an eye out for a sneaky-looking stranger. Unfortunately I couldn't give much of a description since Harry Bruno was so nondescript, and besides, I was still claiming not to have ever seen him anyway.

All my customers wanted in on the community watch action. Milly hit the nail right on the head by saying, "Most of us can tell the difference between a tourist passing through and a no-gooder looking for trouble." A Moraine truism.

Stanley showed up and offered his assistance, too. "We're putting the whole town on orange alert," he said. "And I'd recognize that ugly mug anywhere . . . I mean . . ." I gave him a nudge in the ribs since we hadn't admitted actually seeing Harry Bruno . . . "an ugly mug . . . not that I . . . Never mind."

Stanley was doing a bad cover job regarding our involvement in a certain confrontation on Patti's porch. If the truth got around, the police chief would hear about it, and we'd all be in trouble.

Holly came in and complained about her overstaying guests. "Johnny Jay still hasn't cleared Camilla and Gil to leave town. He better hurry up. Those two are driving me out of my own home."

"How so?"

Holly shook her head. "They aren't leaving the house. All three of them, Max included, are sitting around doing business by phone. I've never seen so many workaholics in one place."

"I know what you can do," I said, adding some sarcasm. "You can actually work a shift here at the store."

"Where's Mom?" my work-phobic sister said. "She can help you."

"Our mother has an appointment at the bank with her boyfriend. They're buying Hunter's house. Or rather Tom is purchasing it, and Mom is going to live with him."

The house news got Holly all squeally, which I felt was a bit theatrical. So I changed the subject and told her about the big explosion on my street.

"Never a dull moment," she said.

"Obviously, Patti can handle her ex. You and I need to focus on finding a killer. Let's go over Nova's carrot juice routine again. Who knew she drank it daily?"

"You," my sister said.

"Besides."

"Me."

"Besides."

"Max for sure."

I took a deep breath. "We're trying to eliminate certain suspects," I reminded her. "Like Max and me and you."

"Camilla and Gil probably. Everybody knew, now that I think about it. Max called ahead with a list of requests. Other than the carrot juice, there was nothing unusual— good wine, no milk products, something about shellfish, tea for Gil since he doesn't drink coffee, that's about it, I can't really remember."

"Where's the list?"

Holly shrugged. "I probably threw it away."

"I still think testing all the gloves over at your place is the next step."

Holly put her hands on her hips. "If the gloves were so important, Sally or the chief would have already taken them."

"Just because those two haven't thought of doing it doesn't mean we shouldn't follow up."

"Why would I help the police find evidence to use against me? I already told you how I felt about that, so let it go."

We locked stares. "Don't even thing about taking them," Holly said.

I shook my head. "That's a big mistake. We should stay ahead of Johnny Jay on this one."

"You've been hanging around with Patti too long," my sister said, and she stalked out of the store.

"Don't ask me for help in the future," I called after her. "Unless you're willing to reciprocate. Our relationship isn't a one way ticket, you know!"

I heard her rev her Jag and roar away.

Spoil sport, I thought, going back to work, making a note to hold Holly's paycheck, since she hadn't earned it. Although she probably wouldn't even notice. I really went out of my way to bend over backward for her, and when I needed something in return, where was she? Gone.

Lori Spandle came in to cause as much trouble as possible. She was really P.O.'d.

"Hunter owes me," she said, her face beet red as usual. "I'd almost sealed the deal with your mother for Clay's house. Hunter's in dangerous water, encroaching on my territory like that."

"Dangerous water, Lori? Why, do you see yourself as a shark?" I had a completely different animal in mind—a leech or wood tick or piranha—something that feeds on humans.

Lori was still griping. "I lost a qualified renter and a six-month lease because of him."

"Too bad you're so snotty. Otherwise, Hunter might have used you as his real estate agent and you'd be sharing in the proceeds." Which wasn't true. Hunter would have handled the sale himself regardless.

"The Hell's Angels might want to rent next door to you," Lori said with a whole lot of implied demon of her own.

"The Hell's Angels would be a refreshing change after your last tenant."

We went back and forth like that for a while until I tired of it. Then she dropped a few cartons of eggs on the floor (a mistake? really?) and stomped out.

"I wish that woman would shop someplace else," Carrie Ann muttered.

"Wouldn't that be great." I took a moment for wishful thinking, then said, "You and I should hang out soon. It's been a while."

"True, but I'm pretty busy," my cousin said, looking content. "Gunnar and I are doing really well."

"Just don't completely forget about your girlfriends."

With Hunter working long hours, Patti gone, my sister and I having a disagreement over gloves, and Carrie Ann spending all her free time with her ex-husband Gunnar and her kids, I was feeling a little lonely. Even Milly hadn't been around nearly as much since she was hanging out at Holly's house, enjoying her new friendship with Effie and whipping up scrumptious delectables.

I don't go around announcing it, but not too long ago I didn't have time for girlfriends. All my energy and effort went into The Wild Clover. I was the only full-time employee and worked morning, noon, and night. Since the store's success, I actually have more free time. Not more money, since now I have to pay staff wages and all kinds of employee and employer taxes, but time is finally on my side.

So I want to enjoy my girlfriends, even if two of

them—Holly and Carrie Ann—are relatives and one of them—Patti—is a psycho.

They add spice to my life, which could turn into too much routine without them. Heck, I would actually appreciate more interaction with some of the problem people in my life.

Like my mother. But she'd abandoned her efforts to reform me in favor of a man's company. And Johnny Jay was preoccupied with other things. He hadn't been around yet today. At the moment, the closest living and breathing thing I had for companionship was Lori Spandle. How pathetic is that?

I went back to restocking, straightening up, and helping Carrie Ann when the line got too long.

When we had a gap in business, I left Carrie Ann at the counter reading a gossip magazine and I took the slow sales time to return a stack of library books, enjoying the short walk down Main Street under my umbrella. I was directly outside the library, ready to climb the steps to the door to make small talk with the director and her librarian daughter, when I spotted Holly and Max's truck coming my way. Holly didn't usually drive it, but maybe she didn't want to take her Jag back out in the rain.

Anyway, that was my first thought.

More likely, it was Chance out and about. I'd like to have a chat with him. He always was an interesting diversion, and maybe he and Effie had noticed something worthwhile to help with the murder investigation.

As the truck approached, windshield wipers slapping, rain beating down harder, puddles splashing out under its tires, I caught a glimpse of the person behind the wheel. It wasn't Chance, but I'd been on the right track—it was Effie driving.

I pushed the library books into the outside return box

and stepped quickly to the curb to flag down the truck, thinking we could have a cup of coffee together, catch up on all the excitement at Holly's house.

Except right when I put my arm up to wave her over, I saw someone sitting in the passenger's seat—Chance?—suddenly duck down out of sight before I got a really good chance to identify him or her.

What the heck?

That certainly wasn't normal behavior.

Effie pretended not to see me on the curb, but there was no way she could have missed me. She stared straight ahead, and the truck kept going. The passenger's seat remained empty. The truck disappeared out of sight.

I was in motion, trotting back to the store for my own wheels, running around to the back parking lot, and blowing out in the same direction Effie had taken, toward my sister's house.

Only I couldn't find the truck. After checking for it at the carriage house, I made several passes through town, and ended up back at the store without ever locating it.

Where had Effie gone?

And who had been her secret passenger?

Twenty-six

"I can't believe you actually compared me to Patti," I said first thing when Holly answered her phone. "She's over the top and isn't sensitive to other people's feelings at all. I'm working to protect us, to protect you."

"Sometimes you just have to let things be," my sister said. "Respect my decisions. But I take back what I said. Patti is way worse."

Oh, okay, at least I'm semi-normal. Right now, at this very moment, I wasn't appreciating my sister's reading-people's-minds skill nearly as much as in the recent past. She should stick to relationship advice and leave the rest of me alone.

"Is Effie having an affair?" I said, blurting out the real reason for my call, leaning way back on the chair in my office, pretty pleased with my assessment of the ducking passenger mystery.

Holly said, "What gave you that goofy idea?"

I told her what I'd seen. The truck, Effie, someone ducking down.

"You could have imagined it."

"No, it really happened."

"With the rain and how dark the day has been, you can't be certain."

"Yes I can," I said with conviction. Then thought, maybe I *had* imagined it . . . but no, if Effie wasn't hiding someone, she would have acknowledged me on the curb. The woman had been obviously ignoring me.

Holly, the amateur therapist, kept going, "Let's work this out, shall we? Was the passenger male or female?"

"Couldn't tell."

"Hair color?"

"Not sure."

"What *do* you know?"

"That I saw somebody slink down in the seat. Is Effie back home? Is the truck there?"

"Let me check . . . Yup, the truck is here."

"Is Chance around?"

"Someplace. Last I saw him, he was working on the dock."

"Do me a favor, go over and look in their windows. If her passenger is inside her home, she's probably not having an affair."

"You want me to look in the window of the carriage house? It's above the garage. How am I going to do that?"

"A ladder."

"I'm calling Mom and telling her you're acting weird."

"That's not very professional of you. If you want to pursue psychology and help people, you can't go tattling to their family."

"I *am* your family."

"Never mind. Forget I called." I disconnected and stood up, making a firm decision. I had to find Patti. She was my one and only partner in crime. That's all there was to it. I grabbed my umbrella and headed out.

First I looked in the vacant house next door to mine, which was my first guess. The house had a lot of possibility as a hideout. Even before Lori changed the lock to one of those Realtor ones, I'd jimmied a window so it would open easily for any future entry needs. Nobody lived there, and it was on the very end of our dead end. Patti could come and go easily without being seen. She wouldn't have to pay for lodging, which would have been a big deal to her. Patti didn't like to spend her money, preferring to mooch as much as she could. Anyway, that house? That's where I would have been if I were Patti.

After slipping inside through the window and searching each room, however, I came up empty. No sign that she'd been there at all.

Next stop, her own house. She could be faking us out, letting us think she was gone while she hid out inside, waiting for some action. But her house was locked up tight, making me wonder how Bruno had managed to get in without breaking anything. Did he pick the lock? Or had she set him up, left it open so he wouldn't see her wiring his car? That second option (baiting him) *was* Patti's style.

I stopped to think things over.

When Harry Bruno came onto the scene, Patti had had him under surveillance pretty darn quick for someone who was supposedly out of town. And she'd been ready with all her equipment. Where was she finding the room to stash explosives?

I walked down to the Oconomowoc River, where raindrops plopped into the churning water. My windbreaker hood protected me and my flip-flopped feet didn't mind getting wet.

Nothing appeared out of place. No camouflaged tent

was pitched on the far side of the river, and I didn't see any human-sized animal holes to burrow into, either.

Standing on the riverbank, I sighed in discouragement, turned, looked up over the roof of my house, saw the last of dark clouds passing overhead.

Suddenly, I had the weirdest, oddball thought. Could P.P. Patti Dwyre be inside *my* house?

It was perfectly Patti.

If she were here, she'd be in the attic, surely. I went inside, climbed the stairs to the second floor, then took the steps which led to the attic.

It wasn't a place I visited often, even though it's not a dark, tiny crawl space, but rather encompasses the entire full length and width of the house. Half of the space had pine flooring, but the other half was unfinished, still with exposed insulation. Besides a few cobwebs, the attic held several boxes of my childhood treasures, old rugs, or furniture that had seen better days but I couldn't bring myself to throw away.

I opened the door. The enormous room was illuminated by several small windows on each of the four sides. Not much available light, since it was so overcast today, but enough for me to see P.P. Patti sound asleep on an air mattress. And not one, but three backpacks flung on the floor beside her.

For an "I Spy" character, it sure did take me a long time to wake Patti up. If I'd been her mobster ex-husband or one of his flunkies, she'd be dead before she knew what hit her.

"Get up, Sleeping Beauty," I said when I finally had her attention.

"Shoot," she said, unpleasantly surprised to see me.

I wish I'd had a gun to shoot her with. Not anything lethal. A BB gun would give her a good sting, and make me feel a whole lot better. "Comfy?" I wanted to know.

"Could be better." She sat up. "Now that you know about my hideout, can I go sleep in your spare bedroom?"

"Depends."

"On?"

"How helpful you decide to be. Come on downstairs, I'll make you a sandwich."

We sat at my kitchen table, drinking herbal tea and chomping on tuna salad sandwiches while I tried to get Patti to admit the truth. She insisted she'd been out of town during all the excitement outside her house. Yet she made one comment inconsistent with that. She said, "You're better off not knowing everything. The last thing I want is to drag you into my problems."

"Since when?" I wanted to know.

"Harry will be back," Patti said, ignoring my question, "and he'll be prepared next time. Men are so dense, you almost have to hit them over the head with a brick to get their attention."

Or in this case, a bomb? "But how far will he go?" I asked.

"Not as far as I will."

That I believed.

"I'm trying to pin Nova's murder where it belongs, on one of the flavorists," I said. "They are lying about their whereabouts, I'm sure of it." Patti had crept upstairs during cocktail hour at Holly's house, so I said, "Have you heard anything about Camilla and Gil that might help me? Did you find anything?"

She shook her head. "I went through their rooms during the dinner, but I didn't have much time."

"Want another crack at it?" I said.

Patti shook her head again. "Harry's my focus right

now. Haven't you noticed that I sort of have my hands full with my own problems?"

"If you solve Nova's murder, you'll get an exclusive and the *Distorter* will have to give your job back."

"The *Reporter*." Patti really hated when I called it the *Distorter*, but if the name fits . . . "Besides, I have to be alive to collect a paycheck," she pointed out.

"I really need my life back the way it was before," I said, putting a Patti-like whine in my voice. That method usually worked for her, so I thought I'd try it. "Hunter and I need more together time to grow our relationship. What he and I need is a vacation far away. If I help you with your ex-husband, will you help me straighten out my issues?"

Patti gave me a not-very-interested shrug, so I rushed on.

"Besides," I said, slam-dunking, "the town is on orange alert. We're all on the lookout for Harry already. See, I'm on it. Together, we'll run him out of town."

Patti smiled, and I knew she was about to reverse her position. "You're my best friend, so I guess. Though we did this before, remember, and you weren't much help to me that time. But if you offer that spare room . . ."

"It's yours."

Then I remembered Hunter, and how he and I live together now, and how I hadn't talked it over with him first. Getting into the groove of togetherness wasn't the easiest thing. I thought about reneging on the bedroom offer, but then I'd have to endure a whole bunch of sneering from Patti about how needy I am, and how I let a man lead me around.

"Okay," Patti said. "I'll search Camilla and Gil's rooms, and this time I'll be thorough."

"But how will you make sure they aren't in those rooms?" I asked. "What if you're caught?"

"No problem," Patti said. "I'm like the Invisible Woman."

Sure, I thought, *and I'm Catwoman.*

Twenty-seven

Back at the store for the afternoon, I found time to call Hunter.

"I ran into Patti," I said, faking nonchalance.

"Really? Where?"

"Uh . . . just around. Anyway, she's afraid to go home just yet and wonders if she can stay with us for a few days."

Hunter groaned.

"Only for a day or two." Was that pleading in my voice? I took a deep breath. "She says she feels more protected with us, you being a cop and all."

I had to lay it on thick. I'd already promised her, but if Hunter thought he had the ball in his court, that he was all big and macho (which he is), and the decision was totally up to him, everybody could go home happy.

"And Patti is our neighbor," I continued. "We have to help her."

"Since when did you become so neighborly?"

Since now, was the real truth. Frankly, Patti hadn't exactly been the friendly block-party type earlier.

"According to my sources, Harry Bruno was definitely in town," Hunter said. "Apparently he's the closest thing to next-of-kin that Nova Campbell had. He insists, though, that he went back to Chicago, that somebody stole his car and dumped it on Willow Street."

"Oh, sure, right. That's likely."

"Dwyre should take a permanent vacation to Timbuktu."

"You want her to run away?"

"He's trouble, she's trouble. I'm positive Patti was behind that explosion. Johnny Jay thinks so, too. And he wants to question her. I'm not hiding the woman or protecting her from the chief."

"Isn't there anything she can do to convince you? It's only for a few days."

Hunter sighed. "She'll have to answer the chief's questions first and to his satisfaction, before she stays with us. And there is absolutely no room for negotiation."

So Patti was just another perp to my cop boyfriend. He always wants to play by the rules. Go figure.

In the end, Hunter approved her for a two-day stay as long as she contacted Johnny Jay immediately and cooperated with him. I pledged to take responsibility for her actions—now I knew how it felt to co-sign for a minor. Scary. I'd have to figure out a way to keep Patti on a short leash.

Next my man said, "You haven't asked a single question about the murder investigation. You didn't even follow up with questions when I mentioned Harry Bruno. Are you feeling all right?"

"I'm fine. I just know you're busy, and not really involved in those issues anymore, and we should stick to talking about us, personal stuff only. Let Johnny Jay handle the problems."

"That's a new twist."

"I'm complicated," I said. With that remark I must have opened up one of Hunter's sex neurons because the next part of our conversation was extremely private, for our ears only. Then he said before signing off, "I have to work late tonight. I'll drop Ben at the house. Take him out to do his business when you get home, okay?"

After disconnecting, I went online and searched Google for images of Patti's ex-husband, which I should have done in the first place. Photos popped up right away and they confirmed that it was in fact Harry Bruno I'd met face-to-face. He hadn't sent a henchman, or whatever they call their employees, to do his dirty work. Harry had planned to handle Patti all by himself. But that was before his pricey car went up in flames. Patti was right, he'd be more prepared next time.

I thought about how many folks move to small towns to get away from the crowding and crime of cities. And here my little burg was with an unsolved murder and a Chicago mobster with a vendetta, both at the same time. Talk about drama!

The last thing I did on the computer was download and print out several copies of Harry Bruno's photograph.

Before my workday was done, I manned—or womaned—the register. A herd of kids came in to buy old-fashioned candy. Local residents also popped in for papers or beer or quick meal items, and we caught up with births and weddings and all the other stuff that makes living in a small town so worthwhile.

With Pattie's ex positively identified, I cut-and-pasted his photo and snazzed it up with a big bold "Wanted—Dangerous" splashed under his chin. Then I called Jackson Davis, the medical examiner, and offered to buy him a drink after work. "I'll meet you at Stu's Bar and Grill," I said when he accepted. I hadn't seen Jackson socially for a long time, and looked forward to it. Although I planned to combine a little business with pleasure, and hopefully learn something new about Nova's murder.

I tacked a wanted poster on the door, freshened up a little in the office, and headed down Main Street.

The happy hour bar crowd had descended. Stu was behind the bar, since he likes to be in the thick of things, which is the best way for an owner to handle a small business. Whoever manages the cash register controls the business. That got me thinking about spending more time at the checkout counter. And also reminded me that Mom commandeered that position every single time she showed up.

I sat at the bar and ordered some of Stu's chicken wings, which are always a popular item. He makes them from scratch and they are delish.

Jackson came in the door, spotted me at the bar, and bellied-up next to me.

"Let me buy you something special," I said to him.

"Think I'll stick to beer." Jackson slid on the stool next to me. "I'm not falling for the same trick twice," he said. The guy can't handle his liquor worth a darn, and there had been a time, not too long ago, when I'd plied him with cocktails spiked with triple-strength booze to worm some facts out of him. But Jackson didn't hold it against me, mainly because I'm pretty sure he has a special place in his heart for me, a certain admiration for me as a woman. I'm not bragging, it doesn't happen to me often enough. But when it does, a woman knows.

The medical examiner likes me, and I like him back.

We both ordered beers. The chicken wings arrived with our brews.

"How's the Nova Campbell case coming?" I asked him after catching up on our significant others, and what we've been doing in our spare time.

"I can't discuss specifics," he said. "But you know I would if I could."

"Let's talk nonspecifics then. Like how long could a person survive after drinking juice poisoned with water hemlock?"

"Okay, nonspecifics then." Jackson took a drink from his bottle of beer. "Depending on the quantity ingested, death could occur anywhere from fifteen minutes up to around an hour or so."

I thought about how the group had been running late, how once they arrived Nova had complained about feeling poorly and had gone down to the river, and approximately how long everyone was at my house before Nova's death occurred. I finished with, "So it's most likely that she drank the poison right before leaving Holly's house for mine."

"It's more than likely." Jackson's facial expression said he was throwing me a bone. "But the water bottle could have been tampered with before that."

That reminded me of the remaining jars of carrot juice that Hunter had taken from The Wild Clover. "What about the box from my store?"

"Not a trace of poison."

Darn! So much for a perfect world. Hunter had been right.

We both took a few minutes to savor Stu's chicken wings, then I said, "Other than saying she didn't feel well, Nova seemed perfectly fine right before she died."

"Was she flushed?"

I thought back and nodded.

"Other symptoms could include seizures, frothing,

nausea, muscle twitching. Next would come respiratory paralysis and/or cardiovascular collapse. Are you sure you didn't witness any of the symptoms I just mentioned?"

I shook my head, realizing the tables had been turned. Our town's medical examiner was examining me!

"Whoever did this knew his stuff," Jackson said.

"Both of the other house guests have that specific kind of knowledge," I told him. "I just don't understand why one of them hasn't been arrested yet."

I gazed steadily at Jackson, waiting for more detail, but all I got was, "How about those Packers?" The Green Bay Packers are a big subject, so everybody at the bar heard that and perked right up and joined our conversation. Talk turned to football and I couldn't turn it back.

Soon after, Jackson took off for some family event. With Stu's permission I tacked another Harry Bruno wanted (or watch out) poster on the bar's door, and wondered what Patti was doing for me, if anything.

I went home and found that Hunter had dropped Ben off. I let him out for a run through the yard.

Patti joined me, stepping out of the shadows, her black garb blending into the background.

"Hunter has a condition to you staying with us," I told her. "You have to talk to Johnny Jay about what happened with the Mercedes."

"I don't know a thing."

"Then that's all you have to say." I figured she was lying, but looking back in time, I hadn't actually seen Patti near the car. Just something big, black, and suspiciously human. "Let's go down to the station and get it over with," I suggested, giving her the benefit of the doubt, though that doubt was a crumb so small a mouse might overlook it.

"I can't," she said. "What if Harry comes back while I'm away and does something to my house?"

"We'll have to take that chance."

"What if the chief doesn't let me go once I'm inside the station?"

A definite possibility. "Then Hunter and I will watch your house."

"You'd do that for me?"

I reluctantly agreed. How had she gotten me so entrenched in her life?

Patti called the chief. He would meet us there.

We walked down to The Wild Clover and took off for the station in my truck.

Johnny Jay has a special interrogation room within the police station, one I've visited enough times to name details with my eyes closed. Bare-bones, heavy wood, lockable door, eagle print on the wall, not much else.

"You stay out here, Fischer," Johnny said to me from a wide-legged stance in the waiting area.

"I came in to answer questions of my own free will," Patti said to him. "And she's my advisor. Story comes along. Or I clam up."

Johnny Jay blustered, but Patti held firm. I'd never acted as an advisor before. Was that something like an attorney, giving legal advice? Whatever it involved, I liked the idea a lot, especially if it torqued off the chief.

Into the room we went.

Johnny Jay is a jerk but he isn't a buffoon. He's wily as a fox, smart, forceful (as in major bully), and tackles a case like a linebacker. But law enforcement officials have to work within some pretty strict guidelines. I understand that. They can't randomly break into someone's house to search for evidence. They can't just haul a suspect in and book them without going through a whole lot of red tape, either.

That's Patti's main argument every time she inserts herself into an investigation and rushes right over the gray area into the black zone. Her moral compass points in a completely different direction than most of ours.

Hopefully she would handle this interview with some semblance of common sense.

"Start at the beginning, Dwyre," Johnny said after swinging his legs up on the table. "And this better be worthwhile."

Patti told him about her marriage to Harry Bruno, how she'd managed to hook up with a mobster without knowing it, and how eventually she got away. And how now Harry Bruno was out to get her, and she needed police protection.

"And why would that be?" Johnny Jay said to Patti. "Could it have anything to do with his second wife dying right next door? You knew her, right?"

Patti's eyes were shifty, but she answered with a half-truth. "I knew *of* her."

"The witness protection program might be a good match for Patti," I offered.

"Did you witness something that could put Bruno behind bars again?" Johnny Jay asked her.

"Not exactly," Patti said. "But I could come up with something."

I couldn't help myself. "If you refuse to do anything," I said to Johnny, "Bruno will murder Patti, and then you can put him back behind bars without any effort at all."

Johnny said, "Stuff it, Fischer." Then to Patti, "Was there anything you witnessed during the marriage that you can offer us?"

"Not really," Patti said.

"Then you can't go into protection to feed off our tax roll."

It had been worth a try.

"So Bruno shows up at your residence," Johnny said,

impatience in his voice. "And for no good reason you torch his car."

"I don't know anything about that," Patti said.

"That would be a really smart reason to be afraid."

Patti shrugged. "I wasn't anywhere near there."

"Where were you?"

"I was on vacation."

"Exactly where were you?"

Patti mumbled something about visiting with friends in a neighboring town, and Johnny said he was going to confirm her story. "Write down their names and address for me," he told her.

"Objection," I said, jumping to my feet. "Is my . . . um . . . friend"—I'd almost said *client*—"being arrested? Charged with any crime?"

"Oh, shut up, Fischer, and sit down."

Like that was going to stop me. I said to Patti, "Don't give him any more information."

Patti pushed away the paper and pen he'd shoved at her.

Then to him I said, "Instead of trying to arrest the victim, maybe you should go after her ex-husband. Arrest him. And what about a restraining order? Get her one of those, too."

"You don't give me orders, Fischer."

"Isn't it obvious what he was up to?" I said. "His car was right outside her house. And he wasn't in the car when it blew. Where do you think he was? Inside her house, that's where. It's a no-brainer." *Even for you*, I could have added.

"Somebody stole the man's car," Johnny said. "According to him."

"Somebody stole his Mercedes and just happened to ditch it outside his ex-wife's house? If you believe that, I have a piece of swampy river to sell you."

"That's his story and he's sticking to it. Legally my hands are tied." Johnny swung his legs off the table. I had a momentary and delightful vision of him hogtied to the table, trussed up with an apple in his mouth. Sometimes I disliked the man so much I felt sick. He stared into my eyes and said, "Unless a witness steps forward and identifies him at the scene, there isn't a thing I can do about it."

I was pretty sure it was too late to step up even if I wanted to.

As we left, I taped up one of Harry Bruno's wanted posters on the cop shop door, hoping it wouldn't come down as soon as Johnny saw it.

Patti really loved the poster.

We came out of the police station into the gathering dusk—cloudy, moonless, humid, the air smelling damp and earthy. At my house, Patti changed clothes, although I wouldn't have known it if she hadn't informed me of that fact. She must purchase all her clothing in multiples. Black tees, black cargos, etc.

After that, she left for parts unknown. I spent the evening raiding the refrigerator and sharing my finds with Ben. Hunter came in after I'd gone to bed, gave me a neck nuzzle, and slid in beside me.

I wasn't sure when Patti got back.

Twenty-eight

I love sunshine. It makes the world seem such a happy place. My bees love it, too. They were humming and buzzing and landing on me, in a friendly, nonaggressive way. Most people don't understand that just because a honeybee lands on you doesn't mean she's out to get you. My little friends are inquisitive creatures, that's all.

Besides, my bees are used to me puttering around by their hives. I'm part of their daily routine. They've even accepted Ben, and he in turn tolerates them.

I donned the bee suit and accomplished the task of gathering all the wonderful, sweet-smelling honey that my honeybees had been so busy making. This was going to be a bumper crop year for Queen Bee Honey.

Stanley Peck called, wanting to come over and watch how I check my hives to make sure they are free from diseases. There are several kinds of diseases that can really hurt them. A watchful beekeeper is a successful beekeeper, as my own former mentor used to state ad nauseam. So I look for irregularities in a hive's patterns, and I make sure the larvae and cells appear healthy and odorless. For example, eggs cells should be pearly white, not yellow or brown.

It all comes with experience, which Stanley doesn't have a whole lot of yet. He's a newbie. So am I, in the scheme of things, but in Stanley's eyes I'm the expert.

When Stanley rounded the corner of my house, right away I saw that he was doing a big no-no in the business. Not exactly a warning that pops up in training manuals, but one that some of us have learned the hard way.

Stanley was eating a banana.

Honeybees have a huge social network, ranging far and wide just like humans do on the web. Only they are more advanced, they communicate with each other by releasing chemicals that other bees recognize and act on.

I've been in beeyards right after a hive has protected itself from invasion, and guess what the air smells like after they've done their chemical thing? Bananas, that's what.

"Ditch the banana," I yelled.

"Hunh?" Stanley said, looking major confused.

Stanley's banana was about to set off a bee alarm.

Oh wait, it already had.

Here they came, all those girl scouts and guards. A whole slew of them. And these girls were out to get my friend. I know I've said again and again how gentle they are. *Normally.* Unless they're provoked. And the smell of banana triggers a hostile response in honeybees. (By the way, coconut hair shampoo and conditioner invokes the same negative reaction. That one I learned the really hard way, too.)

"Throw the banana!" I backed away from him since he

was still coming forward, about to unwittingly share his newly found problem with me.

Stanley, not thinking straight, threw the banana *at* me. Ugh!

"Ow," he said, starting to wave his hands. A dark cloud of ticked off bees had their landing gear out and some of them had found their target.

"Run!" I hollered, taking my own advice.

We made it inside with limited damage, considering the extent of Stanley's mistake. A few bees followed us but made hasty attempts to withdraw as soon as they realized they were inside enemy territory.

Hunter turned from a window where—judging from the amusement on his face—he'd witnessed the whole thing.

Neither of them could believe it when I explained why my bees had gone on the attack.

"We have to get Lori over here," Stanley said. "And gift her with a basket of bananas."

That was one fine idea.

"We'll have to check the hives for diseases another time," I said. "They're too riled at the moment."

"I'm really sorry," Stanley said. "I didn't know."

"Who eats a banana right out in front of the world, anyway?" my boyfriend asked Stanley. Hunter's sparkly eyes slid my way.

And that's how my morning started out.

Not too bad, considering several of the past mornings. A few bee stings and a lesson for my apprentice and one for me—write down every single weird detail regarding bees so I don't forget to pass them on to beginners.

Hunter and Ben left for work, and right after Stanley took off, Johnny Jay intercepted me on the way over to the store. Luckily Carrie Ann was opening that morning.

"I need a word with you, Fischer."

"No way, Johnny."

"It's Chief Jay to you."

"And it's Ms. Fischer to you."

Johnny looked tired this morning, like he'd had a rough night. Being on call twenty-four/seven was starting to accelerate his aging process. There were other dependable officers who could easily pick up some off hours, but the chief is a control freak and has to be involved in every single incident that occurs. It's his fault and his problem. The bad thing for me was that lack of sleep made him ornerier than usual.

He dangled his handcuffs, a trick that has gained my cooperation more than once. But not today.

Maybe it was the "lawyer" side of me coming out of the box again, the same one who had appeared briefly during Patti's interrogation yesterday, surprising the heck out of me. Where did that new me come from? I'd like to invite her over more often.

"You were spying on my house just now," I said, throwing some accusation into my voice. "Weren't you? You waited until Hunter left, knowing I'd be passing this way soon. Are you actually stalking me?"

Johnny chortled like my suspicion was ridiculous, but he turned a teensy shade of pink. "I don't need to stalk you," he said. "You follow the same pattern, day in, day out. The bees, then the store, sometimes Stu's, and in between you snoop where you don't belong."

Was I that predictable? Apparently, since Johnny had hit it right on the head, except for that snooping part. I think.

"We need to talk right now," he said.

"Give me one good reason."

And he did.

His next simple but powerful words were music to my ears considering the source. "I need your help," he said.

The police chief had never, ever asked for my assistance before. Ever.

This had to be really, really good.

How could I resist? But first, caution. "No handcuffs? No interrogation room?"

"Neither."

With that, I climbed into his police chief car. And mind you, not in the back where the doors don't open from the inside and a thick sheet of hard plastic separates the front from the back.

No, this time I sat in the passenger seat. Life was improving.

Twenty-nine

"Where are we going?" I asked, all perky and chipper on the outside, but on my guard on the inside, considering who I was sitting next to. Johnny turned south. At first I thought we might be heading back to the station, that I'd been tricked into the car by his efforts to appear human, but we drove right past the cop shop.

"We're taking a little trip to Waukesha," he informed me. "A nice visit to the morgue."

Okay, then, that's one place I'd never been before. "Does Jackson know?"

"He's waiting for us."

We rode for a while in silence.

"Why are we going there?" I asked, suspicious about his need for my help.

"You'll see. It's a surprise."

I texted Hunter to let him know where I was and with whom, just in case I was never heard from again.

For a law enforcement guy, Johnny sure did drive fast, like he was king of the road, way over the speed limit. Could I make a citizen's arrest? Somehow, in this case, I doubted it.

I breathed a sigh of relief when we pulled up at the Waukesha Sheriff's Department, since that's where Hunter works. Until right this minute, I hadn't even known where the coroner's office was located. I mean, really—how often does an average person go to the morgue? It hadn't been on my radar before now.

We walked in a door marked "8," took the steps to the second floor, and ended up in a room where the first thing I spotted was a sort of bathtub on wheels and more stainless steel than I'd ever seen in one place. Wheeled dissecting tables, instruments . . . I eyed up a saw and felt a shiver run through my body.

Thank God, not a single sighting of blood or gore, though. The room was spotless. But I had to wonder how many bodies had passed through here, and I hoped I never ended up like a slab of beef on one of these tables— naked and stone-cold dead. Morbid morgue thoughts crowded my brain.

Jackson really was waiting for us just like the chief said. Another huge comfort. It always helps to have a friend around when dealing with Johnny Jay, for witness quality assurance.

"Let's go show her," Johnny said, so I braced for the inevitable. I might have slow-dawning issues from time to time, but with the recent murder and all, I put two-and-two together and came up with Nova Campbell.

As we walked down a corridor, I said to the chief, "And you have a point to all this?"

"You aren't coming clean with me. Once you get a reality check and see the consequences of your actions, or your sister's, maybe you'll take this more seriously."

•The three of us continued on to an impressive door (Can we say stainless steel one more time?) and through it into a room that had a horrible lingering odor of decay. Another chill ran through me, this time because it was really cold inside. I knew we must be in the cold storage area where Jackson kept his bodies. For the first time, I wondered how Jackson could do this job, and what kind of personality lurked under his friendly exterior.

I didn't want to look at the table or the body on it.

"Nova Campbell's cadaver," Johnny Jay announced. "Take a good, long look at what's left of her."

Jackson and I locked eyes, and I could tell this wasn't his idea. Johnny Jay had put him up to it. That jerk was *not* getting the satisfaction of seeing me cower, even though I felt a little sick to my stomach.

So I filled my lungs with foul air—through my mouth, I'm not totally dense—and looked over at what was left of Nova.

Part of me wanted to pass right out, but the analytic side discovered, surprisingly, that I could handle this much better than watching Nova go from alive to dead in my backyard. That had been much harder. What I was viewing now was about the same level of difficulty as walking up to an acquaintance's casket and peering inside. Maybe one notch worse.

"That's her all right," I said, as though I was there to identify her, pleased that my voice didn't crack. It remained strong and steady.

"Okay, Johnny," Jackson said. "That's enough. Thanks for coming, Story." He gave me a shoulder squeeze on the way back into the autopsy room. "Chief, why don't you hang around for my next autopsy."

"As appealing as that is, Davis, I'm passing."

Jackson winked at me to let me know Johnny wasn't a frequent visitor and that his stomach wasn't as strong as he made it out to be. "You can take this with you," he said, handing a sealed plastic bag to the chief. "I'm finished with it."

"Where's the report?" Johnny said, studying the item inside—a black water bottle. I took an educated guess that it was the one Nova must've drank from on her last day on earth.

"I faxed the report over to your office," the ME told him. "It should be on your desk."

After glancing at the water bottle, I did a double-take and suddenly felt light-headed. The room swam before my eyes, all the morgue tables undulated, ribbons of overhead lighting flashed at me, the walls spun out of control.

Jackson must have noticed my distress, because he grabbed my arm to steady me, and ended up walking me out to Johnny's squad car. How I got there on my rubber legs, I really don't know.

All the way back to Moraine, Johnny verbally worked me over while I leaned back against the headrest.

"You delivered that carrot juice," he said accusingly. "Now, I don't really think you were part of some mastermind plot to kill Campbell, or even that you were a conscious accomplice. Personally, I believe you were just a pawn. Either your sister committed the murder or her husband did, and you didn't know what you were doing. Why is it that you're always right in the thick of things?"

I didn't have any energy to use up on a verbal duke-out with him. He kept going. "As it stands, the out-of-towners have solid alibis. But your sister doesn't. And she had plenty of reason to want Campbell dead."

His voice droned on. "You just got a glimpse of the results. What do you think of your sister right now? Still want to protect her and that conniving husband of hers?"

The plastic bag containing the water bottle was on the seat console between us.

"What's the matter? Cat got your tongue? It would be the first time. Guess this trip was too much for you. Good. Now maybe you'll cooperate and help put a killer behind bars."

Johnny Jay thought the morgue tour had been too much for me. He couldn't be more wrong. The water bottle was the big problem.

Because I recognized it.

How could I not? The side facing me read "Stalkers Have Rights, Too." I didn't have to see the other side to know it said "I'm Watching You."

The water bottle belonged to Patti Dwyre.

Thirty

I'd been startled speechless and still hadn't found my speaking voice when Johnny Jay deposited me at The Wild Clover. But my brain wasn't one bit numb. Inside, I was yakking up a storm. Thoughts were zinging all over the place, talking fast and loud.

Patti!

My mind slowed down long enough to take a moment to express gratitude. At least, I didn't have to confess to giving it to her as a gift or something like that, which would only keep me in focus with the head investigator. Like I wasn't already in his sights.

This time, I was totally in the clear.

But what was her bottle doing at the coroner's office, carefully wrapped in plastic, now turned over to the police chief?

What the heck was going on? *Had* Patti murdered Nova? Why had her water bottle been found on Nova's night table loaded up with poisonous water hemlock? Sloppy wasn't Patti's M.O. If anything, she was meticulous about undercover procedure, saving her own skin at my expense more times than I like to count, leaving me behind to suffer the consequences by myself.

Yet Patti had been creeping around inside Holly's house the night after Nova died. Sure, she'd said it was all in the name of research and a possible breaking-story exclusive. But what if she'd been just trying to cover her tracks?

Speaking of the devil, my cell phone chimed the special song that notifies me when Patti is calling from the other end—"Tubular Bells," the theme song from the *Exorcist* movie. Somehow it fit Patti to a T.

"I was in," she said. "And now I'm out."

"Huh?" I tried to balance my cell phone between my ear and shoulder because I was rearranging my honey display to include a brand-new honey stick flavor—red grapefruit. My latest creation smelled divine and tasted as good as it smelled, maybe better. But would it sell? I sure hoped so.

I had to stop what I was doing. The shoulder thing wasn't working.

"Do I have to spell out everything to you?" Patti said, not sounding mean, more subterfuge-ish. "Listening ears and all. Remember what we discussed."

"Oh, right." Our agreement to help each other, and Patti was reporting in. Was that it?

"Toys," she said. "If you get my drift."

"Come again?" By now, I was in the back room. "And will you please go someplace where no one can hear you. Otherwise this is going to take all day."

"Fine. Just a minute"

I heard background sounds while I waited. Muffled, unidentifiable, as though Patti had her hand over the micro-

phone. *See, the woman is über-cautious*, I said to myself
in a self-convincing (hopefully not delusional) tone. Plus,
Patti and I had shared a few adventures and caught our-
selves several bad guys (the hard way, I might add). I
couldn't picture her switching sides.

I heard a familiar beep and paused to read a text from
Hunter: "ME says u ok. I agree but 4 dif reason. JJ gone?"

I sent my own text: "☺"

Then Patti was back on the airwaves, just as someone
banged on my office door. "Hang on," I said, and opened
it to find Patti with her phone still to her ear.

We both ended our calls, me more annoyed than ever.
Patti slid past me and slumped down in my desk chair. "I
had to hide in Gil Green's bedroom closet forever," she
whined. "He picked the wrong time to take a nap. And I
had to pee. It was awful."

She unzipped a small black backpack and dumped the
contents on my desk.

"Oh my God," I said, taking in the sight of brilliant-
colored items. "You found all this in his room?"

"Sure did." Patti picked up a stick with a feather on the
end. "A tickler," she said. "For long lingering strokes."
She tried to sweep it over my face, but I was quick. No
way was that thing touching me. Who knew where it had
been.

She pulled it back and said, "I do believe this is an
ostrich feather."

Patti had stolen Gil Green's stash of sex toys? I didn't
want to come in contact with any of them, but I got as
close to the desk as possible to study the props. "Sex flash
cards?" I burst out laughing.

"Of different positions. And look at this game. Twelve
Months of Naughty Nights."

"And love dice," I said, spotting the hot-pink dice and
remembering one particular evening when Hunter and I

had played that game. Very romantic really. All those cute words to act out after taking turns throwing the dice and watching what appeared—"Kiss" and "Chest" and "Neck." Not the throat kind of neck, of course. The action verb.

"I didn't find anything in Camilla's room," Patti said. "These things"—here she wrinkled her nose in either disgust or disappointment or both—"confirm their alibi."

"And how did you arrive at that conclusion?" I argued. "All this proves is that he has sex. Or really wants to."

"There's more proof," Patti said, poking at her phone while I pondered the best way to approach her in regard to a confiscated, personalized, lethal water bottle.

There just wasn't going to be an easy way to bring it up.

But what she showed me next took precedence.

"While Gil was napping, I snuck out of the closet and scored his cell phone," Patti said. "Then I took it back into the closet and went through everything, including photos he'd taken with his phone. Then I sent select pictures to my e-mail."

I tucked in behind her so we could both see.

"Those two hound dogs weren't lying about their sexual encounter," Patti said, using her arrow to move forward. There the lovebirds were, taking turns showing the camera their mugs, in Holly's guest bed, covers pulled up just enough to conceal private places, looking rumpled and ruffled. Patti said, "Camilla had to have taken this one of him. I don't get what she sees in him."

"Or what he sees in her," I added.

"It's almost like they're posing," Patti said.

"Like they know they'll need an alibi," I said back.

"Give it up," Patti told me. "I don't think either of them did it."

"You don't have any proof that they didn't," I pointed

out. I didn't want to accept that. Mainly because it didn't leave many other suspects. Holly? Max? Me? Patti?

"Let's discuss you for a minute," I said, launching into my excursion to the morgue.

"I thought that was you I saw inside Johnny Jay's gumball machine," Patti said.

"Gumball machine?"

"Mobster slang for police car," Patti answered. "What does your morgue visit have to do with me?"

So I told her the rest, how Jackson had handed a particular piece of evidence to the chief and how I'd ID'd the water bottle as belonging to Patti. To be on the safe side, I sidled over to the door for a quick exit, realizing that ID'ing her bottle would be a bad thing if Patti was the killer.

Patti stared at me for so long I started worrying that she'd lapsed into a seated coma (is there such a thing?). Then she jumped up from the chair and came at me fast. I tried to remember some of Holly's wrestling moves, ones she'd used on me to take me down and keep me there. Nothing helpful came to mind.

Next, I turned to get the heck out of the room, but she already had me from behind.

Squeezing the air out of me. Harder and harder.

I screamed as loud as I could while I still had enough breath to manage more than a squeak. "Help!" I said, but it came out as a croak.

She released her hold.

I turned to fend her off.

And she attacked again.

By now, I heard people coming to my rescue. I also realized (belatedly) that Patti was actually hugging me, not squeezing the life out of me. This was the first physical contact we'd ever had. Patti wasn't usually a toucher.

"I just realized something," she said excitedly. "We've finally caught a break in this case!"

Maybe having the wind knocked out of me had also rearranged my brain cells because I had no idea how her water bottle meant a break in the case. Maybe for the cops, but it should have serious consequences for Patti.

Carrie Ann bounded into the room with Stanley Peck right behind her. Stanley wasn't concealing at the moment. He had his handgun out at the ready, pointed in the air. Customers were crowding in, too. Boy, I must have really let out a blood-curdler.

Unfortunately, all those inquisitive pairs of eyes landed on my desk, mouths gaping open as they took in the collection of sex toys.

I heard another voice, one that made my own blood run cold.

"Story Fischer," my mother said. "What is all this . . . stuff?" Then, "For cripes' sake. I am *so* embarrassed."

I try to make my family proud. I really do. Except as I've mentioned before, I have the unfortunate knack of being in the wrong place at the wrong time. Like the time when Lori Spandle and I got in a fistfight in front of Stu's. My mother had witnessed that brawl, too, along with her boyfriend and all of Stu's customers who spilled into the street.

This was another perfect example.

I'd have liked to blame everything on Patti, but she hadn't always been in the vicinity when things went south. Although this one was entirely on her shoulders and she'd better step forward and come up with some explanation to tell all these people, pronto.

I swung my head around, looking for her. Where had she gone? *Crap.*

"These things belong to Patti," I told the roomful of

spectators. "Really . . . she stole . . . I mean . . . you have to believe me . . . Patti, where are you?"

Carrie Ann reacted. "Okay, everybody, Story is fine. Let's clear out."

Stanley put his piece away and practically fled.

My mom stomped off. The customers backed out of the room. Patti's troublemaker face wasn't among them. How did she do it? Hadn't Hunter warned me about her? Multiple times? Wait until this rumor found its way to him. I'd never hear the end of it.

Once we were alone, Carrie Ann started hooting and tee-heeing.

"I'm so glad you're enjoying this," I said, feeling weak in the knees.

"Did Patti really bring these into the store?"

"It's a long story."

"I'm dying to hear it, but let's do damage control first."

"What am I going to do?"

"Hide out for a while."

"K."

"Get rid of these . . . objects first." My cousin's managerial skills were showing themselves, and boy, were they needed. Then I heard music swelling from her voice. "I'm going to tell everybody," she said, "that one of your deliveries got mixed up, that you were expecting a box of candy and when you saw what you opened instead, you were so shocked you screamed."

What a brilliant idea! "I don't know how to thank you."

"That raise I've been asking for would do it."

"It's yours," I said, caving in a moment of extreme vulnerability.

Before Carrie Ann would leave the room to complete her mission to save my character, she made me put her increase in writing.

After that, I scooped the items into a paper bag and slipped out the back door with it clutched in my fist, and a good deal of revenge swelling in my heart.

I called Hunter's cell phone. "Did the cops find adult toys in Gil Green's room?" I blurted right at him since if they had, it might have been going the rounds when they talked shop. At this point, I couldn't believe anything coming out of Patti's mouth.

"Ah, yes, why?"

So she had told me the truth. "I wish you had mentioned that," I said. "You knew about Gil's and Camilla's alibis, too, didn't you?"

By the silence on the other end, he had known.

"We need to talk more," I told him. A little communication from him would have been helpful.

"Let it go, Story."

"One of the flavorists did it, or both. Max said the team didn't get along and neither of them seems too broken up by Nova's death."

"I don't have every single detail," Hunter said, "But the chief seems to think they're innocent. And he's a suspicious guy, as you know. He wouldn't let them off just because. He has a reason."

I whined a little. "All along I've been convinced that Camilla Bailey killed Nova Campbell."

"That's because you want your killers to be unlikeable people, and sometimes they just aren't."

That certainly had a ring of truth to it. Bad people should act bad, right? "What are you saying? That killers can have hearts of gold?"

"No, that's not what I'm saying. Look at sociopaths for example. On the surface they can be friendly and interesting. You have to delve down much deeper to find the dark side."

"That's not always true," I argued. "Lori Spandle's

personality is just as slimy as her heart. On the other hand, you happen to be just as good as you look."

"Thank you, sweet thing. But do me a favor and take a break from your sister and her houseguests and all the drama, okay?"

"I will," I lied.

After hanging up, I considered what Hunter had told me. My main suspect in the Nova Campbell murder had been a flavorist with what I thought was a taste for poison. I'd let myself run wild with assumptions based solely on our unpleasant meeting in a wildflower patch, and as much as I didn't want to admit it, Gil probably hadn't killed Nova, and Camilla Bailey might actually be innocent. Geez, I hate when that happens. Especially to such a nasty woman.

I got into my truck, threw the bag in the passenger's seat, and drove off to Holly's house. On the way up the driveway, I stopped as Holly's jag eased up alongside me going the opposite way. Camilla was with her. "We're going to the antique store. Are you looking for me?"

Good! This was my opportunity to get myself some gloves. "Just socializing," I said. "Don't stop on my account. Have fun." And with that, we went our own ways.

Gil Green was standing on the edge of the garden talking to Chance. Milly and Effie were seated on Holly's patio, acting like the buddies they had become, leaning in, sharing something between them, laughing. I had the bag of Gil's goodies with me.

"Not likely," Gil was saying as I approached. "Well. Hello, Story."

"Hey," I said. "What's not likely?"

"A *loxosceles* recluse," Gil said.

"Brown recluse spiders in the garden," Chance explained in English. "This guy doesn't believe me."

"They're called recluses for a reason," I said, having to agree with Gil Green.

"What are you up to?" Effie asked me when I wandered over.

"Returning a few things," I told her. "I saw Holly leaving. She said to put them away."

I hustled inside with my brown paper bag, took the steps two at a time, then realized I didn't have a clue which guest room was which. I opened a door. Gil's on the first try, judging by the men's shoes and other manly personal effects. I dumped out the toys in the nightstand drawer, and quickly glanced around for gloves. Not a one.

Next I went across the hall and scored again—Camilla's room. I recognized the baggy dress tossed on her unmade bed and the safari hat she'd been wearing when we tangled over wildflowers. I did a cursory search for gloves, not finding any left out in obvious places, then I hurried downstairs, clutching the empty bag.

"I'm putting together a work crew," I lied to the women, noticing it became easier every time. "And we need to borrow some gloves to clean up Main Street."

Which was sort of true. I guess.

"Can I get them for you?" Effie asked.

"Naw, I know where they are." With that, I headed to the outbuilding, helped myself to every single glove I could find, and stashed them in the bag.

Then I went back to Effie and asked if she had any other pairs of gardening gloves. While she was gone to the carriage house for a pair of gloves she'd left inside, I asked Milly, "Were you out driving with Effie yesterday? I thought I saw the two of you near the library."

"Wasn't me. I worked on the newsletter all day."

Okay, then.

I put Effie and her mysterious passenger out of my mind for the time being. I had bigger fish to catch.

Thirty-one

Enough was enough.

Nothing was getting done. Or some things were, but not the right things, like, oh, I don't know, maybe like ruling out my main suspects instead of busting them for murder. If those two flavorists weren't behind Nova's murder, then who was? Patti was MIA since the sex toy fiasco. Her behavior had moved her back onto my suspect list and she'd be on Johnny Jay's, too, once I told him Patti was the owner of that water bottle.

I wasn't going to cover for her anymore. But there was something I had to do first.

The Waukesha Sheriff's Department came into view. I grabbed the bag of gloves and entered the building. According to Jackson's assistant, he was hard at work. The autopsy door was closed. I took a deep breath, knocked on the door to give him a heads-up, and went in.

Wimpy little Story had left the building. The new, improved version was in action.

The ME glanced up from his work, did a double take, and set down some kind of tool that I didn't want to even know about.

"I need to ask a favor," I said, looking up at the ceiling, which seemed the safest place. "But I can't talk in here."

That's how we ended up in his office, which was the size of a postage stamp. And I thought mine was pathetic. I placed the bag on his desk and took a seat next to him, fighting claustrophobia, which I didn't even know I had, that's how tiny his office was.

"What can I do for our Story?" Jackson asked.

I glanced at the bag. "I want you to test the gloves inside here for traces of poison," I said.

Our medical examiner is at the very center of any murder investigation, and Jackson is no dummy. "Let me guess. You want me to test for . . . oh . . . I don't know . . . um, water hemlock?"

"That's right."

He took the bag and peered inside. "Where did you get these?"

"I can't tell."

Jackson leaned back in his chair and studied me. We locked eyes. His said that he really liked me and wanted to help me out. Mine said, so do it.

"All right," he said. "But if I find what you're looking for, then you have to tell me where the gloves came from and turn the evidence over to the proper authorities."

"I'll consider your request," I said, not meaning it, since revealing the source would implicate my sister even more.

Jackson shook his head. "It isn't a request. It's a requirement. Otherwise, no deal."

"All right already."

"You agree to my terms?"

"I said yes."

We shook on our new deal. Even as we did, I was wracking my brain for an escape clause.

My cell phone rang as I headed back to the store. Carrie Ann was on the other end. "You have a visitor. He says he's going to wait as long as it takes. I think you better get here fast."

"If it's Johnny Jay, I'm never coming back."

"Guess again." My cousin's voice lowered, which meant the mystery man was in close proximity. "And bring one of those posters for the newsletter."

What? Did everybody in my life have to talk in secret code? Then I got it. Posters of Patti's ex-husband mobster. A gasp escaped before I said, "Harry Bruno's there?"

"Right."

"Be right there."

One part of my brain was asking a ton of questions. How had he found me? And what did he want? Did he think I blew up his car? Was he hunting us down one by one? The other part answered back, Just go find out. It's broad daylight and you have customers to protect you.

Back at The Wild Clover, my visitor was lounging near the honey display, picking up one item at a time, studying it, putting it down, then picking up another. Since Harry was the town's orange alert and his mug had been prominently featured in my posters, he was also surrounded by customers acting as watchdogs.

And they couldn't have been more obvious. Harry had to know he was under major surveillance. He recognized me right away, and said, "We need to talk."

Nothing good ever comes after that line.

"I didn't blow up your car," I said.

"I know. That's not why I'm here."

To say I was intrigued wasn't a strong enough emotion for what I was feeling. Where to talk, though?

The back room was out. Too private. No way was I going to be alone with this guy.

My colorful Adirondack chairs in front of the store? Too public? I had visions of a mob mobile pulling up and opening fire. Not to mention that the orange alert team might take him out.

"I'll meet you at Stu's Bar and Grill in ten minutes," I told him.

Harry nodded, swung his head around, glaring at his tails, and left the store.

Once he was gone, one of the customers said, "Don't go."

"Go," somebody else said. "And report back."

"Call the chief," I heard down aisle two, then follow-up comments flew through the store.

"But he hasn't committed a crime."

"He will."

"Where's Patti? We should warn her."

"We should warn *him*."

"What if she blows up Stu's?"

"What if a rival gang riddles the place? We need to warn Stu."

I piped up. "Let's not get carried away. Nothing bad is going to happen. The man just wants to talk to me. We're meeting in a public place with lots of witnesses."

"We'll follow you."

"Nothing but trouble," was the last comment I heard before swinging out the back door. I wasn't exactly sure who it referred to.

It wasn't especially reassuring that Harry Bruno knew who I was and where I worked and probably even that Patti was staying with me. But maybe that was his motive for meeting with me—to let me know he meant business and he wasn't going to let a beekeeper with a little store get in his way.

Just to be on the safe side, I took the back way to Stu's instead of marching down Main Street like a moving target.

Thirty-two

"I want my bar and grill to remain in one piece," Stu whispered to me from behind the bar. I couldn't tell if he was kidding or not. Stu isn't easily rattled, and he didn't look rattled now. More amused than anything.

Being a bar owner, I bet he's seen it all. Brawls, busts, secret assignations, the works. Stu has a cool head on his shoulders, a necessary requirement in his line of work. He's scrappy, too, when he needs to be, which isn't often. And clearly nothing important was getting past him, because he did a jerking motion with his head, in the same direction where Harry sat waiting for me. The buzz had beaten me to the bar. No surprise there.

The lunch crowd had dwindled since it was well past noon, but there were still a few customers finishing up, lounging over their desserts and coffees. If I hadn't already known where Harry was sitting, their suspicious, sliding eyeballs would have clued me in.

For the first time, I pondered the wisdom of circulating those posters. Harry might be a tough guy who should reap what he'd sown, but I didn't want to be responsible for his future health. I could name several of our residents, including Patti, who tended to carry things further than necessary.

I expected our infamous mobster to be cradling a highball glass or tipping a martini, but Harry had a coke in front of him. And he rose to pull out my chair, just like a true gentleman, shattering a few of my stereotypical musings.

Where was uncouth and crass? Not here, at least not now.

Glancing toward the entrance, I noticed some of my customers sidling in, and had a warm, fuzzy moment of gratitude for them. They were watching my back.

"How did you know where to find me?" I asked him.

"I could tell you I have connections and leave it at that," he said with a friendly enough smile. "But the truth is, I recognized you from an ad you placed in the local paper for your grocery store."

Well, that was possible. My smiling face usually accompanied any of The Wild Clover's advertisements.

Harry and I talked small stuff while we ordered. He went with a Caesar salad. I couldn't resist ordering a burger, telling myself I needed the extra protein and everybody needs a certain amount of fat in their diets. Right?

Maybe our table topics were a Chicago mob–style rule, not discussing business on an empty stomach, so I followed his lead. Our subjects stayed neutral. We covered local weather and questions and tidbits about Moraine. I felt like a tour guide.

Then we chowed down on what I hoped was his dime. After that, we both ordered coffee, and it was time for business.

"Where is she?" Harry wanted to know.

I sidestepped his question. "You need to go home," I said, still feeling my newfound oats. "She isn't interested in seeing you."

"It's not what you think," he said. "Like that Caesar I just ate. It's not what it seems, either. Did you know it wasn't named after Julius Caesar like everybody thinks? Turns out it was invented by Caesar Cardini, an Italian immigrant like my grandfather. And all along us assuming it was good-old Julius."

Okay, I didn't know that fact about Caesar salads. But where was this going exactly? "So are you saying you're like Julius Caesar? Or you're like the salad?"

Harry must have read my confusion, because he dispensed with the analogies. "I'll admit I was bitter when Patti ran out on me, and maybe I said some things to make certain individuals assume I wanted revenge, but it's the exact opposite. See, like the salad, it isn't what you think. I'm here to win her back. To start new and fresh."

"You think she killed your second wife, don't you? That's really why you came here. To punish her."

Harry threw his head back and laughed. "Nova was second rate, that's for sure. I hated the woman. If Patti got rid of her, she did me a favor. I should thank her."

Sure, Harry was soft-spoken and polite, but I sensed an undercurrent of violence and ruthlessness. I had his number, and I wasn't buying his line.

"Your car blew up," I said. "If I were you, I'd be really P.O.'d."

"What's a car to me? Nothing I can't replace. But my woman is priceless. Patti's always been a hothead."

"From what I understand, she's not your woman anymore, and hasn't been for a long time."

"I only need a chance to convince her." Harry put extra emphasis on the word *convince*, which I didn't like one bit. And then he said exactly what I expected from a no-good creep. Harry said, "I've changed."

My doubt must have showed through.

"What, you don't believe me?"

"I don't know you well enough to have an opinion." I did an inner snort, but kept my expression neutral. *Sleezeball*, I thought.

"Tell her I love her," he said, getting up and throwing a bunch of bills on the table. Then he looked around, said, "And call off the clowns, will you?" and walked out.

At that moment, I intensely disliked Patti Dwyre. For involving me in her crime-family business. For living next door. For every single episode of Patti weirdness she'd ever exposed me to.

My protectors, those buds who Harry had just referred to as "clowns," were on their feet. "Find out what he's driving!" I yelled to them, hoping at least one would follow Harry. I couldn't do it. He'd spot me—or make me, as Patti would say.

From Stu's window with the best view, I called the cop shop and asked for Johnny Jay. And was connected to Sally Maylor instead. "Good deal," I said. "I should have asked for you in the first place. I have information regarding a piece of evidence from the Nova Campbell murder."

"What do you have?" Sally said.

"The murder vessel belongs to Patti Dwyre."

"Vessel?"

"Or conduit or whatever. You know, the water bottle that was found on Nova's nightstand, the one with poisoned carrot juice."

"Ah."

"When the chief gave me a ride, I thought I recognized it at the time, but wasn't sure enough to tell him. It just dawned on me. It's definitely Patti's."

Now, to a casual observer, my tattling might make me seem unlikeable, not exactly friendship material, but I had several reasons for pointing Johnny in Patti's direction:

- It really did belong to her, and I had a duty as a citizen of the United States.

- Johnny would bring Patti in for questioning, probably keep her behind bars as long as possible, and possibly save her from a violent and deadly mob hit.

- Harry Bruno would get wind that Patti was no longer in my vicinity and leave me alone.

- If Patti were in custody, she couldn't do any more collateral damage to my life.

See? Lots of good reasons for squealing on her, most of them for her own good.

I finished with, "I just had lunch with Harry Bruno. He's in town."

"I'll pass that on to the chief."

Right when I hung up, my sister's pickup truck drove past the window.

Harry Bruno was behind the wheel.

Thirty-three

I ran outside and watched the taillights disappear down Main Street, wondering what to do next.

Where should I go from here? Two isolated events—murder and mob—were fusing into some kind of twisted logic, if only I could figure it out.

Patti thought that we finally had a break in the case after finding out that her very own water bottle was at the scene of the crime. She'd seemed excited but I just couldn't see the upside. Was she a viable murder suspect? What if she'd lied about the reason for her divorce? What if Nova had actually stolen Harry from Patti, and wife number one had retaliated?

Holly hadn't killed anyone. That was totally out of the question. But how well did I really know my sister's husband? Not enough to rule Max out, but I had to trust Holly's choice. If nothing else, she was discerning when it came to men.

On the way back to The Wild Clover, I called my sister. She picked up on the first ring. "They're leaving!" she said, all excited. "Our houseguests have been cleared to go A.W.A.Y. Only they couldn't get a flight out until tomorrow. The limo is picking them up in the morning at 9:00 a.m."

"Wonderful," I said sarcastically. Even if they were innocent of murder, I hated unleashing Camilla and Gil before we had a killer in jail. Letting go was hard to do.

"When was the last time Patti was over at your house?" I asked, wanting to shout out about Holly's truck and who was driving it, but needing to ask a few questions first. Once I informed her of the truck's status, she'd be in no shape to answer anything.

"When she was here with you, for dinner." Oh right, Holly didn't know about Patti's sneaking in the other day. Which was just as well.

"I meant before that?"

Holly paused again on the other end. "A week or so ago," she finally said.

I thought back. When had the water bottle been delivered? Around then, I was pretty sure.

"Did she have a water bottle with her?"

"I don't remember? Why?"

"That was her water bottle in Nova's room. The one with poison in it."

Holly squealed. "OMG!" she said. "How did it get there?"

"That's what I want to know! And there's more. Your truck just went down Main Street."

"So?"

"So, Patti's ex-husband, Harry Bruno, the mobster from Chicago, was driving it."

Holly screeched.

"You need to report it stolen."

"I better check with Chance first. There has to be an explanation. Are you sure? You've been wrong about things before."

"I'm absolutely, positively, 100 percent sure."

"Okay, then, I'll do something right now . . ." Holly sounded rattled.

"Let me know what happens with your truck the minute you hear."

"I will."

"And don't let Patti find out Harry has it," I told her. "Or you can kiss your truck good-bye."

While I waited for Holly to report back on the whereabouts of her truck, I called Jackson Davis to check on the results of his testing on the gloves I'd delivered. I'd forgotten to ask him how long before we'd have those results—an hour, a day, longer? Jackson's answering machine kicked in, so I left a message for him to call me as soon as he had something.

Then I made an attempt to locate Hunter to update him on the whereabouts of Harry Bruno and other developing news, but he was in K-9 training today, shaping up canine partners for more crime busting, so I didn't expect him to pick up. Later, if he gave me grief, I could always say I tried to include him but he hadn't been available.

I surprised myself by the enormous relief I felt when he didn't answer his phone. The last thing I needed was a lecture from him about how I should mind my own business and cooperate with the local authorities and blah, blah, blah. I love the man, but sometimes . . .

Next Grams called.

"Hi, sweetie," she said. "I'm calling about that mobster in town?"

"So you know."

"I'd have to be in my coffin not to. Is that girl safe?"

By now Patti might be in custody, so I said, "You don't have to worry about her."

"Such a sweet person to get mixed up with a character like that. He must have good qualities along with the bad or she never would have given him a second look." Grams, even with all that age and experience, still believes everybody is basically good. Even the rats.

"What are the seniors saying about the murder?" I wanted to know. Grams is like the queen bee of the senior citizen crowd. While most of my customers blab about anything and everything they hear, the older set tend to watch and listen, and then instinctively wade through the BS and come away with more of the actual truth than the rest of us.

"They all agree that you are like a trouble magnet."

"Besides that."

"We're sticking up for our own and going with an outsider did it." Which was the usual stance in our town. If a local is involved in any sort of crime, we analyze him up, down, and sideways and come up with a unified plausible temporary insanity reason why it could have happened to this particular person on our watch.

"The only suspicious outsiders have been released," I told her. "They're leaving tomorrow."

"They aren't the only outsiders hanging around, you know. Mabel down the road spotted you-know-who driving your sister's truck."

"Harry Bruno? I saw that, too, but I was on foot and couldn't tail him."

"Don't worry. Mabel flipped around and went after him."

"Good for her." Mabel was one of Grams's oldest and dearest friends, a real pistol just like my grandmother. "But isn't she legally blind? What's she doing driving?"

"Oh that old rumor! She has perfect vision. She picked out the mobster, didn't she?"

"Where did he go?"

"Had the nerve to drive right up your sister's driveway. Mabel is there right now," Grams said. "We sicced the cops on him in case he's up to no good. I'm driving over, too, and making sure my granddaughter is all right."

"I'm not positive he's committed a crime, though. We don't have proof that he took the truck without permission from Holly's hired help. Otherwise, wouldn't he be in hiding someplace other than Holly's house?"

"Some crooks return to the scene of the crime. I saw that on television."

"I'll meet you there," I said, hanging up and racing out the back door.

The first thing I saw when I pulled into Holly's driveway was Mabel's car's rear end. The front end of it had crumpled directly into a mature maple tree. The airbag had deployed. I stopped and ran up to the car. No one was inside.

I drove a little farther and parked next to Johnny Jay's squad car, which had the lights flashing but at least he wasn't polluting the air with noise from the siren. I didn't hear any sirens in the distance, either. A good sign that Grams's friend Mabel wasn't seriously hurt.

Patti was in the backseat of Johnny's squad car, pounding on the window to get my attention. Which was momentarily diverted by Grams's Fleetwood crawling toward me up the driveway. She missed my truck by less than a hair and had to scoot over to the passenger side to get out, that's how close she parked.

Patti was shouting from the inside, "Open the door. Let me out!"

Grams said, "Where is Mabel? Is she okay? What happened to her car?"

"I told you she was blind."

My grandmother's head swung to the noise blasting

from Johnny's backseat. "What is that nice young woman doing inside a police car?"

"I'm not sure," I fudged.

"Let me out!" Patti yelled.

"We better not," I told Grams. "She might be dangerous."

"She looks a bit agitated," Grams agreed.

Ignoring Patti was a hard thing to do, but we left her where she was and headed for the backside of the house, since nobody ever uses the formal front door. Sure enough, a group had assembled on the grass. I pushed through and there was my sister, practicing one of her wrestling moves on Harry Bruno. I noted Max, Camilla, and Gil all staring bug-eyed at the two on the ground. Effie held back from the group. I looked around but didn't see Chance.

Holly is a perfect example of "Eye of the Tiger," which is what she used to chant to herself during high school wrestling events. According to her, everybody has what it takes to win as long as they believe in themselves and stay ultra-focused on the task at hand. That's where "Eye of the Tiger" comes in. When one of those big cats is on the hunt, it has eyes only for its prey.

Holly liked to take the offensive with her game face in place, and if she hadn't met and married Max Paine, she would have made a great professional wrestler. Although Mom would have put the kibosh on that fast enough.

Anyway, right this minute, she had Harry in some kind of paralyzing chokehold.

"Let him up," Johnny Jay ordered her.

"Let me go," Harry said as best he could with Holly's arm pressing down across his throat. He was pinned but good.

"You stole my truck," Holly said.

"Let him up," the police chief said again. "I can't book him on the ground."

Grams said proudly, "That's my granddaughter. She's a spitfire!"

"Let him go, beautiful," Max said, clearly bewildered by his wife's prowess.

Holly kept the pressure on, ignoring the calls to release Harry.

"Handcuffs," I suggested. "Restrain him first, then Holly will let go."

The chief was flustered, or he never would have done what I suggested. But he did, and soon he had Harry on his feet. Over at the patio table, Mabel had an ice pack on her knee. "Lock him up and throw away the key," she yelled. "He deserves life!"

"What happened?" Grams asked Mabel.

"Something zipped right in front of my car. I had to do an evasive maneuver, or I would have hit it."

"So you slammed into the tree instead?" I said, checking out her wound and finding no gushing blood or protruding bones at weird angles. "You should be checked out by a doctor."

"Cheap airbag," Mabel complained.

"I'll drive her to the hospital," Grams offered, and off they went. The blind leading the blind.

So pretty much everybody was accounted for. Max, Camilla, and Gil on one side of what had recently been Holly's grassy mat. Me, Harry, and Johnny Jay on the other. "Somebody should have brought Patti over," I said. "She'd have loved to see this."

"Dwyre is in police custody. She stays where she is," Johnny said to me.

"Where did you find her?" I asked him, hoping he hadn't hauled her out of my house. Although if he had, he would have instantly arrested me, too, on some trumped up charge like harboring a fugitive.

"Coming out of her house." Then to Holly, he said, "Did this guy steal your truck?"

Holly nodded. "I want him charged."

I glanced over at Effie, who remained silent.

"What's with this town?" Harry said. "It's like walking into Dodge without a weapon!"

Johnny Jay marched Harry over to his squad car with the rest of us tagging along. Patti's face came into view, plastered against the window, wide-eyed when she spotted Harry.

Harry's head swung toward the window. "Patti!" he said, spotting Patti before she had a chance to duck out of sight. Then to Johnny, "What did she do?"

Johnny Jay gave him one of his more popular answers. "Just shut up," he said.

"Do I get to sit in back with her?"

Johnny Jay squinted at Harry and read his mind. Actually all of us could read his expression of love and affection. Either Harry was a magnificent theatrical performer or he really had feelings for Patti, however Neanderthal they might be. Maybe he just had trouble displaying them like a normal person. Johnny Jay made a call to headquarters and requested another transport. "Does that answer your question?" he said to Harry.

But Harry couldn't take his eyes off Patti. "Maybe you can book us together," he suggested to the chief.

After that, he glanced toward Effie. I caught a meaningful look passing between them, then a quick shake of the head from Harry.

Soon after, Johnny Jay was gone with his two trophy fish.

Thirty-four

So I had that connection I thought I needed, one between Effie and Harry, which was a total surprise. He'd been the one in the passenger's seat when she was driving, I was sure of it. How did Effie know him? How did the pieces fit together? And where had Chance disappeared to?

Hunter called while I was on my way back to the store. "What's for dinner?" he wanted to know.

"One guess," I said.

"You?" Ever hopeful, that's my man.

"Guess again."

"Okay then, next guess: whatever I bring home?"

That's the beauty of a man who's used to being on his own. He's had to take care of himself, and doesn't expect all of that from his lady. "Correct answer," I told him. "You win the prize."

"And the prize is . . . you?"

"Right again. Just let me check in at the store then I'll meet you at home. I have all kinds of things to tell you."

At The Wild Clover, Mom was ruling the roost, perched behind the cash register in front of a long line of customers, talking with Stanley. Or rather, bossing him around. When he spotted me, he broke free and pulled me to the back of the store.

"What about the customers?" I said. "Mom needs help."

"I have a complaint," Stanley said to me in a low voice. "Your mother is a nice person and all . . ."

Did I hear a "but" coming?

". . . but I can't work with her. She's like some kind of dictator, watching me every second, and if I stop to take a breather, she's all over me about wasting money. You have to change the schedule around!"

"That's Carrie Ann's job," I told him. "Talk to her. Right now, you have to help at the checkout. You're needed."

"I've already discussed it with Carrie Ann. She said I'm low man on the totem pole and nobody else will work with Helen, either, so I'm stuck."

"Where *is* Carrie Ann?"

"She took off as soon as your mother showed up."

"Where are Brent and Trent?" I glanced at the time. Five-ish. Between four and seven o'clock The Wild Clover was one of the town's hottest spots, with residents' attentions turning to that age-old question, the same one Hunter had asked: "What's for dinner?"

Tonight was no exception.

"The twins have classes, same night every week, remember?" Stanley said. "Originally I offered to help out here as a favor to you, but I'm telling you, I might lose control and shoot your mom."

Just then Mom yelled out, "Where's my bagger? Stop lollygagging and get over here!"

Stanley's head swung to the front, then back at me, and his eyes went wild. "I quit," he said. "Right this minute. I'm done. Welcome to the wonderful world of bagging for your mother."

And he stomped out the door, leaving me holding . . . well . . . the bag.

As soon as we had a lull, I called Hunter and told him my plans had changed, that I would be closing up the store tonight, and he was on his own until eight o'clock.

Usually when my mother appears on the scene, I take off for the back room or out the door to work in my beeyard. Speaking of honeybees and the queen in particular, each hive has only one queen. And that's for a very good reason. Because if more than one hatches out, they instinctively fight to the death. There can be only one queen bee.

Instead of escaping, I had to endure "Story this" and "Story that" and "when are you going to listen to my advice on placement." When business really wound down, Mom had time to take potshots at the rest of the staff. Carrie Ann didn't handle a particular situation quite right. The twins used their phones to surf online nonstop, and Stanley Peck was a slacker. . . then back to me . . . and those sexual appliances on my desk in full view of our customers! What was I thinking?

By seven, I was ready to call Stanley and borrow his gun.

But I made it through that last hour with only a slight, but steady twitch above my left eye. I hoped it wasn't permanent.

"Are you and Tom getting along?" I asked out on the sidewalk after we locked up.

"Why would you think we aren't?"

I could have said because my mother was reverting back to the lemon-sucking, snake-tongued, head-swirling control freak from my past, the one who disappeared in a puff of smoke when she started dating Tom. Instead I said, "Well, is everything okay?"

"We have some things to work through," she said stiffly.

"Do you want to talk about it?"

"No."

"Can I help?"

"No."

Okay then. But they better work things out pronto so my new mother can return.

Before I walked home, I called the limo company that Max always used for airport runs. I pretended to be Max's secretary and cancelled tomorrow's trip to the airport. With so many loose ends, I just couldn't let Camilla and Gil get away. Besides, really, what was another day or two in the scheme of things?

Hunter and Ben were waiting for me on the front porch. I was starving but Hunter had prepared for that with sub sandwiches. We dug in. Between bites, I related the latest happenings—meeting Harry at Stu's, his unwise decision to flaunt his presence at Holly's house, Johnny Jay arresting both Harry and Patti. I left out only one irrelevant item regarding my own involvement in Patti's roundup.

When I was through, Hunter gazed into my eyes, making me semi-uncomfortable. "The rest, please."

"What rest?"

"I can tell you're holding something back." Was I becoming that transparent? Maybe. Or maybe Hunter was using his cop instincts on me. So I blurted out the rest—how I had realized that the water bottle belonged to Patti, and how I'd squealed on her. Guilty feelings were starting to eat at my soul.

Hunter made it all better. "You did the right thing," he said. "You don't want to be an accessory, do you?"

"Of course not."

"Withholding information in a police investigation would get you in all kinds of trouble. Don't feel bad. If Patti's innocent, she'll be okay."

Right then, Hunter's cell phone vibrated. "It's Sally Maylor," he said. "I better take it."

And that's how we found out Holly had been arrested for the murder of Nova Campbell.

Thirty-five

❦

Hunter and I took off for the police station on his Harley. As we breezed through the night, my man admitted that Sally had been keeping him informed as things developed, had kept him in the loop as though he was a member of the investigation team. I had guessed as much. I wasn't the only one of us with secrets. Hunter had his share, too. Somehow that fact made me feel slightly better.

When we arrived, the cop behind the counter told us Max and his attorney were already deep inside the bowels with a killer whale named Johnny Jay. That isn't exactly what the cop said, of course, but I easily could liken our chief to Moby Dick. Or Jaws.

While we waited for news, I considered my sister's dilemma and how the facts must look from Johnny Jay's point of view.

Nova had demanded that Holly stock carrot juice, so my sister asked me to bring some over. Then, having researched in advance to find the exact poison to accompany the juice, she concocted the potion from water hemlock she picked along the river's bank (never mind that my sister is afraid of anything having to do with the natural world—small insects, bacteria-infested river water, etc.). Johnny Jay would have decided she killed out of jealousy, that Nova was threatening her nice fancy lifestyle, that Holly was protecting her marital status and future wealth. Holly had no alibi, and she was the only one who'd disappeared during Nova's final moments at the riverbank. "Couldn't handle witnessing her evil work," Johnny would say.

My sister was in so much trouble!

A while later, after what seemed like forever, Sally Maylor came out into the waiting room with Patti Dwyre. "You're free to go," Sally told her, glancing our way, acknowledging us with a nod before disappearing back down the hall. I heard a door slam somewhere.

I really wished I had Holly's skill at takedowns. Hunter must have caught a whiff of my intention to do bodily harm to Patti because he got a firm grip on my wrist.

"What happened?" I said to the traitor, trying to shake him off subtly, and failing. "Your water bottle was involved in the murder. Why would Johnny release you and arrest my sister?"

"Because," Patti said, sounding miffed, which she had no right to be. "I'd left my surveillance bottle in her house. I didn't remember where I'd lost it until you and I talked about it and suddenly it came back to me."

"Just like that you remembered?"

"Just like that."

My heart sunk. "So that's what you told the chief?"

"Why wouldn't I? It's the truth."

Hunter, sensing that I wasn't going to lunge for Patti, released my wrist and picked up a magazine.

A thought struck me. A really disturbing one. If I'd kept my big mouth shut instead of calling the police, my sister would be free right now. Instead, I just had to implicate Patti, who in turn pointed her sneaky little finger at Holly. Why hadn't I seen this coming? Johnny had been dropping hints regarding my sister, but I hadn't taken him seriously, mainly because he always throws around threatening remarks. I didn't really think that time was different.

Then Patti said to me, "Don't go acting all innocent. The chief told me you were the one who squealed on me."

Doesn't it just figure? "I had my reasons."

"And I had mine."

We traded glares. Right now, I couldn't trust anybody, least of all Patti Dwyre. But an old adage came to mind—keep your friends close and your enemies closer.

"Sit down and wait with us," I said to the enemy. "If nothing else, you'll get a good story out of this, maybe even get your old job back at the paper when they find out you have inside information."

Hunter rolled his eyeballs but didn't say anything. He went back to reading.

"Now," I said once she sat down, "what's the scoop with Harry?"

"I'm not going back to him, if that's what you mean."

"I mean, what's with him stealing Holly's truck?"

Patti shrugged. "It's not Harry's style to steal, so I'm guessing he didn't."

"And how does he know Effie? What's their relationship?"

Patti shrugged again, although I caught a hint of surprise in her expression before it slid back to a neutral position. "How should I know?"

Until recently, I'd assumed Nova's death had something to do with the Savour flavorists. Greed. Or competition. Or just spending too much time in the same space with the same project and somebody snapping . . . but what if her death had nothing to do with the team? Had I been chasing a red herring?

"Hunter," I said to the buried nose, "could there be a connection between Nova and Harry and Effie and Chance?"

The look Hunter gave me once he glanced over? I didn't like it. Still, when Patti got up and went to the restroom, I finished my thought. "Harry shows up in town, suddenly Patti's involved in the murder big-time—her water bottle, wet pants and shoes, acting strange . . ."

"She always acts that way."

"Harry then pops up over at Holly's house, Patti fingers Holly as the last person around that bottle, and boom, my sister's in jail."

"I'll see what I can do," Hunter said, not really looking like he was going to act on that comment.

"This is my sister we're talking about!"

To make matters worse, my mother and Grams walked into the station. Hunter really took a major dive into that magazine. I mean really, was a ripped up old copy of *Good Housekeeping* that fascinating?

I told them where everything stood. Patti came out of the restroom and listened in.

Then Max appeared with his attorney. "She'll have to go before the judge tomorrow," he said. "Johnny Jay won't budge on releasing her until then, so I'm staying here close by for tonight."

"My baby has to spend the night in jail?" Mom wailed. (I wracked my brain for her past responses to my own incarcerations. "How could you?" came instantly to mind. And, "What are people going to say?")

Jealousy smacked me right between the eyes. I smacked it back because the two of us have been going rounds for years, and I wasn't going to let it get me down this time. Everybody has family conflicts. Besides, I had Grams on my side—sweet, loving Grams.

Holly might not be my baby, but she's my baby sister. I stood up straight and tall and felt superhuman strength flowing through my veins, and I determined to save Holly in spite of her favored position, and I'd do whatever I had to do to prove her innocence.

I might not trust Patti, but I needed her help.

While Mom sobbed and Grams tried to comfort her, and with Hunter ignoring us and buried in his stupid magazine, I gave Patti a sign she recognized. Eyes darting to the door, a little conspiratorial smile, a barely perceptible head thingy in the same direction as my eyes.

And the two of us were off into the night.

Thirty-six

I hated to ditch Hunter without a word of warning, but he hadn't exactly been sympathetic lately. If living with a man entails constant reprimands and bossy orders and lectures on how I should behave, or react, or feel, then I might as well be back living with my mother.

Part of me, the important part, realized I was acting out in a time of intense stress and who better to take the brunt of my whacked-out-ness than the one I love the most. Well, wasn't that the truth of human behavior? I should be taking my pain out on someone who really deserved it. Like Johnny Jay or Lori Spandle.

The other part of me, smaller but just as noisy, couldn't stop going out and looking for relationship problems. Enough of that for now. I'd committed to a course of action and I would take responsibility, something lots of folks avoid.

The first immediate hurdle to overcome involved transportation.

As in, we didn't have any.

I'd arrived at the police station on the back of Hunter's motorcycle, and Patti had made her grand entrance in the back of a squad car. What to do? Even if I had Hunter's keys, I couldn't drive his Harley. Even if I could, taking his bike would be the stake through the heart of our relationship, dead and gone for sure. Even I knew about certain boundaries and limits.

Grams, on the other hand, had left her keys dangling in her Fleetwood as usual, and my grandmother is the most forgiving soul on the planet.

Grand theft auto! That's me. Patti didn't comment or complain one bit, but she wanted to know about Effie Anderson.

We tore out of the police station with me in the driver's seat, while I gave her my take on Harry and Effie knowing each other, how something had passed between them before Harry was hauled away. We whizzed over to Holly's house with barely a plan of action in place.

"Who should we start with? Or where?" Patti said, getting out and closing the door as quietly as she could. We'd at least discussed and agreed on one thing—hide the vehicle from sight so as not to announce our visit. We walked up the driveway from a copse of dense, sweet-smelling honeysuckle.

"How about Max's study?" I said, trying to place its location in my mind, another one of many of the Clue rooms.

"Good idea," Patti said. With six bedrooms, as many baths, studies, and all those nooks and crannies, it would have taken me a while to find Max's home office, though I shouldn't have worried, because sneaky Patti led the way without making a single wrong turn.

We crept up the stairs, past a guest bedroom, where I could hear certain houseguests carrying on together behind a closed door. Yuck. I banished the image of them from my mind and thought a positive thought. At least we had a clear path.

Holly's husband's study was all manly leather, Persian rugs, and luxury rosewood furniture.

"Locked," Patti announced after trying to pull open a drawer from a credenza that spanned an entire wall. She rummaged around in her pocket, came up with some little doodad, and before long we were staring at a long line of file folders.

We dug in, Patti on one end, me on the other.

I found a file with correspondence between the three flavorists, but the contents were gobbledygook to me. Words like *miraculin* and *glycoprotein molecules* and *carb chains*, a reference to the original fruit they based their research on, and several back-and-forths regarding issues with the FDA approving the product. Nothing to raise my antennae.

I just didn't get why one of that team hadn't already been charged with Nova's murder instead of my sister. I mean, aside from their having alibis, which could have been trumped up. In a perfect world, Camilla and Gil should be charged with a conspiracy to take out a coworker. While I searched, I thought about the case again.

Assuming they were innocent—not a welcome option in my book, but one I had to seriously consider—who else wanted Nova out of the way bad enough to kill her? Not Max. He could just as easily fired her if he'd wanted her gone. Unless she had something on him. But even if Max had murderous tendencies and a rock-solid motive, he wouldn't have invited her to his home for the weekend and then killed her there.

Holly, as I thought before, could also have sent the diva

packing at any time. And same thing: Nobody in their right mind kills a houseguest. Besides, it was clear as day that my sister and her husband adored each other, so that stupid article that ran (and got Patti fired) was absolutely ridiculous.

So what next?

"Chance Anderson," Patti said, as if she'd read my mind and was answering my question.

"What?" I said.

She held up a folder. "I found his file."

Oh, right. The employment records.

Patti plopped down in Max's executive office chair, spread out papers from the file, and selected one. She actually swung her legs up on the desk, leaned back, and started reading while I kept going in the credenza, flipping through folder after folder, finding little except more information on Savour Foods and Max's many business dealings, more than I ever cared to go through. It would take at least a week.

"Chance's employment background fits with this job," Patti said, scanning the file. "Groundskeeper for a lot of years, landscaping, gardening, several local references with contact information, all high praise, no suspicious gaps in time."

"Anything on his wife?"

"Not yet."

She reached over and clicked a button on Max's computer.

"You won't be able to get in," I told her. Patti might be able to pick a lock like a con artist, but hacking into a computer would take more time than we had. Playing with combinations was a complex, time-consuming task.

"Don't be silly," she said, and I watched her dragon tattoo slither on her arm as she used those muscles. "Nobody locks down their personal computer when it's in their own office inside their own house."

She had a point. And she was right on, because the computer beeped and kicked into gear.

I gave up the credenza for more interesting snooping.

Patti went online and keyed something into a search, but her fingers were too fast for my eyes to follow the displays. "Nothing," she said, whizzing back and doing another search. "Humphhh," she said, sounding puzzled.

I could always tell when Patti was onto something because her whole being became supercharged with energy, sometimes so electric her hair seemed to stand up bushier. And her eyes, like now when she glanced at me, went slightly wild.

We were into Max's e-mail, which made me more than a little uncomfortable. "We shouldn't pry into his personal life," I said, feeling more like a busybody at the moment than a respectable sleuth.

Patti didn't look up from the screen. "Based on what I'm finding, he doesn't have a personal life, at least not online. The man is all business."

"No other woman then?" Where had that question come from and why had I voiced it? Geez. Talk about subconscious thoughts popping through. Never once had that idea spent a single second in my head. Okay, maybe once or twice, but no way would Max actually cheat on my sister.

Patti shook her head, lifting my spirits for once. "Not one single personal e-mail. All work related."

"That's the reason they're so rich," I told her. "He's totally focused. When he comes up for air, all he wants is to be with his wife."

"Isn't that sweet," Patti said, dripping sarcasm, her fingers flying. The woman was a certified man hater, never having a single kind word to say about any of them. Maybe Holly could use her psychological skills to help Patti get past her . . . well . . . past. That is, once I got my sister out of this mess.

I tried to keep pace with Patti, but the woman was a computer dynamo. Scrolling, backspacing, clicking away.

My cell phone vibrated, I.D.'ing Hunter. I ignored the call.

It vibrated again. My mother. I didn't answer.

"We better go," I said to Patti, already having abandoned the computer for one more pass through the credenza.

"There must be something here," she said.

"I found Effie's folder!" I held it up.

And heard voices in the hallway.

"Bring it along. Let's get out of here."

"But we aren't through," I said. "I'd like to take a look in Nova's room."

"The cops already did that."

"Maybe they missed something."

A door slammed close by.

"We're out of time," Patti said. "We need to go."

Which was exactly what we did.

Thirty-seven

On the way back to the police station, Patti clicked on the overhead light and skimmed through the single-page resume Effie had turned in for the housekeeping position.

"Not much in her file," Patti said, turning the sheet of paper over and finding nothing on the back side. "She's from Chicago?"

"Effie and Chance met through an online matchmaking service," I told her. "If I remember right, soon after they got married, he applied for the job at Holly's and they moved into the carriage house. Effie took the position of housekeeper."

"Says she used to be a bookkeeper. I don't recognize the name of any of the places she worked, but it's sure a big coincidence that she's from the same city as Harry."

"It's a huge city."

"The world is a small place," Patti countered. "Six

degrees of separation. We're all six or less steps away from a mutual connection. We have Harry married to me, then to Nova, and it seems like he might know the Andersons. Effie coming from Chicago *shouldn't* be a big deal. But. . . ." She trailed off while we thought about that.

"If Effie knew Harry, though, wouldn't you have known her, too? Wouldn't she have known you?"

"Not necessarily," Patti turned off the light. "Harry had his fingers in all kinds of different business ventures. She even could have worked for him after we were divorced."

I thought about that. Harry Bruno had been taken down by Holly right in her backyard, mere yards from the carriage house where Chance and Effie were residing. Chance had been missing in action at the time. And Mabel mentioned something streaking at her, throwing her off course and causing her to veer into a tree. Could it have been Chance, going somewhere in a hurry?

It fit. Sort of.

Were the Andersons connected to Nova's murder?

"Somebody has been setting me up," Patti said. "We have to clear my name!"

"You!" I said, getting one of those stress-induced knee-jerk reactions and even having to correct Gram's Fleetwood because I was busy glaring at my passenger. The car wasn't the only thing crossing the line. "Tonight you implicated my sister. She's the one in custody, not you!"

Good thing we'd pulled into the station. There was only so much of my neighbor I could take in one sitting.

We found Hunter, Mom, Grams, and Johnny Jay all standing outside, watching us get out of the Fleetwood.

"I told you Story didn't steal my car," Grams said to Mom. "She only borrowed it."

"For cripes' sake," Mom said, addressing me. "You can't ask permission like a normal person? I just knew it was you, that you would take our only means of transportation. Shame on you. I've been filling in Hunter on some of your past antics. He should know what he's getting into."

Hunter looked rather sickly, which is what happens to human beings when Mom launches her grenades in their vicinities. Besides, wasn't she supposed to be complaining about me marrying Hunter, not the other way around? That was her usual mode of operation—to diss every single person who means anything to me. If she was confiding in my boyfriend, that could only mean she had finally accepted him into the fold.

I wasn't sure how I felt about this sudden turn of events. I sort of liked the wall dividing our space.

"You didn't let Harry Bruno walk out of here, did you?" Patti said to the chief.

"He's spending the night," Johnny Jay told her.

"Where's Tom?" I asked Mom, thinking he could talk her down from whatever ledge she'd climbed up on.

Grams piped in and said, "They're having a tiny problem."

"Tiny!" Mom snorted, sounding suspiciously like I did when I snorted. Reminding me never to snort ever again.

Johnny Jay inserted himself into our conversation. "I advise you to press charges against these two women," he said to Grams. "Your granddaughter runs wild. She could use a lesson."

That was a big tactical mistake on his part. It's one thing to threaten me in private. It's another to do it in front of my family.

Hunter started working his jaw, a sure sign that he was really ticked off. I gently took his arm and gave him a warning squeeze. Attacking the chief, either physically or verbally, at the police station couldn't result in anything positive. Hunter stepped down, I felt it in the response of his strong arm muscles. "You deserve a reward," I whispered to him. "For good behavior."

Patti heard and snickered.

The rest of my family didn't go as quietly as Hunter. Grams stepped close to Johnny. We never learned what she was going to say to him, because Mom shouldered her out of the way.

"Oh, cram it," Mom said to the chief, passing her sourness around in equal shares. "If you had a brain in your head, Johnny Jay, you might be dangerous. Too bad your position isn't an elected one, or we'd be seeing the back end of you very soon. You might be appointed by the town board, but the board is walking on thin ice, and some of their terms are coming up for vote. I'm going to head a campaign to rid this town of you because, you, Chief Jay, are a nincompoop."

Wow! I couldn't have said it better.

While I was mentally high-fiving the entire group, Johnny gave my mother a good, hard look, opened his mouth to spew something, changed his mind, turned on his heels, and stomped back inside.

"That boy should have been disciplined more growing up," Grams said. "The kid's parents sat down at the tavern night after night like he didn't exist. Poor Johnny Jay. Well, there's nothing more we can do for Holly. Let's go get some rest, Helen."

"Wait a minute," I said to Mom. "What's going on with you and Tom?"

Mom's mouth was in a hard line as she looked from one of us to another. "It's personal," she said, walking away, getting into the passenger's seat and slamming the door.

"Call me," I said to Grams in a conspiratorial voice.

"Patti needs a ride," Hunter pointed out to Grams, since he and I were on his bike.

"We go right past your house," Grams said to Patti. "Come with us."

Grams winked at me as if to say she'd call when she could, and they were off into the night, leaving Hunter and me alone.

My family must have done quite a number on my man, what with Holly in police custody suspected of murder, plus all that time while Mom bent his ear, because he didn't ask a single question on the way home, not even where Patti and I had disappeared to. He didn't ask anything later, either, while we stood in the backyard watching Ben sniff and squirt.

I think he was afraid of what my answers might be.

The only saving grace was that Patti decided to spend the night in her own home instead of ours since her stalker wasn't free to roam.

Thirty-eight

Hunter's job requires irregular hours. He doesn't work nine to five, and he certainly doesn't have many weekends off, which suits us just fine because Saturdays and Sundays at the store are so busy. We'd decided to take at least one day of his days off and spend it together.

And this was our first official one. Carrie Ann and the twins were on the schedule, which was pretty much the only available staff since Mom was moping, Holly was incarcerated, and Stanley had quit. If this kept up, I'd have to hire more help. Or let Carrie Ann worry about it.

As always, I checked on my beehives, making sure all my little girls were happy, while Ben romped around, drinking from the river, snapping at those little bugs that like to float on top of the water. He ended up taking a swim and drying off right next to me, shedding water like a rotating sprinkler.

Why do dogs always do that?

After I'd dried myself off, Hunter and I had our morning coffee on the patio, basking in the warm rays from the sun and planning our day.

Originally, I'd imagined our special day together would consist of catching up on typical chores like laundry, a little housework, and lawn mowing, then some afternoon fun like a bike ride or something equally relaxing, followed by dinner out and a little romance.

Instead, my sister was in jail. We found out early that Harry had been released after his lawyers showed up. He'd scheduled a court date and paid his bail. Holly, on the other hand, was still in jail and likely to remain there until Max and his high-powered attorney could get her out. They hadn't managed that feat yet.

Which totally sucked. Here was a known mobster with a criminal record as long as Main Street running around free, while a woman who never did a single unlawful act in her life was behind bars. Life just isn't very fair.

I was dying to get into her cell and talk to her, ask a few questions about the validity of Patti's claim that she'd left her water bottle at Holly's house, because I wasn't about to trust anything Patti told me. That was for starters. I also wanted to pick my sister's brain about the Andersons.

Last night, I'd considered talking to Max about Chance and Effie, but decided that might only upset him further and I didn't want to be the source of any more of his stress.

"Were you paying attention last night," I asked Hunter, "when Patti told us she'd left her water bottle at Holly's house?"

"I heard her."

"And?"

"And, you just can't stay out of it, Story baby, can you?"

"Do you think I can get in to see Holly?" I asked him next.

"I doubt it," my hot man said, looking particularly smoking today. He had on shorts and nothing else but a five o'clock shadow. I love that look. "Johnny Jay won't want to make either of you two comfortable."

"I have to at least try," I told him. "I couldn't sleep all night just thinking about my little sister caged like an animal."

"Understandable."

"Tell me about that morning before Nova died. You were over there when they interviewed everybody who'd been in the house that morning."

At first I thought he was going to go into one of his "stay out of it" spiels, so I added, "This is my sister we're talking about. She's been accused of murder."

I must have sounded pretty pathetic because Hunter began talking.

Everybody had accounted for their actions between eleven the morning of Nova Campbell's death and the time they rode together to my house. Camilla and Gil stayed upstairs in his room until the last minute. Max had worked in his study, only coming out for coffee refills. Holly was in her room. According to Max, Nova came back from her run and went upstairs to shower.

"Did he see if she took carrot juice up with her?"

"No. He didn't."

"That's when she was poisoned, though," I said, thinking about Nova downing the concoction before or after her shower.

Hunter kept going. "They were due at the house for the tour of your beeyard, so they began to gather."

"They showed up late," I said. "Max called right around the time they were supposed to show up."

"That's because of the women. Max and Gil went out to the car. Camilla showed up shortly after. Holly took her time, so Max called her on his cell and told her to hurry up. But the real holdup was Nova. After waiting about fifteen minutes, Max went back inside to get her. She wasn't in her room. He searched the house for her then returned to the car, to find she had appeared. Later, when questioned, Camilla said she came from the direction of the garden."

"Do you think that's significant?"

Hunter shrugged. "Maybe. Maybe not."

"Where were the Andersons during that time?"

"Chance was clearing brush. Effie had been in the carriage house."

I poured more coffee for both of us from a carafe I'd brought outside.

"It was really bad luck that Nova died where and when she did," I said.

"I'll say," Hunter said.

"Thank you for telling me all this. You get an A+ for cooperating."

"I can show you more cooperation. Come here."

Before we could act on that, Grams's Fleetwood pulled into the driveway, inched up, stopped, then inched up some more. Mom, in the passenger's seat, had her window down and was blasting my grandmother.

"I'm calling the motor vehicle department on you," Mom crabbed. "Old people should have to go through retesting every year, both written and behind the wheel. And eye tests. Look at Mabel. Can't tell a tree from a parking space. You're going to kill somebody, that's what you're going to do!"

Grams popped out of the car, rearranged the fresh daisy in her bun, put on a smiley face (which I don't recall her ever having to force in the past), and headed for me. "We have to do something about your mother," she said. "I can't take one more minute."

Join the club, I could have said. Instead I asked, "Why hasn't she moved in with Tom yet?"

By now, Mom was stampeding our way. Grams swirled, held up a warning finger, and my mother's open mouth actually clamped shut. "Not one more word, Helen," my usually easygoing grandmother said to her.

Hunter had vanished from the backyard.

Grams and Mom parked themselves at the patio table while I hustled into the house to get coffee cups for them. No Hunter in the kitchen, either.

While serving at the outdoor table, I saw a shadow pass on the other side of the cedars separating my house from P.P. Patti's. Patti was at it again, eavesdropping, snooping, stalking. I chose to ignore her presence.

"What's wrong?" I asked Mom, whose lips looked like they had been glued shut. Her arms were folded across her chest in a defensive position.

"She refuses to move in with Tom," Grams explained when Mom wouldn't. "And she waited until after he went to all the trouble of buying her a house to change her mind. A house! Now she won't go. Tell her the rest, Helen."

I stared at Mom, who glared at each of us in turn. Granted, I hadn't wanted her to move in with Tom; I'd been overcome with shock at the very idea. But I didn't want this bitter woman as my mother, either.

"Tell her!" Grams ordered.

Mom's lips slowly peeled apart. "Your father visited me," she said, unfolding her arms to take a sip of coffee.

That's my deceased dad she was talking about, the one who hasn't been around in physical form to talk to us for . . . oh . . . over five years at least.

"In a dream?" I prompted, seeing that she had stopped after that short declaration, while I needed more information. "He came in a dream?"

Mom squirmed. "I'm not sure exactly. It seemed so real. But I know this for sure, he specifically told me he wasn't happy with the arrangement I had with Tom Stocke."

"Dad would want you to be happy," I told her, realizing that was true. "He would definitely understand."

"Well, he didn't understand at all, and I'm not going against his wishes."

"See?" Grams said to me.

"Have you told Holly about this?" I asked Mom, thinking my sister would have some rational advice to offer.

"She hasn't told anybody but me," Grams stuck in there, addressing me. "I don't discount the truth of her words. Maybe he *did* pay her a visit. But, Helen," she turned to Mom, "you read his words wrong."

Which wouldn't be the first time, although hopefully it will be the last with my dad. Mom tends to overanalyze everything anybody says and sometimes her resulting conclusions aren't even close to the actual intent.

"What exactly did he say?" I asked.

"He said, 'Don't do it,'" Mom replied.

"That's it? Don't do it. That could mean anything."

Mom's lips went fine-lining again.

"Would Dad approve if you and Tom got married first?" Was I really participating in this surreal conversation?

Mom's face scrunched up. I saw tears coming.

"Now you did it," Grams said.

I heard Hunter's Harley start up and roar off, while Mom fished around in her purse for tissues, found one, and wiped her eyes. *Thanks a lot,* I telegraphed to Hunter with a big helping of frustration. *What a coward!*

"Tom hasn't"—sniff, sniff—"asked me."

"Ah," I said, realizing the crux of the problem. "You need more of a commitment from him."

That same sneaky shadow on the other side of the cedars caught my attention again. Patti must be slipping. She was usually more covert than this.

"You go see Holly," I said to Mom, patting her hand. "That is, if you can get in. And share your situation with her. She's really good at giving advice."

"That Holly is the spitting image of Ann Landers," my grandmother agreed. "Come on, Helen, let's go."

"Not with you behind the wheel," Mom said. "I'm not riding in the death seat."

I left them there to sort it out.

And that was only the start of my day off from the store.

Thirty-nine

I walked to The Wild Clover just like every workday, but instead of going inside, I went around back and took off in my trusty blue pickup truck, heading for Holly's house.

Where I found pandemonium reigning in the Paine household.

For one thing, Max arrived home about the same time I got there, after having spent the night at the station, hoping for a miracle that would free his wife. What a mess the man was. Hair every which way, rumpled clothing, and tired, haunted eyes.

A week had passed since his houseguests came to visit with the original intention of a work-free weekend filled with relaxation and team-building. That had fallen to pieces (though at least two of them had been able to figure out a new way to "bond," ew).

Apparently Camilla and Gil hadn't been very happy when the limo didn't show up to whisk them to the Milwaukee airport. By the time they called the transportation service and discovered the error, it was too late to make the flight.

Oops.

When I entered the house, Max was in the process of having his ear bent by the unfortunate grounded passengers, who were surrounded by packed suitcases and dashed plans.

"Somebody canceled the limousine," Gil told him. "That's what I was told when I called to find out where it was."

"I'm not staying here any longer," Camilla said, and I wondered what she had to complain about. From my perspective, the only sweat she'd been subjected to wasn't considered actual work in our society.

I smelled something wonderful in the air like pancakes or waffles, and saw Effie and Milly cleaning up. I wandered into the kitchen, but found the griddle had been cleaned and put away. Darn. Not a single leftover in sight.

"Where's the gardener?" Camilla said, still with some of that not-one-more-second tone. "He can take us to the airport. We'll try to get out of here on standby, right, Gil?"

Effie looked up then and said, "Chance is out running errands and won't be back until later this afternoon."

Wasn't that convenient. The man was a virtual disappearing act. "What sort of errands?" I wanted to know.

"Personal ones," Effie said, stone-faced.

"He wasn't here yesterday, either," I kept going, "when Harry Bruno was arrested for stealing the truck. Was he off doing personal business then, too?"

Effie and I locked eyes. "No," she said. "He wasn't."

"I'd take you," Max said. "But I'm only home long

enough to shower and change my clothes, then back to the police station." He bounded for the stairs, and was gone from sight.

"What about Effie?" I said, thinking this would be the perfect time to do a little sleuthing in the carriage house. "Can't she take you?"

"Not her," Camilla said. Since the clean-up crew was running water in the sink, I was fairly certain her words hadn't carried.

"Why not?" I asked back, moving out of Effie's earshot. Camilla automatically followed me. So did Gil.

"I hate to be picky," she said, getting picky, "but your sister did a terrible job training her house help. The woman is surly" (look who was talking!) "and obviously resents her subservient role in life."

"But she can drive?" Gil said to Camilla. "Who cares about her personality?"

"Honestly," Camilla said to me, "tell your sister she can do better than that woman. Even self-absorbed Nova saw right through her. And not only that, she refuses to cook! Flat out refuses. Insubordination like that would never be tolerated in the business world."

"All I care about is getting to the airport," Gil complained, walking away. I heard him in the kitchen. "Effie, we need a ride to the airport."

"Not my problem," she replied. "Sorry, I have other things to do."

"Now do you believe me?" Camilla said. "We ask her to do a simple task, and she refuses?"

"I'll drive you," Milly offered, coming out, wiping her hands on a towel.

Darn. So much for a peek inside the carriage house. I couldn't think of any other ways to stop the two flavorists from flying off, but at least I'd slowed them down. Not that I supposed it mattered anymore.

The next half hour was a flurry of activity: getting the couple's bags into Milly's trunk and that group on their way; Effie finishing up in the kitchen then vanishing, probably to hide out in the carriage house; and Max, refreshed after a shower and change of clothes, getting ready to rush back out to the police station.

I caught up with him before he drove off, and asked, "Did you check the Andersons' references before you hired them?"

Max frowned. "That's an odd question, but yes, of course. Why, is something wrong?"

"No, I'm just getting a bit paranoid, worried about Holly. So they all checked out?"

"Yes, of course, but I have to go. We'll talk later. Okay?"

"Later, then," I said, watching him leave.

Suddenly all was quiet.

I was alone and back at Holly's outdoor table.

I called Jackson. He picked up this time.

"Anything on the gloves?" I asked him.

"Nothing helpful," he said. "Compost. Pollen. That's it. Nothing toxic."

"Thanks anyway, I owe you."

Disappointment set in after we disconnected. I didn't have a single, solid lead. This wasn't the way it was supposed to work. Clues should build up, one after the other, guiding and pointing the way down the right path. Instead, I might as well have beat my head against the wall for all the puzzle pieces I was connecting.

But wait. That wasn't necessarily true. I still had lots of unanswered questions to explore.

Like . . . where was Harry Bruno? He'd been released from jail. Had he left town? Doubtful, I decided, based on the way he'd been sniffing around Patti.

And what about Chance Anderson, also missing in action? My internal radar told me to pursue that thread. I marched toward the carriage house for a showdown with the only other person still on the property.

Effie Anderson had some answering to do.

Forty

I climbed the stairs on the side of the garage and banged on the door at the top.

Nobody answered, so I banged again, this time trying the door. Locked.

"I know you're in there, Effie!" I hollered through the door, plastering my ear against it and listening for sound on the other side.

Nothing happened.

This was ridiculous. Was Effie actually avoiding me?

I stomped back down the stairs, stood outside eyeing the carriage house above me, and wondered if I could find a ladder high enough to climb up there and bash out one of the windows. It really was as high up as Holly had told me when I'd suggested she climb up and spy on Effie.

After searching the inside of the garage, I couldn't find a long enough ladder. I'd have to be related to Spider-Man to get up there.

Next I went to Holly and Max's outbuilding. The Queen Bee Honey–stickered ATV was missing. I'd bet my honey business that Chance had torn off on that exact one yesterday. The work truck was also missing from the property.

Effie said Chance was out running errands, so he'd have the truck. But if he'd come back after Harry had been arrested, then where was that ATV?

I fired up another four-wheeler and drove over to the maple tree that had stopped Mabel's forward motion. Fat tire tracks led off from the grass into a wooded area. The tracks were easy to follow since all the low vegetation had been packed down from the weight of the ATV and hadn't sprung completely back.

It was rough going, and I wondered why Chance had chosen to make his own path instead of using one of the groomed trails. It confirmed for me that he'd left in a really big hurry. As though he'd panicked.

The tracks wove here and there, dodging trees, and came out onto the shoulder of highway E (which is more like a country road than a highway). I promptly lost the trail and had to zoom back and forth on the road, searching for a sign. But the trail was as cold as this case had become.

Where was everybody?

I was sitting on the ATV while it idled, feeling depressed, heading for one big confused funk, when Holly's work truck suddenly roared toward me at about a zillion miles an hour. It wasn't heading for Moraine, either. Exactly the opposite—away from town.

Was that Harry Bruno in the driver's seat? Oh my gosh, it was! And he had a passenger. A woman, I thought, or a long-haired man. Was it Effie?

So what? I thought next as the truck blew by. Big fat deal. Let them all disappear—Chance, Harry, Effie, throw in Patti, too—and may their spaceship never return.

Although, speaking of Patti, where was she? Shouldn't she be snooping around by now, inserting herself and all her crazy ideas into our lives, looking for, or causing, trouble?

I drove back to Holly's empty house and called 9-1-1. "Harry Bruno has my sister's truck again," I told the officer who answered. "I'm reporting it stolen. Again." He put me on hold. Johnny Jay came on the line. "You're making this up, Fischer," he said.

"Honest. I just saw it with my own eyes. He's heading south, he's with someone, and he's traveling fast."

"I'm on it. Unbelievable. Where are you?"

"Why?" Suspicion always pays off when Johnny Jay is involved.

"I have a few follow-up questions for you. I'll expect you at the station in the next half hour."

"I'm busy."

"That not what they told me down at your store."

Johnny Jay had been out looking for me? That wasn't good. "It's my day off," I told him. "I'm not spending it down at the police station."

"You will if I say so."

Who did he think he was? What a pompous, arrogant, control-freak bully. Ha! Maybe I'd just hang out here at Holly's house all day. Later I'd call Hunter and have him meet me on the dock for a boat ride and a little fishing. Surely Holly had a nice bottle of wine inside her wine fridge. And cheese and crackers. Yes, that sounded like a great idea. And maybe when Holly got out of jail, which I hoped would be sometime today, I'd be here to welcome her and Max home. The four of us could go out to dinner at Stu's Bar and Grill. A wonderful evening with loved ones.

With that plan in mind, I hung up on Johnny.

After rummaging around in the house, I found a pad

of paper and pen and poured a glass of lemonade from a pitcher in the refrigerator. Pausing with the glass at my lips, I dumped the contents down the sink drain and popped open a can of diet soda instead. One can never be too cautious in a kitchen that produced a toxic drink that actually killed a human being.

Back outside, I started to make a bullet list of things to follow up with. Then something lodged in my brain. Nagging at me, poking, saying things like—*everything doesn't always have to be what it seems.*

Well, that was really helpful. I have to say that my intuition could be more . . . well . . . intuitive. Or more helpful in weeding out the quack grass from the rose bed. More user-friendly. Instead, it makes me try to sift through stuff and that never works well.

Everything doesn't always have to be what it seems.

What the heck did that mean? That I should try making an assumption that Nova Campbell wasn't really dead?

She was dead all right. I'd witnessed the whole sorry event. Not to mention viewing her body in the morgue. Okay, but I'd already decided I may have misjudged the motive. That maybe it wasn't work related. Let's see. I made a Beginners 101 list of possible motives based on TV shows I've watched:

- Jealousy

- Revenge

- Greed

- Rage

- Fear

- Love

I crumpled up the list.

I had to be missing an ingredient, something other than carrot juice and water hemlock. So what if the motive really wasn't obvious?

I was making scribbles and cryptic symbols all over my paper pad, tearing them out, crumpling them up, tossing them into a pile.

I wrote down Patti's name in capital letters, since she was on my main suspect list. It was her water bottle that had been poisoned, and she'd been in the river while Nova breathed her last breath. And she had a powerful connection to the dead woman.

But why would Patti leave behind a bottle that so clearly could and would eventually be traced back to her? I mean, really, how many people put "Stalkers Have Rights, Too" on their water bottles? And "I'm Watching You." It was only a matter of time before Johnny Jay would have been all over her even without my help. Patti certainly was an obvious choice.

Almost too obvious.

Thinking of Chicago and Patti's past brought me to Harry Bruno. Harry certainly had the background and history to pull off a homicide and get away with it. Right? But he and Nova had already divorced. If he was going to kill her wouldn't he have done it before now? And how would he get his hands on Patti's bottle? Besides, Harry was obsessed with Patti. Why would he frame her?

What about the Andersons? Something had sent Chance packing in a great big hurry. I didn't believe Effie when she said he was out running errands. Especially now that Harry Bruno had sped past me driving the same truck Chance was supposed to be out and about in. And I was almost certain he had a woman, probably Effie, with him. No, I believed Chance had taken off on the ATV yesterday, almost collided with Mabel in his hurry, and hadn't returned.

I glanced up at the carriage house again.

And that's when I ruled out Effie as Harry's recent passenger.

Because she was coming toward me with a pitchfork.

Forty-one

It wasn't as though Effie was rushing at me with rabid foam dripping from her mouth, or with the pitchfork's deadly prongs aimed directly at my heart, or anything like that. She was probably about to work in the garden and my so-called intuition was going off on a tangent. Since she wasn't netted head to foot, the spider invasion must finally be under control.

"Hey, Effie," I called out, as friendly as can be, considering the enormous weapon at her disposal. "I was just looking for you. Come sit with me."

I would have loved to add, "And ditch the pitchfork, please," but even I can recognize overreactions when I see them.

Effie stopped, jammed the tines of the pitchfork into the grass at the end of the patio, left it standing upright, and joined me empty-handed. My inner mouse sighed in relief.

"Why are you still hanging around?" Effie asked in a

light voice that matched mine. She glanced at the pile of
crumpled paper before sweeping over to my most current
written musings, which I hid by laying an arm across
them. Nonchalantly, coolly, I might add.

"I love this view," I said. "The peacefulness, the quiet.
I don't get much personal space in my life with the store
and all." Which wasn't untrue. Just try to have a moment
of peace with "I Spy" living next door and Hunter always
after the bennies that come with living together.

"So you're hiding out for a while?"

I nodded.

"That's too bad that you have to hide to find personal
space."

"Yes, but what is, is. By the way, didn't you hear me
knocking on your door a little while ago?"

"No. I must have been in the shower."

"You don't have to lock up your home in broad daylight. Not in Moraine anyway. I know Chicago is different, but here, you're safe in your own home."

Effie looked up sharply at my reference to her hometown then nodded as though she was going to take my
advice in the future. "Old habits," she said.

"When is Chance coming back?" I asked, thinking
fast. "I have a landscaping problem he might be able to
solve for me."

"Not until later."

"Did he take the truck?"

"Yes," she said, either lying through her teeth, or maybe
she really didn't know that Harry had it in his evil
clutches. If the latter was the case, I clued her in.

"I saw Harry Bruno driving the work truck going south.
He had someone with him, a woman. I thought it might be
you, but . . ." No sense stating the obvious, which was that
I'd been mistaken about the identity of the woman.

At this point, Effie should have seemed more concerned

about her husband's actual whereabouts if the errand thing was true. Instead, she looked off toward the lake. "Is that right?" she said.

"How do you and Chance know Harry?" I said, doing my best to sound firm, determined, with a no-nonsense tone that implied I wasn't likely to accept any fabrications on her part.

"What makes you think that we do?"

"You let him use the Paines' truck. And he was staying with you." I wasn't certain of that last part, but it made sense. Where else would he have holed up? That did the trick. Sometimes guessing pays off.

"If you must know, I used to work for him. But Harry Bruno is a bad man," she said. "That's why I left his employment. He showed up here and said I owed him a favor and that he wanted a place to stay for a few days. I was afraid to say no."

"How did he find you?" I leaned back, pretty proud of my interrogation skills. I'd done much better than Sally or Johnny. Wait until they all heard this.

Effie certainly seemed fearful. "He has resources, that's what he told me."

"If you worked for him, you must have known his wives?" Why hadn't any of this come out earlier? Was Harry that scary?

She shook her head. "No, I didn't know either of them, not until after Nova Campbell died. Harry or Patti did it, one of them had to. I'm so sorry for bringing that bad man into your lives."

Poor Effie. She seemed nervous, intimidated by Harry Bruno, and sincerely apologetic.

Still, I couldn't help asking, "Where were you that morning? Where was Chance? And can anyone vouch for either of you?"

Immediately Effie became visibly agitated. "Are you

implying that I or Chance had anything to do with Nova's death?"

"Of course not." Okay, I was doing a little wishful thinking. Better one of you than my sister. Although Harry would do just fine. I wasn't so sure how I felt about Patti being the murderer, though.

"I'm sure you want to get your sister off," Effie said, sort of huffy, "but don't go making accusations against us. She's in jail for a reason."

And with that, Effie got up, walked over to the pitch-fork, pulled it out of the ground (I went on guard momentarily), and stomped out to the garden.

Geez. Did I believe her? She still hadn't accounted for her husband's whereabouts. Should I go after her? Ask more questions?

On the side of the rose garden, Effie began using the pitchfork to dig into a pile of compost, lifting and turning the fertile matter the same way I work mine. Roses (actually all flowers and vegetables) love organic compost, and last year I'd convinced Holly to insist on keeping a compost pile going. It was good to see that she still was following through.

I called Patti's number. She didn't pick up. I tried calling Hunter but only got his voicemail. I was annoyed that he snuck out earlier, but still I left a message to meet me at Holly's house for some fun in the sun. "And bring Ben," I said to the machine, "since he loves a good swim, too." Maybe we could salvage our day after all.

Speaking of the sun, it was really turning out to be a hot one today, but it was still comfortable in the shade with a bit of a breeze blowing off the lake. I went inside and opened another soda. Then went back to writing down more meaningless junk.

And that's when more than just Harry in Holly's truck started going south.

Forty-two

Johnny Jay's police car pulled up alongside my truck. I spotted it instantly from my peripheral vision. He climbed out, hitched his bossy pants, shoved on a pair of mirrored shades, and headed my way with his usual swagger.

I seriously considered hightailing it out of there. The chief isn't much of a runner. I'd beat him in foot races so many times growing up, I'd lost count. Some of the time we were having competitive races with other kids, seeing who was faster, and I'd won my fair share. But some of the time I had to run to save my skin when I'd caught Johnny Jay bullying some poor kid. Wanting to redirect his focus to me, I'd thump him in the back of the head, not hard, it didn't take much to get his attention. Trust me when I say the guy really can't run.

However, these days he had a gun within easy reach on his hip and was probably an expert marksman. I might be rather impulsive, acting before thinking an action all the way through, but I'm not a total idiot. Johnny just might dislike me enough to shoot to kill.

"How did you find me?" I wanted to know, when he came to a frowning halt.

"You called our emergency number when you reported the truck stolen again. Your cell phone pinged off a tower not too far from here," he said all proud of himself. "A little triangulating got me close enough to figure out where you were. It's high tech all the way for Moraine law enforcement."

Damn my phone. Or rather damn modern technology and whoever decided to make an innocent person's cell phone into a homing device for overzealous law enforcement officials who had nothing better to do than stalk the very citizens they were supposed to be protecting. Was nothing sacred anymore?

In the garden, Effie stopped working and rested on the pitchfork. Her eyes were glued to us. I hoped they stayed that way. Johnny Jay didn't always operate within the law, but he only committed abusive indiscretions when he didn't have an audience.

I thought it best to point out that fact.

"Effie Anderson is right over there," I said to him, glancing in her direction. "So mind your manners."

Johnny Jay turned his head and made note.

Effie wiped her brow, which reminded me just how hot it was out in the sun, without the benefit of the shade I was enjoying. Then she dug the pitchfork into the earth same as last time and headed for the carriage house.

Something about the rose garden and spiders started taking root in my brain, sprouting a little web of new ideas. *Not what it seems* played in my head again.

"I'm going to hook everybody up to a lie detector," Johnny said to me. "You included. I'm here to escort you to the station." He pulled out those same stupid handcuffs he always threatens me with. "You can come along quietly or . . ."

I sighed. "Let me put these things away first. I'll be with you in a minute."

While Johnny waited near his car, I picked up the crumpled pile of notes and the empty cans, took everything inside, and dumped them in the garbage. I also discarded my dream of an afternoon in the sun with Hunter.

Soon, Johnny would know everything I knew, every single last connection between all these people, including the one between Effie's past employer and Nova's ex-husband. I'd leave him to sort through the convoluted mess. I couldn't do any more than I already had.

Then out of nowhere, I remembered several comments about the night the flavorists had arrived. At the time, it had seemed insignificant, but now that I had more information regarding Effie's past, it made some sense. Nova had rubbed Holly the wrong way, but she'd also had a run-in with Effie the night before her death. I tried to remember back.

Holly and I at her outdoor table, me meeting Nova for the first time, Holly saying that Effie had had a strong reaction to Nova the night before. And Camilla right before she left for the airport, dissing Effie. Something about even self-absorbed Nova seeing through the housekeeper.

I walked out of the house, actually looking forward to the upcoming interrogation with Johnny Jay. Pieces of the puzzle were falling into place, and some of us had more explaining to do.

That's when I saw Effie coming at me with . . . Oh My God . . . was that a Taser?

Forty-three

Giant bolts of electricity hurtled toward me. The pain was excruciating, like nothing I've ever experienced before. I heard a scream far away then realized it came from me. My muscles went rigid, and I keeled over.

Later I learned that the agony inflicted by a Taser only lasts about five seconds, but that was the longest five seconds of my entire life. When it finally ended, I struggled to sit up.

"Get up, or I'll use it again," she said.

"Where did you get a Taser?" was all I could think to ask. Was I slurring?

"The police chief is a generous guy," Effie said. "Get up."

I wobbled to my feet, unsteady, and spotted my cell phone on the ground where it must have fallen from my hand. Effie kicked it away, motioning me toward the squad car. I stumbled over. Johnny Jay sat slumped in the backseat, looking like I felt, an indication that he'd had the same treatment. Effie opened the back door. "Get in," she told me, then to Johnny, "Don't try anything funny, or I'll Taser you again."

Both of us complied. I would have done anything to stay clear of more of that torture.

I've been in Johnny's backseat before, but this was the first time I'd seen Johnny Jay in the rear of his own vehicle. It has standard vinyl seats, bulletproof glass—which doesn't matter because Johnny was minus his weapon— steel plating on the back of the front seats to discourage stabbing attempts, and a tough plastic screen between front and back. Did I mention the doors can't be unlocked from the inside?

We sat next to each other gathering our wits. My body felt weak and feeble, but my mouth had plenty of energy. I said to Johnny, "Let me get this straight. Effie Anderson Tasered us with your own stun gun? Then she helped herself to the weapon in your holster, and now we are locked in the back of your squad car?"

"Shut up, Fischer."

"What's your plan?" I wanted to know, opening and closing my hands, my fingers tingling. "How are you going to regain control of the situation?"

"I can't think while you're yapping."

Just then, Effie got into the driver's seat, and turned her head to smile at us through the plastic partition. "Comfy?" she said.

"Not really," I said back. "Does all this mean you're the one who killed Nova Campbell?"

Johnny Jay groaned. "Nice hostage tactic, Fischer. If you don't mind, I'll handle things from here."

"Be my guest," I told him. "You've done such a great job of handling things so far."

Effie started up the car.

"You even left the keys in the ignition?" I said to Johnny, stating the obvious. "You really mucked it up this time."

Effie drove over to the outbuilding while I tried to think of a way out of this situation. Let me see. I'd told Effie I was hiding out, so she was well aware that nobody other than the chief knew where I was. She'd seen my notes, heard my questions, and had probably decided I was getting too close. Then Johnny had showed up, and for all she knew I'd called him over to convince him to arrest her for the murder of Nova Campbell.

No wonder she'd gone on the attack. We were both going to get a bullet to the brain.

"You can blame this on her, Chief," Effie said, apparently meaning me. She drove inside the building and parking next to the ATVs. "Her and her twenty questions. Wanting to know where Chance went, mentioning my Chicago connection, calling you, plotting against me." Effie gave me a hateful glare.

"Where is Chance, anyway?" I still wanted to know and finally had a chance to find out.

But Effie ignored me completely. "I had to kill Nova Campbell," she said to Johnny. "I couldn't believe it when she walked into the house that night. Then later she came to the carriage house and threatened to expose me to the Paines, and tell Harry where I was."

So Effie had lied when she said she didn't know Nova.

Then I remember Holly telling me that Nova had gone upstairs early claiming a headache when in fact, she snuck out to hassle Effie.

"Does Chance know about this?" I asked.

Effie kept right on talking, directing her remarks to the chief. "I'd taken some money from Harry's business, a little at a time. Why not? He had so much and I had so little. Then one day an auditor showed up to go through the books. I had to get out of town. That's why I married

Chance, for a new name and a new home. Harry never would have found me if his ex-wife hadn't shown up."

I doubt that, I thought, since I figured Harry could've easily found Effie if he'd wanted to, just like he'd found Patti. But this wasn't the time to bring that up.

"Maybe we can cut a deal," Johnny told her. "It'll go easier on you if you surrender and make a full confession."

"I'm confessing right now," Effie said with crazy eyes. I wondered why I hadn't noticed them before. "She promised she'd give me a little time to make it right with Harry on my own. That bought me a little time to plan on how to get rid of her. I knew about the water hemlock, so I poisoned the carrot juice. But she'd lied to me and called Harry that same night. There he was, right at the door demanding his money back, threatening to torture my husband, make me watch. A very bad man."

"What happened to Chance?" I inserted again.

"Harry was threatening to hurt my husband, so I had to tell Chance who Harry was. I told him to get away while he could, before Harry came back with the truck. Instead, he asked all kinds of questions, until Harry pulled in and Chance finally got it through his head and took off."

"Where did he go?"

"He drove the ATV clear to the other side of the county and holed up with his uncle. I'll have to leave him behind."

"You need to let us out of this vehicle," Johnny said.

"Killing a cop doesn't bother me," Effie said.

I had some serious hyperventilating going on after that remark. Here I was, about to lose my life, and with Johnny Jay of all people!

"Do something," I mouthed at him. He shrugged back, at least three shades paler than normal. So much for his usual bluster, the buffoon.

Effie got out of the squad car, leaving the motor running, slammed the door behind her, and walked out of view.

"I told you to back off my family," I said to Johnny. "If you hadn't been so obsessed with bringing down one of us, we wouldn't be in this situation."

"I'll think of something," he said, without a trace of confidence.

"You better make it quick."

Effie pushed a button and the overhead door descended. Then she was back, leaning in the driver's door. She didn't have Johnny's gun in her hand. A good sign. "I'm not sure what I'm going to do with your bodies yet," she said. "But I'm very resourceful. By the time they find them, I'll be long gone."

"You aren't going to shoot us?" I asked.

"I hate the sight of blood," she replied. "I'm giving you a break. Carbon dioxide is supposed to be painless." She ducked out and was gone, leaving the driver's door wide open and the car pouring out emissions.

I pounded on the plastic separating us from freedom.

Now, or very soon, would be a very good time for nosy Patti to show up. Or Max and Holly. Hunter would be around later, looking for me. But he would be too late.

Johnny just sat there like a big slug.

"Kick out the window," I advised him.

"Bulletproof," he said.

I looked over at him, saw the defeat in his eyes. We were doomed.

Forty-four

Regarding Johnny Jay's complete meltdown: I was
good friends with a nurse once who worked in a hospital.
She handled blood and guts every day. But when I accidentally almost whacked off a finger with a cleaver while
she and I were in the kitchen together, she fell apart,
became more than useless in the emergency. Later she
explained, "I'm used to it in a clinical setting, not in my
personal life."

So that must explain the cop I was trapped with. I've
seen Johnny Jay in full control of a dangerous situation
more than once, and he can be formidable. Now that he'd
been forced to give up that control, he'd reduced down to
a big, fat quitter.

Surprisingly, although my muscles felt sore, I was
back in control of them.

I yanked on my seat back, hoping it would fold down
so we could get into the trunk, maybe find a tool that

could help us. No such luck. It wouldn't budge. The smell of exhaust fumes wafted my way.

"Where's your baton?" I said to him, eyeing up the plastic barrier keeping me from the front seat. "We can bash our way out."

I glanced over. Johnny hadn't moved or looked up.

I said, "Let me guess. You gave that to her, too."

"I never liked you, Fischer," Johnny said.

"Tell me something I don't know." I threw my shoulder at the door. And only hurt my shoulder. "Do you mind helping out here?"

"It's useless," he said. "Give it up. You know why I never liked you?"

I slumped down next to him.

"Because you were so mean." This was Johnny talking to me?

"You're kidding, right?" I said, in disbelief. "I'm not the one who picked on weaker kids!"

"I needed a friend back then, and I reached out to you. You pushed me away every time, mocked me in front of our classmates. You were a mean girl."

I have to admit, looking back, I wasn't always kind and considerate to others. But still! "So this really doesn't have anything to do with me turning you down for prom?" That's what most of my friends and family thought. If I had accepted his offer way back then we'd be friends now.

"You know how long it took to work up the courage to ask you?" he said. Okay, it did have something to do with prom.

"I'm sorry," I told him. "I didn't mean to hurt your feelings."

"I didn't go to prom. Six rejects. Can you imagine what that did to my ego?"

Johnny Jay has a crushed ego? Yeah, right. "I didn't

reject you six times," I told him, getting down on the floor and peering under the seat.

"Not just you, six different girls rejected me, but yours hurt the most."

What was this? Deathbed confession time? "I've said I was sorry. Can you give me a hand down here? See if you can loosen these bolts holding the seat back in place. If we can just get into the trunk maybe we can find a way out."

Johnny Jay squished down beside me and reached way down and toward the back. He grunted so I knew he'd put some effort into it. "I can't get a grip," he said. "My fingers keep slipping."

I pulled off my T-shirt and handed it to him. "Wrap that around it."

It seemed like forever, but must have only been a minute or two, when he finally rose up with bolts in his hand and his eyes on my bra. I grabbed my top and whipped it back on.

Johnny put some muscle into the back of the seat. By some miracle, it pulled away, exposing a pathway to the trunk. He slumped after that.

"Are you feeling dizzy?" he said to me.

"Not yet," I said, light-headed now that he'd mentioned it. "And quit talking. You're using up our air."

I scooted through the opening, since Johnny was too big for the job.

"Where's the tool kit?" I yelled to him.

"It doesn't matter," he said back.

"I'm sick and tired of your quitter attitude," I said, getting extra anxious over having to deal with Johnny and what was fast turning into the hopeless situation he'd predicted.

With the squad car running in the closed up building, how long would it be before we succumbed to the toxic fumes?

"Johnny!" I said loudly.

No answer.

I twisted around and poked my head out. Johnny was lying back with his eyes closed.

So I slapped him. Hard.

His eyes flew open.

"I don't know what to do next," I said, close to tears. I didn't want to die yet, and I especially didn't want the chief's face to be my last image of life. "I don't want to give up, too."

"It doesn't . . . matter," Johnny said again, all dramatic.

"Shut up, Johnny," I said, using his line.

Then I thought of something Hunter had told me in case I was ever trapped in a trunk.

At the time, I thought it was a big joke. Like I'd ever be trapped in a trunk. Right? But Hunter was always giving me trivial pointers.

Here's what he said: Some of the newer model cars have an emergency trunk release inside. Don't ask me why that stuck, but it did.

And Johnny's car was pretty new. Where would a release like that be?

The trunk was dark. I fumbled around in a panic, finally found something that felt like a latch, pulled on it . . . and watched the trunk swing open from inside.

I scrambled out and made for the garage door.

As if we hadn't been through enough, the overhead door was locked. So was the side door.

Nothing can be easy. I raced back and opened the door on Johnny Jay's side. He flopped out onto the floor. Geez. The guy had a lot of weight on me. Why was he the first to go down?

We were out of the car, but obviously not out of the woods yet.

I turned off the squad car, found a crowbar in the

trunk, and actually managed to pry open the side door. It's amazing what a person can do under pressure.

I pulled and prodded and slapped at Johnny until finally, with a little help on his part, I got him outside, where we crawled onto the other side of a thick bush, fell side by side, facing the sky, and sucked up fresh air.

If Effie had been watching, she would easily have caught us coming out, and we would have been goners.

Instead, she'd obviously been too confident, too sure that she had us trapped, because she was a no-show, thank God. Because I didn't have any more tricks up my sleeve.

Except we still didn't have any means of contacting the outside world for help. I'd dropped my cell phone, and Johnny had surrendered his equipment. Not only that, Effie had an arsenal of weapons at her disposal.

"Can you swim?" I said to Johnny.

"Better than you, Fischer," he said, not too far gone to challenge me.

"Then let's get out of here."

And that's how we made our escape, slinking through the yard, staying in the shadows, wading into the lake, and pushing off for the next house down the line. And in this neighborhood, that was quite a swim.

Forty-five

Thankfully they were home, didn't flip out and shoot us when we rose from the lake like monsters from the depths, and did a bang-up job of calling for police backup and wrapping our shivering bodies in blankets.

Later, I found out why Johnny had been overcome with the fumes first. He was in worse shape than I was, and I don't mean just aerobically. Thanks to Effie's efforts to kill us, and Johnny's subsequent visit to the ER in the back of an ambulance, the doctors discovered that his ticker needed a little maintenance.

So you might say I had a hand in saving his life more than once. Even so the ingrate threatened to arrest me for assaulting a police chief. Hopefully, he'll forget about those slaps over time. Ha, not likely.

But that came later. After our phone call for police backup, Effie put up quite a fight.

The Critical Incident Team handles the big stuff, not the local police, and Effie sure did qualify for special treatment after attempting to murder a cop (I counted, too, but not nearly as much). Since Hunter is part of that team, he, several others, and K-9 superhero Ben went in for the takedown, leaving me at the other end of the driveway, biting my fingernails.

A shot rang through the air. I said to Sally Maylor, "Was that one of us firing?"

She shook her head, and I took that to mean she had experience determining type of weapon sounds, and this one wasn't one of ours. Effie then, had taken the shot.

Silence ensued and time passed. I stayed back on the perimeter per orders, holding my breath, craning for a view, my heart beating overtime, thinking, what if the absolute worst happened and I lost Hunter?

Next I heard Ben bark and a high-pitched female scream.

Pretty soon, the team came into view, Ben dancing in the lead as though he'd had the time of his life, Effie trussed up like a bird ready for the spit, and a piece of cloth wrapped around her wrist where Ben had taken the chief's gun away from her.

We watched the other team members shove Effie into the back of a squad car. I was glad it was someone else's turn for a change.

"My truck is still here," I said to Hunter. "Come home with me."

Hunter waved off the rest of the team and everybody took off, leaving us alone.

"I'm grilling a burger for you tonight," I said to Ben. Hunter thought I meant him, gave me a big, loose grin. "You, too," I told him, proud of my guys.

"The Illinois police picked up Harry as soon as he

crossed over the Wisconsin border," Hunter told me. "He had a hostage with him. Patti."

"Patti?" I said, wondering how long Harry would have been able to contain her before she cleaned his clock. And wasn't it a good thing I hadn't counted on her to rescue me? She's rarely around when she's needed the most. Then I remembered the shadow on the other side of the cedars while my mom was having her meltdown. That must have been Harry, stalking her. Patti must've been the one I saw in the truck's passenger seat.

Hunter followed up with, "Harry also had a metal box with him, filled with hundred dollar bills. He swears it's his money. He's being held for kidnapping Patti. They're letting her go even though it will be a crime against humanity."

As we walked up the drive toward the house, I laughed at that, the first time in recent memory. "And Holly?"

"She'll be on her way home within the hour."

I studied my man. "When that shot went off, I was so scared."

"Ben saved the day."

Ah, what a canine champion. I paused to scratch his head. "Sorry about how our day together turned out," Hunter said.

"It isn't over yet. I want to do a little digging in a garden."

Hunter looked confused by that, but he followed me into Holly's rose garden. I pulled out the pitchfork that was sticking out of the ground and went to work using it like a rake around the rosebushes.

A soiled pair of gloves emerged from the earth. I'd bet my blouse that Jackson Davis would find evidence of water hemlock when he examined them.

Spiders, my foot.

We also found a hole in the ground, about the right size for another rosebush to go in. Or for a metal money box to come out.

We invited everybody involved over for burgers. Master griller Max would handle the hamburgers, cooking them to absolute perfection. Holly made the concession to actually enter my backyard. Of course that was only after I reminded her that bees don't fly at night.

Milly, shocked to learn that her new friend was a murderess, recovered enough to volunteer to bring her potato salad, which is the best in the world.

Carrie Ann and the twins weren't overlooked, either. We were prepared to feed them once they closed the store. "Bring Gunnar and the kids, too," I told my cousin.

Hunter went over to The Wild Clover and picked up the meat and buns. Ben approved of his selection, and later had the burger I'd promised him.

Stanley Peck showed up with his homemade honey mead, which he makes in his bathtub. I failed to mention that fact to the others, considering it might turn off a few of the guests. I even went out on a limb and sampled it myself. Delish.

Max showed off his company's latest flavor experiment by picking a bunch of endive from my garden and sprinkling it with Savour Foods' latest discovery. I thought I tasted extra sweetness, but the product has a ways to go. Great concept, though.

Patti slipped through the cedar hedge. In spite of her annoying ways, we were all grateful she was okay. "I'd have gotten free eventually," she said, and we all believed her.

While we ate, Hunter and I filled in a few holes, some of those holes of the rose garden variety.

"Effie didn't want anybody to notice the area in the rose garden where she'd recently dug," I said, "so she made up the spider story."

"Which really worked," Holly added.

I went on. "She buried the gloves she'd used to pick the water hemlock in the same general area where she also buried some of the cash she'd stolen from Harry. Fifty grand of it. Harry claims she took more than that, but if she did, she isn't saying."

"How did he find out where she was hiding?" Stanley asked.

"Nova," Hunter told us. "She made good on her threat that very first night." Hunter looked at me and said, "Phone records prove it, and Harry confirmed the call."

I hadn't liked Nova, but felt a pang of sadness for her. "If only Effie had known that she was too late. Nova would still be alive."

Hunter looked over at Patti. "Effie knew exactly who you were the entire time."

Patti shook her head. "I never met her when I lived in Chicago."

"No, but she knew you and used that to her advantage, setting out to frame you. It sure helped that you'd forgotten your water bottle over there. What could be more believable than one ex-wife killing the other?" Hunter reached over and took my hand in his.

Holly jumped in. "That's amazing how she put together such a complicated scheme in only one night. Imagine if she'd actually preplanned. I can't believe a murderer lived in my carriage house!"

"I can't believe I considered her a friend," Milly said sadly. "What happened to Chance? Is he okay?"

"He has a brother in Waukesha," Hunter told us. "He's staying there for the time being."

I still had one more question. "How did Effie get Nova to drink out of Patti's travel mug? I mean, she wasn't exactly the pro-stalker type."

As always we looked to Hunter for the answer. "That morning when nobody could find Nova," he said. "She was meeting with Effie in the carriage house. Effie begged her to reconsider her threat to expose her, Nova laughed in her face, not bothering to mention that she'd already set Harry in motion."

"Maybe she was afraid Effie would run," Patti added.

We all thought that was probably one of the reasons, but I could see Nova mocking her just to be nasty.

Hunter continued. "Anyway, Effie already had the poisoned juice in the water bottle, and she knew exactly how Nova would react when she mentioned that she'd helped herself to the juice in the refrigerator."

Holly piped up, saying, "Nobody, but nobody, touched Nova Campbell's juice. Or her personal belongings, or anything else that she owned. She was ultra-selfish. That's why Gil put her name on the jar, to keep the peace."

Max shook his head at that. "I can just see her, grabbing the bottle away."

"Which she did," Hunter said. "Then told Effie to stay away from things that didn't belong to her. And drank it right down in front of Effie, actually throwing the empty bottle at her. While you were gone, Effie placed it on Nova's nightstand."

Patti leaned in. "She must have really hated it when the cops went after Holly instead of me." Her eyes went to Max, then back to Holly. "You aren't going to really sue me, are you? Once I get my job back, I'll write something nice to make up for it."

Holly laughed. "The only way we will consider letting it go, is if you promise *not* to write anything more about our family."

Patti thought that was a pretty good deal.

So that's what went on at my house following the arrest of Effie Anderson for the murder of Nova Campbell and a whole host of other charges for attempting to kill Johnny Jay and me.

May she rot in jail.

Oh, there was one more incident worth mentioning.

Right before Max threw the burgers on the grill, Grams Fleetwood pulled up on the street out front. I couldn't see her from the backyard, but when metal hits metal and Grams is expected, there's only one conclusion.

We rushed to the street just as Mom was getting out of the passenger's seat. Grams had run right into Lori Spandle's realty car as Lori and a new perspective buyer stood in the yard next door.

I won't go into how potty mouth Lori is, or how Mom went to town on everybody in sight, including the poor people who'd just wanted to look at the house (they decided against buying it, obviously), and I won't mention some of the threats that were flung around or how Stanley almost went for his concealed weapon.

The important part is when Tom Stocke pulled up, rushed to my mother right in front of everybody, got down on his knee, and proposed to Mom right on the spot.

Just then, at that exact moment, Hunter moved up behind me. He wrapped his arms around me in a big bear hug, and while we witnessed Mom's blubbering and Tom's pleading, in the end, Mom said yes.

We were one big happy family again.

For now.

The Wild Clover
❧ Newsletter ☙

Notes from the beeyard:

• Honeybees are the state insect in seventeen states, including here in Wisconsin.

• Hives should be placed facing the southeast so honeybees wake up to sun. They love it as much as we do.

• Busy, happy bees mean pollination equaling higher yields in your vegetable garden.

Wildly simple concoctions:

• Make rose honey by picking rose petals, any kind, even wild. Then lightly pack them in a jar. Pour in honey and cap it. For at least the next few days shake the jar gently to mix the flavors. The longer it melds, the better it will be. Serve with popovers (recipe below).

• Moisturizing facial mask—2 egg whites, bit of flour, add honey to form thick paste, apply for few minutes, rinse with cold water. Your skin will be silky smooth.

Popovers with Pumpkin Pie Honey Butter

FOR THE POPOVERS:

2 eggs
1 cup flour
1 cup milk
1 teaspoon vanilla
½ teaspoon salt

FOR THE HONEY BUTTER:

Mix together ½ cup butter at room temperature, ½ cup honey, 1 teaspoon pumpkin pie seasoning.

Preheat the oven to 450 degrees, and warm 6 custard or muffin cups with a dab of butter in each.

Beat the eggs slightly, then mix in the rest of the ingredients until smooth. Distribute the mixture evenly between cups.

Bake at 450 for 20 minutes, then reduce temperature to 350 and bake 10 additional minutes.

Serve piping hot with pumpkin pie honey butter.

Honeybee Bars

1 cup granola
1 cup quick cooking rolled oats
1 cup chopped nuts
½ cup craisans
1 egg, beaten
⅓ cup honey
⅓ cup cooking oil

¼ cup packed brown sugar
½ teaspoon cinnamon
½ teaspoon apple pie spice
½ cup mini chocolate chips (optional)

Line an 8x8 baking pan with foil. Grease foil, set aside.

In a large bowl, combine granola, oats, nuts, flour, and craisans. Stir in egg, honey, oil, brown sugar, cinnamon, apple pie spice, and chocolate chips.

Bake in a 325 degree oven 30–35 minutes or until lightly browned on the edges. Use foil to remove from pan. Cut into 12 bars.

Notes from the garden:

• Instead of using chemical herbicides, spray weeds with vinegar.

• July is the perfect time to start more basil from seed. It goes so well with September's tomatoes.

Milly's Potato Salad

3 pounds of red potatoes, skins on or off, chopped
6 green onions, chopped
½ cup minced chives
1 cup mayonnaise
Salt and pepper to taste
6 hard-boiled eggs, chopped

Boil the potatoes, then let cool to room temperature. In a large serving bowl, mix potatoes, onions, chives, mayo, and salt and pepper, then fold in the eggs. Chill for several hours.

Arugula & Garden Tomato Salad

2 tablespoons white wine vinegar
2 teaspoons Dijon mustard
3 tablespoons extra-virgin olive oil
8 cups arugula
1 cup thinly sliced red onion
16 small tomatoes cut in half, or quartered

Whisk together the vinegar and mustard, then gradually add in the olive oil. Toss in the arugula, onion, and tomatoes. Serves 8.

Isabelle "Betts" Winston loves teaching the secrets of mouthwatering country food in her hometown, Broken Rope, Missouri—but when an all-too-current murder threatens the start of tourist season, Betts must find a way to solve it without getting burned . . .

FROM NATIONAL BESTSELLING AUTHOR

PAIGE SHELTON

If Fried Chicken Could Fly

A Country Cooking School Mystery

At Gram's Country Cooking School, Betts and Gram are helping students prepare the perfect dishes for the Southern Missouri Showdown, the cook-off that draws the first of the summer visitors. Everything is going smoothly until they discover the body of local theater owner Everett Morningside in the school's supply room, and Everett's widow points an accusatory finger at Gram. Now, Betts has to dig deep into Broken Rope's history to find the modern-day killer—before the last wing is served . . .

Includes delicious recipes!

"Each page leads to more intrigue and surprise."
—*The Romance Readers Connection*

"A breath of summer freshness that is an absolute delight to read and savor . . . A feast of a mystery."
—*Fresh Fiction*

facebook.com/TheCrimeSceneBooks
paigeshelton.com
penguin.com

M1106T0712